Obsession 3:

Bitter Taste of Revenge

Obsession 3:

Bitter Taste of Revenge

Treasure Hernandez

www.urbanbooks.net

Urban Books, LLC
97 N 18th Street
Wyandanch, NY 11798

Obsession 3: Bitter Taste of Revenge

ISBN 13: 978-1-60162-648-6
ISBN 10: 1-60162-648-7

First Trade Paperback Printing March 2015
Printed in the United States of America

10 9 8 7 6 5 4 3 2 1

*This is a work of fiction. Any references or similarities
to actual events, real people, living, or dead, or to real
locales are intended to give the novel a sense of reality.
Any similarity in other names, characters, places, and
incidents is entirely coincidental.*

Distributed by Kensington Publishing Corp.
Submit Orders to:
Customer Service
400 Hahn Road
Westminster, MD 21157-4627
Phone: 1-800-733-3000
Fax: 1-800-659-2436

Obsession 3:

Bitter Taste of Revenge

Treasure Hernandez

Chapter 1

"Oh my God! Somebody please help me. I can't have my baby born in this place." Secret was curled up into a tight fetal position. She looked as though she was inside of her own mother's womb instead of a mother about to push a baby out of hers.

Her knees were rammed into the bottom of her protruding belly. Her toes were pointed stiff, more so than a ballerina performing the *Nutcracker*. Her arms were clenched tightly around her stomach. She was going to keep that baby inside of her at all cost.

"Urghhhh!" she cried out as another sharp pain cut through her midsection.

"Will somebody come help this bitch please? Ain't nobody got time for this shit. A nigga tryin'a sleep. Damn!"

Secret's cellmate showed no empathy for the excruciating pain she had been going through since lights out. Secret couldn't have cared less though. She didn't need empathy. She needed someone to come in with a great big needle or a pill potent enough to take all this pain away, without harming her baby of course.

Secret had suffered enough pain in her short eighteen years for both herself and her unborn baby. Secret was seventeen when she got pregnant just about to turn eighteen. Now she had long turned eighteen. On her next birthday she would be nineteen.

She never wanted her daughter to live the painful life she had. There were plenty of nights she just lay on her jail cot, held her stomach and stared up at the ceiling, praying to God that her baby would skip the generational curse of the Miller family. It was a curse that included a miserable life with miserable parents being raised in the streets of Flint, Michigan.

Within that prayer Secret always told God, "And please don't let it be a girl." There had been Secret's grandmother, who Secret's mother Yolanda had sworn was the worst mother in the world. Secret begged to differ, not because the grandmother she knew had been as sweet as pumpkin pie, but because Secret felt that Yolanda was the worst mother in the world. In her defense Yolanda said her own mother had made her that way. Would Secret be giving that same excuse years from now to her own daughter? And then would her own daughter be using it for her own daughter, and so on?

Tears would slide out of Secret's eyes and onto her paper-thin pillow at just the thought of having a girl child. The women in her family all having had children in their teens hadn't made things any better. It had only made the struggle of raising a child worse. Secret just knew for sure if she had a boy the curse would end there. Not only that, but she felt that a boy would have a better chance of surviving the streets of Flint, seeing that no matter how hard Secret had tried, she was never going to be able to escape the city. She'd been born and raised in those streets and it definitely looked like her child was about to be as well.

"Owwwwweee. Jesus!" A strong cramp ripped through Secret's lower abdomen. They were coming with vengeance in what seemed like every five minutes now.

At first the cramps that woke Secret up out of her sleep were bearable. They weren't any worse than bad menstrual cramps. As a matter of fact, when the cramping first started, Secret was able to close her eyes again and sleep through it. But that was when they were minor and only about an hour apart. Through the night they had gotten stronger and closer together.

Secret couldn't take it anymore. She had waited this thing out as much as she could. She had lain there and tried to hold that baby inside of her so that it wouldn't come into this world with the stigma of being born in a jailhouse. The baby was in control now and it was coming out whether Secret liked it or not.

With sweat pouring from her body, her gown sticking to her like toilet paper, Secret managed to sit up on the edge of the cot on her top bunk. "God, help me," she repeated three times. She breathed in and out deeply. She took her hand and wiped her forehead to keep the salty sweat from rolling into her eyes and stinging them. Her hair was drenched and matted. There was no combing that mess out. She'd have to get it shaved, she just knew it. But this was no time to be concerned about hair care. She had to get out of that bed and go over to the door and yell for help. Her lazy cellmate sure wasn't getting out of her bed to do it.

Just as Secret was about to hop down another cramp ripped through her. At the same time it felt like her insides were falling out. She let out the loudest roar ever.

Her cellmate, who'd had her pillow over her head trying to drown out Secret's wails, snatched it off. She leaned her head from out under the bunk to yell at Secret for making such a ruckus. "Will you shut the fuck—"

The gushing water that poured from the top bunk halted her cellmate's words.

"What the fuck?" Her cellmate jumped up. "Did this bitch just fuckin' piss on me?" she asked, wiping the moisture that had hit her face. She then looked down at her wet hands. "I'm 'bout to fuck this bitch up!"

She got up from the bottom bunk and went right for Secret's jugular. Before she could do any real damage to Secret, the cell door flung open and two guards came storming in.

"What the hell is going on in here?" the female guard asked.

"Looks like Mel is trying to get some of that pregnant pussy," the male guard said and laughed.

Mel, Secret's cellmate, had spread Secret's legs apart, not to try to have sex with her, but to have a better position at putting her hands around her throat. She'd had every intention of choking the life, and the baby, out of Secret had the guards not shown up.

"Pregnant pussy is the best," the female guard agreed.

"How the fuck you know?" he asked his coworker.

She only winked and smiled.

"Nasty-ass dyke," he said under his breath as they both went over, taking their own sweet time, to get Mel off of Secret.

"No, fuck that!" Mel resisted as the two guards subdued her. "That bitch pissed on me."

"Aww, poor baby," the female guard teased. "And since when don't you like a little golden shower?"

The two guards hollered out in laughter as Secret hollered out in pain. This made the guards turn their attention to Secret.

"Oh, shit!" the female guard yelled out when she saw the condition Secret was in.

Secret was sitting on the edge of the bed with her legs cocked open. She was drenched, clutching her belly and clearly in pain.

"I think she's in labor," the female guard said.

"Hel . . . hel . . . help me," Secret managed to pant out. "My baby. My baby." The tears wouldn't stop flowing.

"Help me get her down," the male guard said as he pulled out his walkie-talkie. With the assistance of the female guard, he managed to get Secret down as he called in the situation. "We have an inmate going into labor. Looks like the baby could be born any minute. Give the infirmary the heads-up. Prepare for her arrival in five." He ended the conversation, put the device away, and was now able to fully assist with getting Secret out of the cell. Once they got Secret through the threshold they closed and locked the cell back up.

On one side of the door Secret was screaming her head off. On the other side Mel was lying back down on her cot saying, "Good, now a nigga can finally get some sleep."

Secret's screams echoed off the walls of the corridors as the guards half carried, half forced her to walk to the infirmary. For Secret, the five-minute trek felt like a walk to death row instead of the hospital bed that was waiting for her once the guards carried her into the cold room. The immediate what felt like glacier temperatures hitting Secret's wet skin was sure to cause her to catch pneumonia. Her catching a cold to the tenth degree wasn't of importance right now, but getting that baby from between her legs without incident was.

"How far apart are your contractions?" Secret heard the voice of the female doctor ask her.

Secret had placed the corner of a sheet in her mouth and was biting down on it as a contraction hit her hard. She couldn't have answered the doctor if she'd wanted to. She didn't want to. There was no time for 101 questions. Her water had broken, her contractions felt like they were coming every second.

The hell with questions; just get this baby out of me! Secret screamed in her mind.

"Damn it! Will you answer the doctor? She's trying to help your ass!" The female correction officer spoke more out of fear than anger. She'd never been in this situation before and didn't know what to do. Secret looked more like she was about to die than to give birth.

"I can take it from here," the doctor looked to the female correction officer and said. She didn't want the CO's negative and nervous energy making things worse for her patient.

The female CO just stood there frozen, stunned by the excruciating pain the young female was somehow able to endure. The doctor's words hadn't been able to melt the ice.

"I said I can take it from here." This time the doctor's tone was sterner and she looked to the male CO, signaling for him to get his partner and go.

He too had been mesmerized by the whole idea that Secret was about to give birth to a live human being. Having no children of his own, no baby momma to stand beside in the delivery room, he'd never experienced anything like this either. He wasn't frozen in fear, though, like his counterpart. He was more in awe. He did, in fact, acknowledge the doctor's words. He pulled his attention away from Secret and looked at the doctor. "Oh, okay." He looked back to Secret while tugging his coworker's arm. "Come on. Let's go."

The female CO, feeling his hand on her arm, was able to snap out of her trance. She looked from her coworker to Secret as he slowly began to pull her away.

The doctor was doing all she could do not to yell, "Get the fuck out already!" She turned her attention back to Secret as the two COs exited the room. "I need you to work with me here, Secret, so that I can help you." The doctor had seen Secret before so she knew her name. She'd given her a checkup or two during Secret's past month of incarceration, "Can you do that for me?"

Secret nodded vigorously. She'd do anything she needed to do for help right now.

"I need you to turn over onto your back. Okay?"

Secret had been most comfortable, for lack of a better word, lying balled up on her side. If lying on her back meant the doctor could do something to help the pain go away, she was more than willing to change positions. If she could.

Upon seeing Secret struggle to turn onto her back, the doctor immediately began to assist her. Secret moaned and groaned with every movement.

"It's okay. I know it hurts. I know it hurts," the doctor consoled her. Once she had Secret on her back, she took some plastic gloves out of the pockets of her white jacket and placed them on her hands. She spread Secret's legs open just as a contraction hit. The doctor's eyes nearly bulged out of her head. This wasn't her first time at the rodeo, but it was the first time an inmate had been this far along before being brought in for help. "Okay, Secret. Grab on to the rail of the bed and squeeze it whenever the pain shoots through, but don't push. Not yet."

The doctor walked over to the phone on the wall and picked it up. She hit a couple numbers and then began talking. "Where are you? I need your assistance. I have an inmate down in the infirmary. She's in labor." There was a pause and then the doctor yelled, "I don't give a shit about you giving an inmate with a migraine some damn pills. Did you hear what I said? This inmate is about to have a baby! Get your ass back here now if you want your job when you do decide to return!" The doctor slammed the phone down and mumbled under her breath, "Giving an inmate with a migraine headache some pills my ass. More like giving an inmate some head."

Secret was in far too much pain to make out what the doctor was fussing about. She just did as she was told, clenching the bars on the bed for dear life.

When the doctor returned to Secret's bedside, she had two cold, wet white towels. She placed one on Secret's forehead and another on her neck. She then went back to the foot of the bed to continue checking Secret out. "Secret, I'm just going to slide your underwear off." The doctor slid Secret's drenched panties off and then laid them on a silver rolling tray that was only about a foot away. She used her gloved hands to gently spread Secret's legs apart. She inserted her fingers into Secret, best guess to see how much Secret had dilated. A few seconds later she closed Secret's legs, pulled her gown down and walked back over to the phone while removing her gloves and pitching them into the trash.

Just as the doctor started talking to someone on the phone, the worse contraction ever hit Secret. It made her upper body rise up and a curdling howl escape her throat.

The doctor quickly finished her call, hung up the phone and walked back over to Secret's bedside. She spoke as calmly as she could. "Secret, your water has broken and you are fully dilated. I could feel the baby's head." Actually, she could see it, but didn't want to freak Secret out too bad. "Nurse Caine was assisting another inmate but is on her way down to help me." She grabbed Secret's hand. "I called for help for you to be transferred to the hospital, but, honey, this baby is coming and is going to be born here."

Secret grabbed the doctor's hand and squeezed it almost as tightly as she had been squeezing that rail just a couple minutes ago. "No," Secret said with both passion and authority intertwined. "I cannot have my baby in this jail." Tears poured from Secret's eyes. "Please don't make my baby have to live with that its whole life. Please, Doctor. Wait for the ambulance and let me have my baby in a real hospital like a mother should."

"Secret, I can't—"

Secret cut her off by squeezing the doctor's hand with her other hand as well. She was pleading like a prisoner being held captive begging for their freedom. "Please, Doctor. I can't have my baby in jail. I'd rather die. I'd rather it die." The tears continued to stream. She trembled. A contraction hit her, but she clamped her teeth together to bear the pain. Only the doctor telling her what she wanted to hear would give her peace of mind.

"This baby is not going to wait, honey. There is nothing I can do," the doctor told her. "It's not really up to me. That baby is coming when it's ready. Now I have to get you prepped so I can assist your little one." The doctor eagerly went to walk away. Not only did she need to help bring Secret's baby into the world, but she could no longer stand to look into Secret's eyes. There was too much desperation and pain for her to witness.

"No, please." Secret refused to let go of the doctor's hands. "Don't do this to me." Secret shook her head back and forth.

The doctor had no idea what was going through her patient's head, but she could only imagine. Who wanted their child to walk around for the rest of their lives with the stigma attached of being born in jail? But her hands were tied. It was in God's hands. He was the one who decided when a life would come into the world. She was just there to help.

The doctor leaned down close to Secret. "I understand how you feel, I really do. But if I don't help get that baby out of you, it will die. It will lose oxygen and die and maybe so could you." The doctor lifted up and went to walk away.

Yet again, Secret refused to let the woman go. She pulled the doctor back down to her. With a trembling lip and meaning every word that escaped her mouth she said to the doctor, "Then let us die."

The doctor just stood there for a moment. Secret's words had penetrated her soul, splintered her soul. She knew what she had to do as guilt instantaneously flooded her being. She hoped she wouldn't live to regret her decision. She hoped her patient and her patient's unborn baby wouldn't suffer the results of her decision.

Chapter 2

"The head is out!" the EMT shouted just as the ambulance pulled up to the hospital emergency room doors. "I told that idiot we needed to deliver there." He then seethed under his breath, "Frickin' jailhouse quack."

"Oh, God! My baby! It hurts!" Secret was torn between the feeling of pleasure and pain, kind of like how a girl might feel when she's losing her virginity. Secret wouldn't know about all that because when she lost her virginity, there was no pleasure in it at all. There was just pain, humility, and disgust. She'd felt so violated like she was being raped. She hadn't known the man on a personal level she'd lost her virginity to, but she had willingly given her body to him. That's what her daddy had wanted her to do. For years she'd longed to be a daddy's girl to her father whose coming in and out of her life wasn't even as consistent as her monthly menstrual cycle. She just wanted to please his heart, which was why she agreed to lie on her back and give up the most precious thing she possessed. She allowed the stranger to run up inside her right there on his kitchen floor while her father waited in the alley behind the house in his car.

He'd owed people money, bad people. They were going to kill him if he didn't pay them. According to the spiel he had given his daughter, he'd been doing anything and everything himself to gather money to pay off his debt and now he needed her to do the same. At first Secret refused, but she couldn't allow her father's blood to be on her hands. Besides, this would be the ultimate act of showing her father how much she loved him. The little girl inside of her just knew if she did what Daddy wanted, he'd come around more. He'd be indebted to her. So she slept with the man who offered her alcohol and Kentucky Fried Chicken as if on a cheap date. But he wasn't cheap. After he'd had his way with Secret, not only did he give her an envelope full of cash to give to her father, the man he'd purchased her pussy from, but he'd also given Secret a li'l somethin' somethin' for herself. That was Secret's first time tricking, first time having sex, and first time getting pregnant. Now she lay in the back of an ambulance suffering the consequences of it all. She was alone.

"Just everybody calm down," the female EMT said, who was also in the back of the ambulance with Secret and her coworker. She was specifically talking to her partner but wanted to remain as professional as possible and not call him out.

"You're the one who agreed with the dumb-dumb back at the jail to transport her instead of just letting her give birth there first," he spat as he tended to Secret as best he could.

The female EMT opened her mouth, but nothing came out. There were no words to defend why she insisted on transporting Secret to the hospital instead of them just assisting in the delivery of the baby at the jail and then transporting a healthy mother and baby to the hospital. But the pleading of both Secret's and the jailhouse doctor's eyes had swayed her to go against what she knew was more medically sound: "My baby can't be born in jail, please!" Secret's pleas had penetrated her heart.

Her coworker had fussed the entire time from the minute they transferred Secret to their gurney up until now.

"If anything happens to mother or baby . . ." His words trailed off at his warning, or perhaps it was a threat. He said none of this out of anger, but out of fear that something, anything, could go wrong.

The female EMT looked down at Secret and their eyes just happened to lock. She squeezed Secret's hand, an unspoken gesture that everything was going to be okay.

"What do we have?" Another voice shouted through the ambulance. It was a man.

"Doctor, we have an eighteen-year-old female in labor, water broke, fully dilated, baby's head coming out," the male EMT said to the middle-aged Caucasian man.

The doctor didn't reply. He just climbed into the back of the ambulance and went right over to Secret. The nurse who had come out with the doctor waited outside the back of the vehicle.

The doctor did a quick check on Secret and then looked to the EMTs. "Surely this all didn't just happen in the short period of time you transferred her."

The first responders remained silent as they stared at one another. The male EMT's look was burning a hole through the female.

"Yes, we know, Doctor," the male EMT said, not throwing his counterpart under the ambulance like he wanted to.

The doctor hopped off the ambulance as he started shouting out orders. Both the EMT and nurse scurried behind the doctor who did a light jog back through the emergency room doors. The nurse was right behind the doctor paying close attention to his direction as the EMTs carted a screaming Secret.

Right as they bust through the swinging doors into a chilly room, Secret's upper body shot straight up as she spread her legs as far as she could. She let out an ear-piercing yelp. To her it felt like a million people were scrambling about the room and they were speaking in unknown tongues. Everything felt so surreal.

There was some tugging, some pulling, someone was wiping her forehead with a white towel. Someone was asking her questions that she couldn't comprehend. There was the clinking of medical tools as the doctor called out what he needed. There was a stinging between Secret's legs as if she'd been ripped and not surgically cut with one of the tools.

"You're doing good, sweetheart," the nurse who stood by Secret's side told her. "One more push, I promise."

Secret hadn't even realized she'd been doing any pushing. That baby was so ready to come out, surely it had been doing everything it could on its own to escape from her dark womb and into this dark world.

For nine months Secret felt like she'd eaten a basketball that wouldn't digest and pass through her intestines. Well finally in the matter of two seconds the basketball exited her body and she felt the weight of the world being lifted from her. Maybe not the weight of the world, but seven pounds six ounces of weight had been lifted from her.

The sound of a faint cry brought a peaceful hush over Secret. This sound had instantly changed her life. It changed who she was completely. She was now a mother. God had just given her the huge responsibility of bringing a life into the world and nurturing it. There was probably a woman somewhere right now wishing the Almighty would bless her womb with a child of her own. Instead He'd blessed a young girl who was just eighteen years old without a pot to piss in or a window to throw it out of. A young girl who couldn't take care of herself, let alone a baby. God had gotten things twisted somehow, so instead of feeling blessed, Secret felt what all the women in her family had been: cursed.

"It's a girl," the doctor called out.

Tears flowed out of the corners of Secret's eyes. It was a girl, confirmation that she was cursed indeed. Her baby was cursed by default, poor thing, and all because she had been born to a Miller woman. If Secret was in a position to do so, she'd protect her baby from everything, everyone. She wouldn't even let her out of the house, home schooling her. She'd do whatever she could to keep the street's paws off of her baby girl. But she couldn't. Unlike the woman who God should have blessed with the baby who had a big house, car, and a husband waiting for her and baby to come home from the hospital, Secret was going back to jail and her baby was going God knows where.

Secret hadn't talked to her mother, Yolanda, since the day the two had a knock-down drag-out fight and Yolanda put her out, which was somewhere around six months ago. Even if Secret had been in touch with her mother, there was no way she would have wanted that evil bitch to raise her baby. Her father was out of the question. He'd figure out a way to sell the baby on the black market for money: either money he needed for drugs, or money he owed to some bad guys because of drugs.

The only other family Secret had was Shawndiece and strangely enough, Secret hadn't heard from her in over two weeks. The first and only one to come visit Secret in jail for the month she'd been locked up so far, Shawndiece had promised to be there for Secret and now she was ghost. That concerned Secret. Worry set in when she had tried to call Shawndiece on her cell phone and it was turned off. Shawndiece wasn't blood family, but being Secret's best friend since she was ten years old, Shawndiece had been more like a sister than just a friend.

Secret had been living with her grandmother in Farmington until she passed away. Farmington was a nice suburb, nothing like the apartment complex Secret had to move into with her mother. It was culture shock for Secret, but Shawndiece's little ghetto tail had been there to show Secret the ropes and take her under her wing. Shawndiece never could put the hood in Secret, but the hood respected Secret nonetheless. At least nobody ever tried to mess with her. Secret didn't know if it was because she kept to herself and didn't bother anybody, or if having the roughest female in the hood as her best friend had something to do with it.

The two best friends were complete opposites. Oil and water for sure, with Shawndiece's sharp tongue being a hint of vinegar. "We balance the universe out," was what Secret had once told her high school counselor, Mrs. Langston, when she'd asked her why she hung around that ratchet girl. Secret had laughed first hearing the older white woman use a slang term surely one of the other students had taught her. If anyone else had said it, Secret would have probably been offended, but she knew her counselor meant no harm. Mrs. Langston was just looking out for Secret. She'd looked out for her all four years of high school.

"There's something different about you from most of these other kids," Mrs. Langston had told Secret one day in her office while she helped Secret fill out some scholarship applications. "You don't belong here. College is going to take you away to the land of opportunities. And if nothing else, it will take you away from this town."

That's all Secret had worked hard toward throughout her schooling: to get a scholarship so she could get the hell out of Flint and as far away from her family curse as possible. A scholarship to OSU was going to be her golden ticket. So when Yolanda broke the news to Secret of the letter that came denying her the scholarship, Secret gave up on her dreams. There was no other way she could afford to attend without scholarships. And then when Yolanda put her on the streets pregnant, she couldn't even afford to live. So she resorted to doing what her father had introduced her to: tricking.

Not that it made it any better, but Secret only tricked with one guy in particular, Lucky. Although Secret never straight-out asked Lucky and he never straight-out told her, she knew he had his hands in the streets. For lack of better terms, he was a baller, street pharmacist. The plan was that she'd pretend she liked him, sleep with him, and then tell him that the baby she was already pregnant with was his. She'd at least have a baby daddy with a bank roll to take care of her. It worked for all of ten minutes. Secret's conscience wouldn't let her go through with the scheme, especially once she started to fall in love with Lucky. But the day the cops pulled them over in Secret's car that had a trunk full of dope that Lucky had put there, Secret's luck ran out. Lucky, unwilling to take the blame for the dope, since the car was in Secret's name, she went down for it and went to jail. Now here she was giving birth to her child while she waited on her trial to start. She had no idea how much longer she'd been in jail. What was even worse, she had no idea what she was going to do with her baby when she went back to jail.

Chapter 3

"The mother's blood pleasure is dropping by the second. We can't stop the vaginal bleeding. Get her upstairs, stat!" the doctor yelled as two of the nurses handled the baby and two other nurses helped him tend to the patient.

Upon the doctor's orders, one nurse opted to assist with the situation going on with Secret. The new born baby was in good hands with a single nurse.

"Go give the staff on two the heads-up," the doctor said to the nurse who had just come over to assist. "Let them know the situation and to prep accordingly. Looks like we're going to have to do an emergency procedure to stop the bleeding." The doctor was turning red with fury. "If anything happens to this patient and her baby, those EMTs . . ." He shook his head.

The nurse receiving the instructions nodded and whizzed out of the room after acknowledging with, "Yes, Doctor."

Secret just lay there in and out of consciousness. She was moving her lips and every now and then a faint, "My baby," would manage to escape her lips, but it wasn't loud enough to be heard over all the commotion going on in the room. Among the commotion, though, there was one thing that Secret noticed she didn't hear; her baby wasn't crying anymore.

If Secret didn't know any better, she would have sworn someone was playing with the light switch. Light, then darkness. Darkness then light. She fought to keep her eyes open, to stay awake. She could not fall into a sleep without first knowing if her baby was okay. She was feeling weaker and weaker by the second. It was becoming a losing battle.

"My ba . . ." She couldn't even get the last word out she was so weak. The next thing she knew, it felt as if someone was spinning her around and around when hospital assistants entered the room and began to wheel her from the room. Light then dark. The world was spinning. Dizzy. "My baby," she managed, still too faint to be audible.

"You're going to be all right, baby," an older African American nurse leaned down and said to Secret as the roller coaster of a ride continued through the hospital corridors.

All Secret could do was stare at her with heavy, fluttering eyelids. She was pleading for answers with her eyes. All she wanted to know was if her baby was all right. She couldn't have cared less about herself. Was her baby all right? Was she alive?

God's will be done.

Those words her grandmother used to say all the time flashed into Secret's head. Secret had cried out to God and prayed that her baby be spared of the generational curse. She didn't want her baby to have to live the same life she had lived. To suffer some of the things she'd suffered in her lifetime. She didn't want her baby to have to live in the streets of Flint, Michigan, raised by those streets that had their own twisted way of nurturing kids. Her baby could not live that way.

A wave of heat followed by a freezing chill flushed through Secret's body. Had God actually answered her prayers in a way she'd never meant for them to be answered? Since she didn't want her baby to have to live this way or that, had God decided to take care of that by not allowing her baby to live at all?

"Ahhhhh!" The cry of agony at the mere thought of her baby left dead back in the delivery room in the arms of a stranger, a nurse, had no problem escaping Secret's throat.

"It's okay, baby," the comforting nurse consoled Secret again. "We're almost there."

The elevator doors closed. The whirlwind of a ride Secret was on was becoming harder and harder to withstand. Dizzy. Faint. She just wanted to close her eyes and let her body rest. But she couldn't rest, not until she knew the state of her baby. Then after that, God's will be done as far as her life was concerned.

"Hey, I know her." A team of nurses had been waiting at the elevator bank for the arrival of Secret. Apparently one had recognized Secret's face.

The nurses on the second floor immediately took over and relieved the nurse from the ER. The nurse who had been consoling Secret relayed Secret's situation for their own confirmation to the nurses. She then watched Secret be wheeled away, getting back on the elevator along with the assistants, returning to their assigned units.

"What's happening?" Secret moaned.

"Yes, honey, what did you say?" One of the nurses leaned down, placing her ear as close to Secret's mouth as she could while at the same time keeping up with the moving bed.

Secret couldn't repeat her words. It had taken more strength than she'd had to get them out the first time. She just shook her head as tears seeped out of the corners of her eyes, creating wet spots on the sheet beneath her.

The nurse stood after a few seconds of Secret not responding. She looked down at her and saw the tears. "Don't worry, Li'l Muffin, it's going to be all right. Just . . ." The nurse's words trailed off, from both her mouth and Secret's ears.

Secret had heard that nickname before. She'd heard that exact same voice calling her by that name before. Was she going crazy? Was she losing it? Was her mind going back in time, as if her life was flashing before her eyes?

"I know her," the nurse said, the sound of her scrubs brushing together as if they were about to start a fire. That's how fast her petite legs were moving in order to keep up with the hospital aides who were wheeling the bed. Standing only five feet and three inches tall, it wasn't as easy of a feat as one might think.

No one acknowledged the nurse's comment for yet a second time, as they wheeled Secret into the operation room where another doctor and two more nurses waited with faces masked and hands gloved. There was some mumbo jumbo, from what Secret could hear, among all the voices in the room. Whether the nurse knew or simply thought she knew who Secret was, was no longer relevant. There was a life that needed to be saved. As far as Secret knew, two lives.

There was a prick in Secret's arm. Within seconds, no matter how hard she tried, she could not get her eyes to open. The lights were out. She was in the dark. The voices faded. She was clueless as to what was going on. Was she falling asleep, or was she dying? She didn't want to do either without first knowing what had happened to her baby. But she was at the mercy of the doctors, the nurses, and whatever that liquid sleeping pill was they'd injected into her veins.

Seconds later Secret opened her eyes. She felt groggy. She felt empty. She went to place her hands on her belly. Her arms weren't yet privy to the fact that they couldn't move as fast as her brain was. They stopped midway. Her body was stiff. An immediate wave of pain shot threw her just from the small, quick movement. She flinched and her face scrunched up. Her brain got on the same page as her body and this time she slowly went to place her hands on her stomach. They still stopped midway. She looked down. Handcuffs. She was handcuffed to the bed. She looked at her belly that, the last time she'd seen it, had looked as though she was toting around a beach ball. Now it was somewhat flat. Her baby, it was gone.

Panic set in and Secret began to wriggle her wrists, as if she could escape the metal bracelets with a few strategic movements. She looked around. She wasn't in her jail cell. She looked to be in a hospital room. She hadn't even worn handcuffs in jail. Why did she have them on in a public hospital?

She began to rack her brain, still trying to free her wrists from the cuffs; then everything started to come back to her. Her mind took her all the way back to sitting on her bunk in the jail and her water breaking. She was in an ambulance and then in a hospital delivery room.

It's a girl.

She heard the baby cry. The lights kept going on and off. The room was spinning; the world was spinning.

Li'l Muffin. She'd remembered hearing those words, and it hadn't been the first time.

The lights went out again and now they were back on again. And even though it had felt like only seconds between the last time they went out and were just now on again, it had been hours, two to be exact.

"Li'l Muffin."

Secret heard the voice again. This time it wasn't in her head. It was right there in her room. She turned her head and looked toward the doorway, where a petite woman wearing scrubs was entering. Why was that nickname so familiar? Why was that voice so familiar? Secret squinted her eyes and tried to focus. The face, there was even some familiarity to that, but why? Where did Secret know this woman from? With the tone of endearment behind the woman's words, clearly she wasn't struggling to recall where she knew Secret from.

The woman's lips spread into a smile as if she'd been waiting to see Secret again. She stepped over to Secret's bed. "How are you feeling?"

Secret blinked. Her eyes were still a little heavy, so it was a slow blink. She wet her whistle by allowing as much saliva as she could to form in her mouth. She thought it might take away the pain in her throat caused by dryness. She spoke. "Okay." She really wasn't. In her body she was okay. She wasn't suffering from any type of unbearable pain, just discomfort. But her spirit wasn't okay. She was anxious and concerned about her little one. "Where's my baby?"

"Your baby is just fine," the nurse said as she began to check the IVs in Secret's arm.

Secret's entire body went as limp as a noodle. The tension had released itself all at once.

"She's in the nursery stealing all the shine from all the other babies. It's her mother we were all concerned about." The woman took out a machine and took Secret's temperature with it. Secret would have asked more questions about her baby, but it would have to wait. She now had a thermometer in her mouth. But as the thermometer rested between her lips, she couldn't help her mind from wandering, trying to place this nurse.

There was a beeping sound. The nurse removed the stick from Secret's mouth. She popped the little plastic piece off the stick and then pitched it into the trash.

Secret licked her lips and tried to moisten her mouth again.

"I'll go get you some water, but let me grab your blood pressure first. After all, that's part of why you ended up here in the first place." She wheeled over a little machine to take Secret's blood pressure. "Your blood pressure dropped so low. You were losing mad blood. The doctor did an emergency procedure on you that I'm sure he'll be in to explain more thoroughly than I can," she informed Secret.

"When can I go see my baby?" Secret asked.

The nurse looked down at Secret's handcuffs and then back up at her patient. "Well, you can't," was her reply.

Secret's blood pressure would have skyrocketed had the nurse not continued talking.

"They'll bring her down to see you. I'll let them know Mommy is up and ready to lay eyes on her little one." She smiled. She announced Secret's blood pressure. "Much, much better," she said, then wrapped up the machine and rolled it back into its proper place. "Now let me go get that water." She was out of the room in seconds.

Secret was so pleased to know that her baby was okay and that in a few moments she'd get to see her. Now the next thing that bothered Secret was the fact that she couldn't figure out where in the world she knew this nurse from.

Chapter 4

"She's so beautiful," Secret said, using her hand to push the button to adjust the bed upright. She wanted to get as good of a look as she could of her newborn baby who was being rolled into the room.

Her tiny self lay bundled in a pink blanket as she lay inside of the clear plastic mobile bassinette-type bed. The nurse rolled her to the left side of Secret's bed and parked the bassinette.

"She is a cutie," said the nurse who had brought her up. She reached into the bed and lifted the baby out. She walked around to the other side of Secret. She placed her as much onto Secret's lap as she could without being on top of Secret herself. Because Secret was cuffed and couldn't hold the baby herself, the nurse held the tiny infant in position.

Secret's eyes filled with tears just staring at the life that had grown in her stomach for the last nine months. The baby just lay there sleeping like a little princess, like she didn't have a care in the world. But soon enough, this cruel world would try to eat the helpless thing alive and give her plenty to occupy her mind with. What pained Secret the most was that she wouldn't be there to fend for her.

With her motherly instincts, Secret went and reached for the child, only to be reminded that her hands were cuffed to the bedrails. She looked from one wrist to the next and then to the nurse.

"Someone is supposed to come take those off," the nurse said. "I asked the officer who is posted outside of your door."

Secret just shook her head. She couldn't believe the state was wasting money for a police officer to guard her door. She wasn't some serial killer or had connections to a mafia that could help her do a jail break. She was just a young teenage mother who wanted to hold her baby. She refused to waste these precious moments with her baby mad at the world. Instead she decided to take in every detail about her little one that she could with her eyes, while her body longed to reach out and pull her close.

"We always suggest mothers nurse their babies, even if it's just for the three days while they are in the hospital, but with your health emergency and . . ." She looked to the handcuffs. "Well, we've been feeding her Similac."

"She's so beautiful," was all Secret could say. Complimenting the baby might as well have been like complimenting herself, because the baby looked like the spitting image of Secret. She had all of her facial features. "Has she opened her eyes yet?" Secret asked the nurse.

"One or twice," the nurse said.

Secret swallowed hard as a horrible thought flushed through her mind. The baby clearly had that Miller nose and Secret's lips. But what if . . . what if she had eyes like the man who helped make her? Secret would know his eyes anywhere. She knew them that day she ran into him outside of the Chinese restaurant at the strip mall. He'd stopped to open the door for her. He hadn't recognized her eyes at all. Good thing, because next he probably would have noticed her belly and possibly done the math. But what would he care? He was just some pervert who had paid to sleep with another man's daughter. Secret didn't take any chances though. She hustled away from that restaurant quick, fast, and in a hurry.

Her baby daddy and that whole night with him was something that Secret had long pushed to the back of her mind. Something she wanted to forget forever. But if this baby had eyes like his, she'd forever be reminded of him, of that night.

"Let me see," the nurse said. She eyeballed Secret, examining her face. "Yep, she has eyes just like yours." The nurse smiled. "She is your mini me all day long."

Secret smiled, and cried, and thanked God in her head.

"I just want to hold her so bad." Secret wriggled her hands hoping she could reach just a part of her baby.

The nurse positioned the baby so that her tiny head was by Secret's hand. Secret stroked her head full of black straight hair.

"You have to smell her," the nurse said, lifting the baby to Secret's face. "There is nothing in the world like the smell of a baby, until they get bigger of course. Then you can't tell their stanky little behinds from the family pet."

Both the nurse and Secret let out a chuckle. This was the first time Secret had laughed since she could remember.

Secret put her nose to her baby's cheek and inhaled. "Baby lotion," she said. Her nostrils were filled with the smell of that pink baby lotion. She closed her eyes and inhaled another lovely whiff of her little one.

The nurse watched the longing on Secret's face to just cup her baby in her arms and pull her into the safety of her bosom. "Where are they with the key to unlock these handcuffs?" she mumbled. "I don't see why the officer out there can't do it. He's the one who put them on."

"Ms. Miller, congratulations on the birth of your new baby."

Secret's eyes opened at the sound of the deep male voice booming through the room. It caught Secret and the nurse off guard and startled the poor baby out of her sleep.

The nurse pulled the now whining baby to her chest.

Secret's eyes followed. "Is she okay?" She panicked at the sound of hearing her baby cry. She felt like a bad and useless mother not being able to take the baby in her arms to comfort her, to let her know that everything was going to be okay. That's what mothers were supposed to do, even though that's not what Yolanda had done when she found out Secret was young and pregnant and needed all the help she could get to raise the baby. But Secret was not her mother. She was going to be a better mother, the best mother she could be. But how could she do it in handcuffs? This motherhood thing was already off to a bad start in more ways than one.

The man, dressed in black slacks, a white dress shirt with a tie, and shiny black shoes, looked to the nurse. "Can you excuse myself and the patient please?" He pulled out a badge and flashed it. "Police business."

This must have been who they were waiting for to remove the cuffs from Secret. "Please take these things off," Secret pleaded with the officer.

"I will." He paused for a second. "But like I just told the nurse here, I need to speak with you first." He had more of an authoritative tone this time around when he said it.

The nurse shifted her eyes to Secret, to the baby, and then back to the man who had just entered the room. "Well, uh, of course."

The nurse walked back around to the other side of the bed. She placed the baby back in its bassinette and looked to Secret. "I'll be right outside the door." She glared up at the six feet six inch tall man. "Along with the other officer." She said it in such a way to let Secret know that this man in the room had backup, and so did Secret.

The nurse exited, closing the door behind her.

"Ms. Miller, I've been meaning to get down there to the jail to visit with you, but you know how things go. You get busy. Life happens. You get caught up." He let out a sinister chuckle. "Look at me preaching to the choir. I'm sure you already know quite a bit about getting caught up."

Secret could tell this guy had an agenda, but she wasn't quite sure what he was getting at, yet. So she just listened. He was taking the scenic route, but he'd get to where he was going eventually. So she just stared at him, not replying. She was just along for the ride. The baby cooed, snatching both Secret's and the man's attention away from each other.

"Cute little baby you got there," he complimented her. "Pink blanket so I'm assuming it's a girl." He stared at the baby a little longer. "What's her name?"

Secret was stumped. She'd hoped for a boy and had only come up with a list of boy names. She hadn't thought to think of names for her new baby girl. Her entrance to the world had been so traumatic, that Secret, for a minute there, wasn't even sure if there would be a baby to name. She just wanted to make sure her precious seed was alive and well. She could name her later.

Already lying there in handcuffs, officially an inmate of the state of Michigan, Secret was in a good running for the worst mother of the year award. The fact that she hadn't even thought enough to name her child would have made her look even worse, so she said the first thing that rolled off of her tongue. "Dynasty." She was kicking herself inside. Where in the hell had that name come from? "But I'm going to call her Dina." She said it as if she'd had everything planned out all along.

"Dina. Cute. I was thinking it would be something more like Shaquanda or Qualeequa. You know how you people like to be fancy with names." He laughed.

Secret didn't laugh. Was this white man throwing a dig at her race? The ride was getting bumpy, not that it was smooth to begin with. Secret was ready to get out of the car. "I'd like to hold my baby, sir." Secret wriggled her wrists. "Can you remove these please?"

"Oh, absolutely. I'm getting to that." He looked down at the baby. "I can see how desperately you want to hold your little one." He nodded, still staring at the baby. "I know all about desperation. About wanting something, someone. Being just that close to them." He held his index fingertip and thumb just centimeters from each other. "You almost have them." He squinted his eyes as if the thing was so minute he could hardly see it. "And then bam!" He clapped his hands together. The baby jumped, but didn't cry out of her sleep. "They are no longer in your reach." He looked at Secret.

Once again, Secret just listened.

"Your baby girl is right there. She's right within your reach. You can see her, but you can't get to her." He shook his head. "Awful feeling, isn't it?"

Secret felt like she was riding around tied up in the back seat of a killer's car. She was ready to escape. "All I want is my baby."

"I understand that." He looked at her and sternly said, "And all I want is Lucky."

Chapter 5

Just hearing his name sent a heated wave through Secret's body. She didn't give a shit about Lucky, no more than he gave a shit about her the day he watched the police haul her eight-month-pregnant self to jail. "Look, Officer—"

"It's Detective, Detective Davis," Flint's finest corrected Secret.

"Detective Davis," Secret continued. "I haven't seen or heard from Lucky since I got arrested and brought to jail. I'm still in jail as you can see." She yanked at the handcuffs. "So you have a better chance of getting Lucky than I do."

"I hear what you're saying. Sure I can go find him on the streets, shoot the breeze with him, drink a forty ounce of Colt 45, maybe play a little one on one, but that's not where I want to meet up with him." Detective Davis leaned down to Secret and seethed. "I want him exactly where he should be and where you shouldn't be: in jail." He rose up and returned to his normal voice. "You know damn well those drugs the officers found in the back of your car that day belonged to that lowlife son of a bitch. Why you insisted on taking the fall for him, I'll never know. And you don't have to tell me either. After all, the only person you really owe an explanation to is that little girl right there."

Both Detective Davis and Secret were staring at the sleeping baby.

"Damn shame," Detective Davis said, shaking his head. "I see women day in and day out putting men before their own children."

"I would never do that," Secret said in her defense.

"You've been doing it for the past month," he spat. He looked at Secret with disgust. "You'd rather your baby be born in a nasty, roach-and-rodent-infested prison than to see your little boyfriend carted off to jail."

"Dina wasn't born in no jail." The name now seemed to fit the little girl. It sounded fitting, like Secret had planned on naming her that all along.

"Might as well have been. After all, jail might have been better than what's in store for her."

The detective's last comment had Secret's interest piqued. What did he know about where her baby was going to end up? "What do you mean?"

"You know exactly what I mean. You're from the streets. You know what goes on out there. You know what happens to young girls who do have a mother to help guide them through life, so you can imagine what will happen to one who doesn't."

That detective might as well have taken out his gun that was in his holster around his waist and shot her in the heart. That's what his words had done anyhow: pierced Secret right in the largest muscle in her body. Secret began to conceive all the worst-case scenarios that could occur in little Dina's life. Rape, molestation, drugs, stripping, abuse, and so much more. What had she been thinking by keeping her baby in the first place? Abortion would have been a quick and easy death versus a long-suffering one out here in this coldblooded world.

But Secret never imagined in a million years this chapter would be a part of her life's book. She was supposed to be a freshman at The Ohio State University living the life of a typical college kid. She should have been cramming for tests during the week and going to parties on the weekend. Maybe even pledging a sorority. But this right here, being handcuffed to a bed after having delivered a baby was not supposed to be part of the plan, ever.

"Makes you sick just thinking about it, doesn't it," Detective Davis said.

He was right; it made Secret sick to her stomach as she felt fluids come up out of her throat. Before she had enough time to ask the detective to hand her the trashcan or the tray hospitals give patients just in case they get sick, her mouth was full of vomit. She couldn't hold the burning liquid in her mouth any longer as she spit it out all over herself.

The detective just stared at her unfazed. Surely he'd seen worse than throw up in his line of work.

"Can you get me something to clean up with, get the nurse or something?" Secret asked.

"Oh, yeah, sure," he said. He took a step toward the bathroom but then stopped in his tracks. He turned back to Secret. "Why don't I just let you do it when I uncuff you?"

Secret straightened up, excited by his words. She wanted her hands free. She knew she wouldn't be alto-gether free in the sense that she was legally a prisoner, but for now just having use of her arms would suffice. Then not only would she be able to clean her own self up, but she'd be able to hold her daughter, also.

The detective walked over to Secret's side and pulled out some keys, presuming the keys to the handcuffs. He fiddled around with them for a few seconds. Secret wanted to jump up off that bed and clobber him upside his head because he was taking so long.

"Ah, here it is," he finally exclaimed and not a moment too soon for Secret. He placed his index and thumb on a single key, started to move his hand toward Secret but then stopped.

Secret's eyes were glued to his hand the entire time. When it remained idle in the air for a few seconds, Secret finally looked up at the detective. He was staring down at the key.

"What? What's the matter?" Secret asked.

"I almost forgot. This is what you wanted, for me to free you. Right?"

Secret nodded. She didn't know what kind of game this cop was playing, but it was going to make her go crazy.

"But I don't have what I want, which is Lucky."

Secret exhaled and threw her body back against the bed. "I already told you, I don't know where Lucky is. I haven't heard from him since the day I got thrown in jail. And if you all wanted him so bad, why didn't you take him the day you took me?"

"We would have if your dumb ass would have just told the cops who that dope belonged to," the detective snapped.

Secret was shocked and confused by the way he was coming at her. She was not Lucky's keeper. As a matter of fact, she had been his kept woman.

"Like I said, I know where he's at. That's not the problem. What I want is Lucky thrown in jail for the rest of his life." The detective tried to bring it down a notch because he was starting to get real intense. "I need someone who knows what a creep he is and hates him just as much as I do to hand him over to me on a silver platter."

"I do hate Lucky for what he's done to me, for what he's done to her." She nodded to Dina. "My baby was almost born in a jail cell, a jail cell that I'm going back to; and God only knows where she's going. And there is nothing that I can do about it." Secret was furious. Tears of anger and helplessness rolled down her face.

"But there is something you can do about it. You can get out of here and be with your baby and take care of her. Can't you see that's what I've been in here trying to tell you?" He threw his hands up as if to suggest this was all a piece of cake.

Secret was exhausted. How many times did she have to tell him she had no connections to Lucky? "Look, Detective . . ." There was so much going on in Secret's mind that she'd forgotten his name just that quickly.

"Davis," he finished for her.

"Detective Davis, what exactly is it you think I can do to help you?"

His lips slowly formed into a sinister smile. "Play Lucky the same way you played him the first time; only this time finish the job and come out on top."

"Huh, what do you mean?" Secret was now even more confused than ever.

"Let me just break this down to you, Miss Miller. We've been watching Lucky for some months now. That means we've been watching you. We needed to get your story, figure out who you were. It didn't take long for us to realize that you were harmless. You were just a kid fresh out of high school who got herself knocked up, didn't know who the father was so you slept with the first guy who you could pin the crime on." Detective Davis raised an eyebrow, signaling Secret to correct him if he'd told a lie.

Secret remained silent, so the detective continued. "You couldn't even do that though. No, your heart was too good, so you told him the truth knowing that you were risking losing everything: the place Lucky was helping you live in by paying bills, buying furniture, the car, the shopping sprees, fancy purses, red bottoms, and whatever else you gold diggers like scooping up into your buckets."

Secret glared at the detective.

"Oh, not you." He put his hands up in defense. "I'm talking about the other gold diggers, the real ones. You know, like your friend Shawndiece."

"Shawndiece?" Secret was shocked to hear him bring up Shawndiece's name, but then she realized that if they'd been watching Lucky, they'd been watching her, and if they were watching her, surely they'd been watching Shawndiece, the only other person she spent time with outside of Lucky.

"Yeah, now that girl could teach you a thing or two about hustling a fella." He chuckled.

Secret knew he was telling the truth. Shawndiece was the one who had coached her on how to pull the wool over on Lucky's eyes. And the detective was right. Secret could have pulled it off if she was really built that way. Shawndiece, on the other hand, was born that way.

"Yeah, that best friend of yours is something else indeed." He shook his head then focused back on Secret. "But not you. You're a good girl." He paused before saying, "So for the life of me I can't figure out how you got caught up with the worst piece of shit walking the streets of Flint, Michigan."

Secret closed her eyes and swallowed hard. *Me either,* she said to herself in her mind. *Me either.*

"But I'm offering you a chance to walk out of here with your baby a free woman. All you have to do is everything I tell you to do."

Secret raised an eyebrow. "Which is what?"

Detective Davis rubbed his hands together as if he was about to sit down to a Thanksgiving dinner feast. "Now here comes the tricky part, but I think you can pull it off. This time it's not just about you."

"It was never just about me," Secret said. "Every choice I've made these last few months have all been about my baby."

"Clearly, with the predicament you're currently in, I could beg to differ, but I won't," Detective Davis said. "But anyhow, now it's a matter of life and death that your every decision, your every move, be about that baby." He pointed to Dina. "You living a good part of your life in jail, while your baby is subjected to death out here on the streets, I say this decision trumps all the others, wouldn't you?" The detective smiled. He looked to be enjoying having Secret between a rock and a hard place way too much.

Tired of the game of Ping-Pong that seemed to be never ending, Secret decided to cut to the chase. "Detective Davis, just tell me exactly what you want me to do."

The detective licked his lips as if he'd just demolished the entire meal, grinned at Secret, and said, "I thought you'd never ask."

Chapter 6

"So, if I agree to do everything you just said you wanted me to do," Secret confirmed after spending the last few minutes listening to Detective Davis run down the plan he had for how Secret could help him set up Lucky, "I can walk out of here with my baby a free woman?" Skepticism laced her voice.

"Well, not walk out of this hospital and into the free world," Detective Davis said.

Secret sucked her teeth and went limp. She knew this was too good to be true. Here Detective Davis wanted her to help set up Lucky, but he was the one setting her up, for disappointment.

"You have to be processed out of jail," Detective Davis said. "It shouldn't take long, just a day or two." He shrugged. "There's a little paperwork involved."

"But I don't have a day or two. Where will my baby go while I'm back in jail?"

Detective Davis thought for a minute. "Don't you have any friends and family she can stay with?"

"Detective, I don't even have friends or family I can stay with, let alone my daughter."

He sucked his teeth. "What about your mom?"

Secret shot him a look with her lips poked out and her head tilted sideways.

"Oh, yeah, that's right. Your mom is one hell of a bitch." He locked eyes with Secret. "Sorry."

Secret shrugged it off. Yolanda was a bitch. She damn sure couldn't argue against that.

"Hell, I hate to say it, because it doesn't help my case none, but the only place you do have is jail. At least you have a roof over your head, clothes, and three meals a day."

What little of Secret's spirit that was intact slowly diminished. Better off in jail. What a life.

"Do you mean to tell me that there is not anyone you know who could help you out?" the detective said to Secret.

She once again thought for a moment. Just then the hospital door cracked opened. "Hello, how's my patient doing?"

Both Secret and Detective Davis turned to face the door.

"Hey, Li'l Muffin, you all right?" said the nurse who had seemed to be on a personal basis with Secret from the moment she hit the maternity floor.

Secret looked at the nurse and a smile soon crept on her face. "I'm feeling much better now that you're here," Secret said to her.

"Good, because that's just what I'm trying to hear," the nurse said and stepped fully inside the room.

Secret looked up at Detective Davis. "Detective, I think this is going to work out after all."

He got excited at hearing those words. His eyes lit up.

Secret honestly had no idea just how badly and for how long Detective Davis wanted to shut Lucky and his drug operation down. In all Detective Davis's years, though, no one in Lucky's crew, or even former members of his crew, ever wanted to play informer. Secret hadn't been the first to go to jail when it was Lucky who should have been behind bars. But if Detective Davis had anything to do with it, she'd be the last. The fact that Secret was willing to help get him what he needed in order to take down Lucky had made his day. If all went as planned, it would not only make his day, but his career as well.

Detective Davis using Secret's newborn baby as a pawn to convince her to work with him was a new low for even himself. But he knew she would be his hole in one. For a minute there, though, he thought his efforts would be in vain since Secret didn't have any family or friends to help her and the baby out. Jail had definitely been starting to sound like a better predicament for her. But obviously someone who she felt could help had popped into her mind.

"So you know someone who can keep the baby for a couple days and then help you when you get out?" Detective Davis asked Secret.

"No," she replied. She looked at the nurse who was pulling over the blood pressure machine. She then looked back at the detective. "But there is somebody who knows me."

Secret looked back over at the nurse and the detective's eyes followed. After a few seconds the nurse realized she was being stared at.

"What?" the nurse asked, shrugging her shoulders. She looked totally oblivious to the conversation taking place in the room. Before anyone could answer, the nurse looked down at Secret's soiled gown from where she'd vomited. "Sweetie, what happened to your gown?" She immediately went over to the sink to grab some paper towels, wetting them first. She began wiping Secret down the front of her gown. Frustrated she looked up at Detective Davis. "Why is she still in these handcuffs? Have you ever thought she might need to go to the bathroom or anything? Besides, it's not like she has forever to spend with her newborn baby. Are you seriously going to deny her being able to hold her in the little bit of time she does have? Who is your superior? I have a phone call to make."

"No need to make any phone calls," Detective Davis said. "I was just about to remove those cuffs." He shook the keys in his hand. "Something tells me I can trust Miss Miller." He shot Secret a knowing look as he inserted the key into a cuff. "There you are," he said after removing both cuffs.

Secret rubbed her wrists but then turned her attention straight to her little one. She looked up at the nurse. "Can I hold her?"

"Sure, but don't you want to change out of that gown first?" The nurse frowned.

Secret looked so desperate, like she couldn't go one more second without holding her baby.

"Hold on," the nurse said, grabbing a towel and placing it down the front of Secret and over her shoulder. "There, that should work. Just lay her on the towel." The nurse lifted the baby out of her bassinette and into Secret's arms.

The damn broke and tears flooded from Secret's eyes.

The detective started to feel a little uneasy and awkward standing there in the middle of this mother-infant bonding session. He cleared his throat. "I'll just be right outside the door," he informed them and then exited the room, closing the door behind him.

"My baby," Secret cried, rubbing her hair. "She's so beautiful."

"Just like Mommy." The nurse smiled. She looked up at the blood pressure machine realizing she hadn't yet taken Secret's blood pressure. *It can wait,* she told herself as she admired mother and child. "She's such a little thing. No wonder I couldn't even tell you were pregnant that day at the gas station."

Secret looked up at the nurse, whose eyes were glued on the baby. She looked at her nametag, which read RAY. Secret didn't know a Ray from a gas station.

"Gas station," Secret mumbled under her breath. She thought for a moment and then it hit her. It came back to her where she knew the nurse from. "You're the Good Samaritan. The day I got into it with my mom and she put me out; you let me use your cellphone to call for help. And you even waited around until my ride came and picked me up."

The nurse smiled. "Yep, that's me. It was the middle of the night and you were dressed in a miniskirt, not to mention you looked like you'd just lost your best friend. I knew something wasn't right."

Secret was excited that she'd finally been able to figure out who the mystery woman was. She looked her up and down again and stared at her face for a few more seconds. "Raygiene, that's your real name, but you said your friends call you Ray." Secret nodded toward her badge. "Just like your nametag says. You even had on your hospital scrubs that night."

"Yes, I had finished up my shift at the hospital and stopped for gas. I'd told myself before leaving work that I had enough to get home and to just do it the next day on my way to work. Call it an instinct or an inner voice, but I went ahead and got it over with. Good thing, too. I was there for you when you needed me."

"Yes, you were," Secret said out loud and then thought, *and hopefully you'll be here for me again.*

Chapter 7

Ray had spent the last ten minutes giving Secret instructions on caring for her baby. "I know some people insist on beating the baby on its back to get them to burp, but a nice rub really will do the trick."

"I see," Secret said as she did as the nurse instructed after feeding her little one about an ounce or so of milk.

A tiny burp echoed through the room.

"I see," Secret reiterated with a chuckle. "Mommy's baby is a greedy gut," she cooed. "Yes, she is."

"Right now, because she's so little, sponge baths will be fine. It's not like she'll be going outside playing and needs a bubble bath or anything. Another nurse will be in to help you with all that. They'll show you how to wash her little scalp to prevent cradle cap and all that."

"You sound like you're the pro," Secret said. "How many kids do you have?"

"Who me? Oh please, I don't have any." She shooed her hand and looked away.

Secret didn't miss her attempt to downplay not having children. "But you want them don't you?" Secret began wiping Dina's mouth.

Ray smiled. "Yeah, Ivy and I have talked about kids. We've been together for about four years now. It would be nice to hear the pitter patter of feet running about."

"So what's stopping you guys?" She kissed Dina on the forehead.

"I work at the hospital and Ivy's band is just really starting to make a name for itself in the music industry. I want kids now, but Ivy doesn't think the time is right just now. She wants to see how this music thing pans out, and I can't—"

"She?" Secret snapped her head up, now giving Ray her full attention. Two seconds after she'd said the word "she," Secret realized how rude that might have come out. Secret had been too busy paying attention to Dina to realize Ivy was a female name, so that Ray had been talking about a girl, and not a guy, this entire time.

"Yeah, Ivy. She's my life partner."

Secret looked down at Dina. "I kind of understand where your girl is coming from a little bit. When I found out I was pregnant with Dina I had so many ambitions and aspirations. I felt guilty that for a minute there I wasn't even going to have her. How could I take care of a baby while living out the dream I'd worked so hard for, which was going away to college?"

"Gosh, you really do sound like Ivy." She began to mock her. "'How can you finish medical school to become a doctor and me win a Grammy if we're changing diapers?'" She rolled her eyes playfully. "But look at you. You decided to have your baby anyway. And I'm sure going to school and taking care of a baby is not easy, but—"

Gloom covered Secret's face. "I ended up not going to college."

"Oh, I'm sorry."

"It wasn't because I was pregnant. I had been banking on this full scholarship to The Ohio State University. I mean, I had worked my butt off, sacrificed enjoying everything most high school students enjoyed in their high school years. I was always studying and doing extra-credit work so that I could earn a full ride to college."

"What happened?" Ray asked.

Secret shrugged and shook her head. "I don't know. You tell me." Secret stared off for a moment thinking about what could have been, how her life would have been completely different had she gotten that college scholarship. For one, she wouldn't have had Dina. The only reason she changed her mind from getting an abortion was because she hadn't gotten the scholarship. The main reason she'd wanted the abortion was because she wouldn't have been able to take care of a baby and go away to college. She'd never had a job during high school. She didn't have time to work and focus on her grades like she needed to. So she didn't have any money saved up to even pay for a textbook.

Asking her mother for any type of assistance when it came to college was out of the question. If Secret didn't know any better, her mother was a coconspirator right along with Satan to see her fail. Her mother refused to help her in any way, shape, or form when she'd learned of Secret's pregnancy. So Secret found herself alone and on the streets. It was Lucky and Shawndiece who had conspired to see Secret make it in life.

Ultimately Lucky had turned on her though and Shawndiece was MIA. Now here stood Ray, who had sort of kinda conspired in a way to help Secret out. After all, if she hadn't been there that night at the gas station for Secret, no telling what could have happened to her.

"Well, it's never too late to go back to school," Ray tried to encourage Secret.

"But way too soon to go back to jail," Secret said sadly.

That was inevitable. There was nothing Ray could say or do to take that burden from Secret.

"If you don't mind my asking, what are you locked up for anyway?"

Secret sighed and proceeded to tell Ray the short version of what happened that day in the car when she and Lucky were pulled over by the police while she was driving her car.

"Ma'am, I'm Officer Hawkins with the K-9 unit. Booser here is a dog trained to sniff out drugs. We have reason to believe drugs might be in that bag. Do we have your permission to check out the content?"

Secret felt cornered as both officers glared at her. "Ye . . . yes . . ." Secret started.

The officer with the K-9 unzipped the bag while the other kept Lucky detained up against the car. The dog started barking wildly.

"Good boy." The officer pet his dog, took something out of his pocket, and fed it to the dog. The dog lost interest in the duffle bag and began devouring the snack. "Look what we have here." He held up a plastic bag full of white stuff to his partner.

"It ain't mine." Those were the words Lucky said and would be forever embedded in Secret's mind.

"You're not going to sit here and tell us that all those drugs belong to your pregnant girlfriend are you? Because unless you tell us the drugs are yours, well . . ." The officer shrugged. "The car is in her name. The bag was in her car. As far as we're concerned, the drugs are hers then. So either you man up or we handcuff your girlfriend and haul her and your unborn baby off to jail."

"They ain't mine," was all Lucky said as he then watched the police officer drag a shocked Secret over to his car and place her in the back seat.

"Li'l Muffin, I don't even know what to say," Ray said after hearing Secret's story.

Reliving that moment brought tears to Secret's eyes. "I couldn't believe he let them handcuff me and take me to jail while I was eight months pregnant." Secret shook her head. "For the past month I have been lying in that jail cell thinking every night that this was the night his conscience would get to him, not let him sleep. Then every morning I'd wait for the guard to come do like they do in movies." Secret deepened her voice as if trying to sound like a man. "'Miller, you're out of here.'" She sighed. "But that never happened."

"I don't understand why you just don't tell them the truth yourself," Ray said. "Why are you waiting on some knight in shining armor to come rescue you? Rescue yourself."

Secret nodded. "I know; that's pretty much what Detective Davis out there said. Said I can be a free woman if I help myself."

Ray got excited for Secret. "Then it's a no-brainer. Tell them the dope was really his and testify against him in court."

"Well, it's not that simple. They actually want me to help set him up. Kind of go undercover like I want to get with him again, play on his team, you know. In short, they want me to get information that could put him away and feed it to the police."

"How?" Ray looked confused.

"They want me to act like everything is all good with us again, get him to trust me and then turn on him. They'll drop all charges against me and I won't ever have to worry about jail again." Secret looked down at Dina and kissed her on the head. "Then I can spend all the time I want with this little one right here."

"I don't know." Ray shook her head in doubt. "That sounds kind of dangerous. I mean, do you really want your daughter around that situation? You know this guy better than me, but is he violent or anything? What if he suspects you of setting him up? I've heard guys in drug rings are ruthless."

Secret chuckled. "It's not like that with him. He never laid a hand on me, at least not in a way I never wanted him to." Secret gazed off for a moment as if thinking about the good times with Lucky. "And the cops are trying to say he's the big man on campus in the dope game, but I swear I never saw any proof of that. I mean, I knew he probably did a little something something illegal, but nothing on the grand scale that the cops are trying to say."

Ray swallowed before she spoke. "Look, don't take this the wrong way, but from the way it sounds to me, you're still protecting him somewhat. Girl, you should be pissed! Who gives a damn whether he is what the police think he is? Turn his ass over to them on a silver platter and keep it moving with you and your baby girl. Shoot, wouldn't have to ask me twice. I'd be like where is the paperwork so I can sign on the dotted line."

"I would, I mean I want to," Secret stressed.

"Then what's stopping you?"

Secret paused for a moment. Was this the door she'd been trying to push open? The door of opportunity? This entire conversation with Ray had been Secret knocking, was Ray now opening it? And should Secret walk through it?

"Well," Secret started, "Detective Davis said I could be out of jail as early as tomorrow."

Ray gave her an "I told you so" look. She clapped her hands together. "See, so what are you waiting for? Let's get that detective in here and handle this so that you and your little girl can go home." Ray headed toward the door.

"Wait, hold up." Secret stopped her. "That's the problem. I can't go home." Secret's voice became very solemn. "I don't have one." Secret was almost certain the apartment she'd been living in prior to going to jail was no more. At the time she landed the apartment, she'd been living out of a hotel that Lucky had put her up in. Considered homeless and pregnant, she ended up receiving low- or no-income emergency housing. The police had probably ransacked her place and reported her to the landlord who in turn had probably reported her to the housing authority.

Ray's excitement vanished just like that. Her hand stopped mid-reach for the door. "But where were you staying before you went to jail?"

"It was a place the government subsidized. I'm sure the police have confiscated everything I had in there since I'm this big drug lord." Secret used her fingers as quotation marks and rolled her eyes. "I don't even know if the landlord has evicted me. I'm just not sure whether it's safe to take the baby there, or if there is still even a 'there' to go to."

"Damn," Ray said under her breath. She thought for a moment and then snapped her finger. "I got it! You can come stay with me, at least until we can figure everything out with your housing."

If Secret could have, she would have jumped out of that bed and done the Holy Ghost dance she'd witnessed members of her grandmother's church doing when she was a little girl. It used to scare her to death. She thought those people were possessed the way their heads used to bob up and down with their arms flailing wildly.

"Are you serious? Are you sure?" Secret didn't want to appear too excited and come across as if she'd been waiting for Ray to say that all along, even though that's exactly what she'd been waiting for.

"Sure." She looked down at Dina. "Like I said, I'd love the sound of a little one in the house."

At first that put a smile on Secret's face, but then it suddenly turned to a frown. "But what about Ivy?"

Ray shooed her hand. "Ivy is on tour with her band. She'll be gone for the next two weeks."

"But what if it takes longer than two weeks to look into my place, get on my feet, and get situated?"

"Doesn't today have enough worries of its own? We'll drive ourselves crazy if we concern ourselves with two weeks from now, don't you think?"

If it was only Secret fending for herself, she would have agreed with Ray. But she had another life she was in charge of. She didn't want to find herself thrown out on the streets, homeless with a baby. If that was the case, perhaps Dina would be better off going to a foster family or something.

Seeing the doubt and worry in Secret's eyes, Ray walked over and put her hand on Secret's shoulder. "Knowing your story and the fact that I'm in a position to help you but didn't, I wouldn't be able to sleep at night."

Secret thought Ray could teach Lucky a thing or two about having a conscience.

"Please, let me help you. At least let me get in touch with someone who can. Your mother, best friend, father, anybody."

"Negative," Secret said, shaking her head. "My mother is the one who kicked me out onto the streets in the first place, after trying to beat my baby out of me."

Ray gasped.

"My father, he's either dead, somewhere with a needle in his arm shooting up drugs, or he's dead somewhere with a needle in his arm. Or he's at his home away from home: jail. My best friend, she came to visit me when I first got locked up but I haven't heard from her since. I've been so worried about having this baby in jail that I haven't had time to worry where she is at. But knowing Shawndiece, she's okay. If anybody is a survivor, that chick is." Secret let out a soft laugh. "She's probably over in Paris right now with some guy spending all his money." Secret's eyes filled with sadness. For the first time ever it hit her that she had nobody, not a single soul. It was just her and Dina.

"Well, you have me," Ray said almost as if she'd heard Secret's thoughts out loud.

Secret looked up at Ray and smiled with teary eyes. She placed her hand on top of Ray's that rested on her shoulder. "Thank you," Secret lipped, trying to keep from breaking down into her ugly cry.

For the past month she'd been living a nightmare and now it felt like a dream was coming true.

Chapter 8

"Whoa, this is a really nice place you and Ivy have." Secret set down Dina's car seat that held the sleeping baby.

"Thank you," Ray said, closing the door behind the three of them.

Secret stood in the middle of the foyer with hardwood floors and did a quick spin.

"Girl, why you acting like Belle in the movie *Beauty and the Beast?*" Ray laughed.

"Because this place is like a castle. Dang."

Ray nodded. "Yeah, Ivy and I like to think of it as our little palace."

Secret took a step into the opening that was the entrance to the large great room. "I used to live in Farmington with my grandma when I was little. She had a really nice home, but I don't remember them being this big."

Ray looked around and admired her own dwelling. "Yeah, we had this built from the ground up."

"Well, when I grow up, I want to be just like you."

Ray smiled at the compliment. She then clasped her hands together. "So, let me show you yours and Lady Di's quarters," Ray joked with a bow.

"Hold up," Secret said as she walked over to the fireplace. On the mantel there were pictures of Ray hugging a girl. She actually looked a couple years younger than Ray. "Is this Ivy?"

Ray looked over at the picture Secret was pointing to. Her eyes saddened as if she missed her. "Yep, that's her."

"You two must be made for each other. You even look alike," Secret said.

"Yeah, I get that a lot." Ray put her head down. "Well, come on. Let me show you two to your room."

The two women scooped up Dina as well as the supplies the hospital had sent home for the newborn. Being a worker at the hospital, Ray hooked Secret up with a lot of extra formula, diapers, wipes, and other odds and ends. All Secret's belongings from jail fit in a single clear plastic bag.

"I have to work two graveyard shifts in a row, but the first chance I get I'll take you into the city to see what's going on with your welfare, housing, and whatnot."

As they headed up a winding staircase, Ray stopped, turned around, and faced Secret. "Did they sign you up for that program where you can get free milk for the baby and stuff?"

"Yes." Secret nodded.

"Cool." Ray turned around and continued up the steps. Once they arrived at the top, they found themselves in a nice cozy loft that had a bay window overlooking the huge backyard.

"This is too cute." Secret walked over to the window and sat on the built-in twin-sized bed. She bounced on it a little bit. "Much better than both the jail cot and the hospital bed put together." She laughed. "This will work just fine."

"I'm sure it would," Ray said, "but that is not where you'll be sleeping. I mean, you can come out here and lounge and whatnot if you want to." She pointed to a rocking chair that sat across from the bed. "I love getting up in the middle of the night sometimes when I have a lot on my mind, grabbing a book, then sitting in that chair and escaping into another world thanks to one of my favorite authors."

"Escape from the real world, huh?" Secret asked. "I wish it was as easy for me as picking up a book."

"Oh, but it is, or even writing a book," Ray said excitedly. "I've been working on a book of my own for the past year."

"Oh, yeah?"

"Yeah, I mean, it's just a little something." She shrugged. "But I think it's pretty decent."

"In that case, you'll have to let me read it one day."

"It's a deal."

Ray led Secret to the room where she and the baby would be staying. It was a huge guest room, the size of the living room at Secret's old apartment. It had a king-sized bed, a chest, and dresser that matched the headboard of the bed. The color scheme was a light blue, yellow, and white. Secret felt like she had walked into the season of spring.

Ray helped Secret unpack her few items. She then gave her a tour of the house. With baby in arms wrapped in a blanket, Secret followed Ray through the four bedroom 4,500-square-foot home. Their final stop was the backyard, which was about a half an acre in itself.

"This is a lot of land," Secret said as she looked at the groves of trees, bushes, and flowerbeds. She looked around at the beautiful, sturdy, and expensive patio furniture. It was situated by a beautiful brick fire pit.

Ray went and sat down on the dark brown wicker couch. "We call this our outdoor living room."

Secret nodded in agreement with the nickname. "I can see why. It's so cozy."

Ray patted the seat next to her. "Sit."

Secret looked down at Dina. It was May and there was a chill in the air. "Maybe another time. I better get her in the house." Secret kissed Dina on the forehead and began rocking her. "Plus I need to wake her up to change her and feed her. All she does is sleep."

"That's a newborn for you. And speaking of eating, let me whip us something up while you go take care of her."

Ray led Secret back into the house, closing the door behind them. Secret went up to her room while Ray shuffled around in the kitchen, putting together a meal for them. Fifteen minutes later Secret returned to the kitchen with Dina in her baby seat. She fixed her a bottle and sat down at the table to feed her while Ray put the finishing touches on her pasta Alfredo dish.

"Looks good," Secret said when Ray placed a plate in front of her. "Thank you so much."

"You're welcome, Li'l Muffin," Ray said as she joined Secret at the table with a plate of her own.

The two began to eat, in silence at first before Ray offered Secret something to drink. "I've got tea, punch, or soda pop."

"Punch is fine," Secret said.

A few seconds later Ray returned to the table with a can of soda for herself and a glass of punch for Secret.

"Thank you," Secret said. She took a sip of her drink and then looked at Ray, who was steadily eating her food.

Sensing Secret staring at her she looked up and with a mouthful of food and said, "What's wrong? You don't like your food?" She swallowed before completely finishing chewing her food.

"The food is great," Secret assured her. She then looked down at her food and played around in it with her fork a little bit.

Ray took one more bite of her food then pushed her plate aside. "Look, if we're going to be roomies, then we have to be able to tell one another what's on our minds. When you let things build up, that's a sure guarantee for—"

Secret cut her off. "It's nothing bad, nothing like that at all."

"Good or bad, speak." Ray waited for Secret to gather her thoughts.

"I guess I'm just a little overwhelmed is all. All of this just seems too good to be true. Three days ago I was in a jail cell going into labor. It was the scariest time of my life. Then I was in the hospital giving birth trying to hold my baby with handcuffs on. Now I'm here." She raised her arms and let them drop. "It's surreal." She looked down at her baby daughter. "Three days ago I had no idea where my baby was going to end up when I got carted back off to jail, but now we're both safe and sound, and together."

Secret was still in awe of how all the pieces of the puzzle just began to fall into place. Both she and the baby were allowed to stay in the hospital for three days. Secret opted to return to jail the next day after giving birth in order to get started on her release papers. After signing a deal with the devil, Detective Davis, to be a State's witness against Lucky—that was, after she helped them set him up—she was released from jail the same day Dina was being discharged from the hospital.

Ray had promised to keep a watchful eye on the little one for Secret. That was the only way Secret had been able to rest for those days she was apart from Dina.

Ray had given Secret her phone number to call her collect to get updates on the baby. This afternoon when Secret was released from jail, Detective Davis took her right to the hospital, giving her instructions on what she needed to do for him along the way.

"I know you're a new mother and you have to spend time with your baby, heal, and all that. So I'll give you a week or two to get situated. After that, you're going to have a chance run in with ol' Lucky boy." Detective

Davis shook his head. "What I wouldn't give to be a fly on the wall when he sees you're out of jail." He laughed.

"Won't you be watching me?" Secret asked.

"No. He sees me and he'll know it's a setup. I've made it clear, face to face, to that punk-ass lowlife how I won't rest until I personally throw him into prison and bury the key beneath hell."

Fear set in on Secret. "So, I'm on my own."

"For the most part. I have a couple other boys on it. Well, should I say, a boy and a girl. But don't you worry about that. Besides, he'll never hurt you."

Secret turned and looked out of the window while whispering to herself, "He already has."

Lucky had been the only person to take Secret in when she'd been down and out. And now here was Ray. She was grateful, but she only prayed things ended better with Ray than they had with Lucky.

"Safe and sound together is where mother and baby belong," Ray told her.

"But if it hadn't been for you, God only knows."

"I'm just glad I could help."

"But why?"

Ray was a little stumped. "Why I'm glad or why I helped you?"

"Why you helped me. I'm practically a stranger and you let me into your home, your beautiful home. You know the only reason they let me out is because I have to set Lucky up. I have to be a rat. Pretend to be something I'm not, and yet you still trust me here. How do you know I'm not setting you up? That when you come home from work one day your place won't be cleaned out?" Secret shook her head. "I just don't know if I could trust anybody like that."

Clearly Secret was now going to be a victim of trust issues, thanks to Lucky. But perhaps this was what karma looked like. After all, when she first got with Lucky it was to play him. Even though she opened up to him and shared the truth, she was still the one who got played in the end.

"How old are you? What, about twenty, twenty-one?" Ray asked Secret.

"Eighteen," Secret replied. "I'll be nineteen in a few weeks."

"Take it from someone who will be thirty before they know it. Trust is an issue you're always going to have to deal with in life. You can't walk around being a prisoner of it. If you did, just think about all the relationships you could miss out on. Hell, you could have been setting me up that night at the gas station for all I knew, but I still chose to help you, and now look what that has led to."

Secret nodded. Ray had a point.

"Have I been burned before?" Ray asked. "Sure, and back in my day when I was young, dumb, and just didn't give a fuck, I burned some people too, ruining relationships that I regret every single day. But we can't live in the past; if we do we can't enjoy the present and won't be able to thrive toward a future. I'm choosing to go with my gut, to go with my instincts."

"Oh, yeah?" Secret asked. "And what are your instincts telling you?"

"That you're going to be all right, and I'll be able to sleep better at night knowing that I had a hand in it and didn't watch you get thrown back into jail while Dina got dumped in the system somewhere. I would have never been able to live with myself or even think straight. It would have constantly been on my mind."

Secret smiled. "Well, thank you. I know that's not nearly enough to show my gratitude for what you have done for me, and I don't know how I'll ever repay you."

Ray smiled and leaned closer to Secret, placing her hand on top of hers. "Don't worry, Li'l Muffin. I'm sure we'll think of something."

Chapter 9

As promised, the first chance Ray got she took Secret downtown to get her state case situated. Secret was happy to find that her welfare benefits had not been interrupted and were still in effect. Due to the birth of the baby, her monthly check was even increased. Ray also took her to the office of the place she'd signed up for in the hospital that would help her out with milk and dairy products for her and the baby. They had to take some type of iron tests where their fingers were pricked.

"Thank you for spending your day off driving us around," Secret told Ray. "Detective Davis said he's going to see about getting my vehicle back."

"No problem," Ray said, "But first things first; let's go see about getting your apartment back."

Secret gave Ray the address to the place she was staying before she went to jail. Ten minutes later they were on the doorstep.

"Well, at least there is no huge orange eviction sticker on the door," Secret said as she dug in her purse for her keys. She fiddled around with them.

"Do you remember which one it is?" Ray asked her.

"It's only been a little over a month. Unless having a baby gives a woman amnesia, I better remember." She laughed, finding the key and unlocking the door. She slowly opened it not knowing what to expect. She looked around and everything seemed to be in the same condition as it was the last time she was there. No furniture was turned over.

The chair by the door was in place. The couch, the coffee table, and the television all in their same positions. The two-seater table set in the dining area off of the living room and before you get to the kitchen appeared fine. Papers weren't thrown all over the place. It looked as though it hadn't been touched.

"Does it look like the police have been here at all?" Ray said, looking around.

"Not from what I can tell," Secret said.

"That's probably because they knew better than to waste their time. They knew that dope wasn't yours, that you weren't no drug dealer."

Detective Davis had told Secret that he'd been watching Lucky and therefore had been watching her. A wave of anger dispatched within Secret's being. It had just hit her at that very moment that those cops knew she was innocent all along. They knew that duffle bag full of cocaine wasn't hers. They'd probably watched Lucky himself place it in the back of her car. His luck wasn't that bad to have just so happened to get pulled over riding dirty.

With Dina in her car seat in hand, Secret headed through the living room, to the small dining area and into the kitchen. She hated to admit it, but she probably would feel a little better if the police had turned over a table, pulled out a few drawers or something to back up their case that they believed she was a drug dealer.

The closer she got, the stronger the smell got that was assaulting her nose. "Uhgggg!" Secret moaned out just a couple seconds later after entering the kitchen.

Ray rushed into the kitchen. "What's wrong?"

"This." Secret pinched her nose and pointed to the garbage can that had maggots crawling around on food that had been scraped into the trash.

"Jesus!" Ray ran over and opened up the cabinet underneath the kitchen sink. She dug around until she found what she was looking for. She slipped the long rubber gloves onto her hands and then went back over to the trash can. "Open the door," she ordered Secret.

Secret went and opened the back door. Ray pulled the bag out of the can, tied it up and placed it in the back alleyway. Secret stood in the doorway watching.

"Thank you so much," Secret said as Ray came back into the house, removing the gloves. Secret shook off the creepiness she felt.

"Girl, in my line of work, I've seen maggots on people's bodies before."

"You know you just made me throw up in my mouth, right?" Secret fake gagged.

The two shared a laugh.

Ray put her hands on her hips and then looked around. "If li'l bit is going to stay here, this place needs to be cleaned from top to bottom and sanitized first. You can't subject a week-old baby to all these wandering germs. I'm going to have a friend of mine named Gene send her crew out. She owns her own cleaning company. They do excellent work. Ivy and I have them clean our house every few months."

"No wonder your home is so spotless. I wondered how you managed to keep it spic and span with all the hours you put in at the hospital and with Ivy on the road."

"Well, now you know my secret." Ray winked. "Do you want to grab anything? Clothes or something while you're here?"

"That's a good idea." Secret headed out of the kitchen and to the stairs. "Keep an eye on her for me, would you?" She pointed to Dina sitting in her seat and then went upstairs to go get some things. She paused the moment she hit her closet. Sitting right by the door was the overnight bag she'd packed for when she went into labor. Next to that was the Coach diaper bag Shawndiece had bought her filled with all the things the baby would need its first

few days in the hospital, including the beige outfit, fit for
a girl or a boy, to wear home.

Secret shook off the thoughts of how things should have
played out, opened her closet, and grabbed a suitcase. Ten
minutes later she made her way down the steps with her
overnight hospital bag, the diaper bag, and the suitcase.

"Gene said they can come out and take care of this
place next week," Ray said as she slipped her cell phone
into her pocket once Secret had come down the stairs.
She looked down at all the stuff Secret was toting. "So you
really don't have to bring a month's worth of stuff." She
laughed.

"I know, right." Secret laughed. "I figured it was better
to have more than enough than not enough at all. For
the last four days I've been at your house I've had to
keep rinsing out the same three pair of panties." Secret
had the pair of panties she'd actually had on while she
was arrested. She bought two pair off of another inmate
whose husband had purchased and sent her a pack.

"Uhhh, TMI. I don't need to know your drawers look
like that trash bag: all kinds of critters crawling around
in them"

They both shared another laugh.

"Humph, if only you knew," Secret said. Thank God
the hospital had given her a nice supply of heavy duty
pads to capture the bleeding she would be having. With
no money, the last thing she wanted to do was have to ask
Ray could she borrow some dang on sanitary napkins.
Fortunately she'd had a nice supply of her own under her
bathroom sink that she'd packed in her suitcase.

"You ready?" Ray asked Secret.

"Yep." She looked around the room. She couldn't wait
to return and start a new beginning. This time she'd be
sharing the place with her baby girl. Having to camp

out at somebody else's place wasn't exactly what Secret would have wanted for her and her child, but it beat any other options, which were slim to none. It made Secret feel good inside to know that she was at least capable of providing a roof over her child's head.

"Here, give me the baby bag and I'll carry the baby, too."

Secret handed Ray the baby bag. She opened the front door and Ray walked out with Dina and the diaper bag. Secret locked up and then followed Ray to the car with the suitcase and duffle bag. After putting the items in the trunk, she got in the passenger seat and as Ray pulled off she looked to her apartment and mumbled the famous last words, "I'll be back."

When Ray walked into the house it was after midnight. She hadn't been home in two days. One of the nurses called in sick and so she had told Secret she volunteered to take her shift as well. It wasn't unusual for doctors and nurses to have to camp out at the hospital on some occasions.

"Because I'm not married and don't have kids, I'm usually the one everyone looks to, to volunteer to fill in," Ray had told Secret over the phone the night she called her to tell her she wouldn't be home from the hospital.

Exhausted, Ray made her way into the kitchen to try to find something to eat before she turned in for the night. The house appeared to be dark except for the nightlight air fresheners plugged in throughout the house. Once she entered the kitchen, it was more so dim than dark. It had a tad more lighting than what the nightlights had produced.

"What the . . . ?" she said as a look of wonderment took over her facial expression.

"Surprise," Secret said in a whisper. The baby was upstairs sleeping, and although nine times out of ten she wouldn't have heard her voice, she still didn't want to take any chances.

"What is all of this?" Ray said as she walked over to the island that separated the kitchen area from the dining area. Laid out on the island was a smorgasbord of finger foods such as chicken tenders, meatballs, cold cut rolls, and a relish tray. There were cheese crackers and a fruit tray as well. Ray's eyes wandered to the bottle of Moscato in an ice bucket with a long-stem candle on each side that sat in the center of it all.

Secret followed Ray's eyes to the bottle of wine. "I hope you don't mind. I'm under age and couldn't buy alcohol on my own. I found it under the bar downstairs."

Ray just stood their speechless.

"Tah dah!" Secret spread her arms wide. "It's for you."

Ray put her hand over her heart and her eyes lit up. "What? Why?"

"Do you really have to ask?" Secret said. "Besides the fact that you work your butt off and you've let Dina and me stay here almost three weeks?" Although Secret's apartment had been cleaned last week, the cleaning crew spotted what they thought were mice droppings. This was reported to the landlord who had the place exterminated. Secret had just gotten the word today that the exterminator had returned to her apartment to do a check, and the coast was clear. She and Dina were safe to move back in.

"But, I wanted to help. I told you that already." Ray looked at the spread again. "You really didn't have to do all this. It's late. You need to rest when the baby is resting."

"Like you said, I figured out a way to thank you and this is it."

"Oh, and I do love it." Ray, with her arms spread open, walked over to Secret and hugged her. "Thank you, Li'l Muffin." She squeezed Secret in tightly. When she pulled back her arms were still around Secret. Secret was staring into her eyes smiling. Ray smiled back. Before she knew it, Secret was getting closer and closer until her lips pressed against Ray's.

Secret gave her a quick but soft peck. Ray stood there, not really returning the kiss, but not refusing it either. Before she could even reply one way or another, Secret's lips were pressed against hers again. This time it wasn't a quick peck. This time Secret allowed her lips to relax on Ray's then she slightly slid her tongue into her mouth.

For some reason Secret anticipated Ray rejecting her, maybe pushing her away, but surprisingly, Ray took in her tongue and began to suck on it. Secret had no idea what she was doing. Never in her life had she even fantasized about being with a woman. Even as she put together this setup for Ray tonight, her intentions were merely to thank Ray for looking out for her and Dina these past three weeks, not to make a move on her. Ray had never once given Secret the impression that she wanted to get with her or that she had a hidden agenda. It's just that tonight, with the candlelight, the atmosphere mixed with Secret's genuine feeling of gratitude, somehow these feelings for Ray surfaced in Secret's being.

With her arms over Secret's shoulders, Ray placed her hand on the nape of Secret's neck and pulled her into her even more. The women swirled their heads and tongues in sync so that their mouths would be in a perfect position for their tongues to make love. Secret's arms were positioned under Ray's arms with her hands rubbing her shoulder blades.

"Mmm," Ray moaned as Secret now sucked on her tongue. Ray allowed her hands to slowly glide their way from Secret's neck, to her back, to her buttocks. Ray moved her hands to Secret's hips then allowed them to grip Secret's ass cheeks. This made Secret moan. With a mind of their own, Ray's fingers walked toward where the good Lord had split Secret then down toward her secret garden. Suddenly Ray stopped. She pulled away with a twisted up face and then pushed Secret away.

Secret knew exactly what had caused this type of reaction from Ray and she couldn't help but bust out laughing.

"Girl," Ray said with a disgusted look on her face. "How you gon' try to get freaky with somebody wearing that big ol' mattress between your legs?" Ray said.

"I am so sorry," Secret said between laughs. She placed her hand over her mouth to try to silent it, but she couldn't help it. The look on Ray's face was priceless.

Eventually Ray allowed her face to fall into a smile. After watching Secret howl in laughter, it became contagious and she started laughing too.

Secret and Ray laughed hysterically, turning the once intimate moment to a comical one. It wasn't clear whether they were laughing off or away the entire kissing incident or the fact that Ray had tried to cop a feel of Secret's bootie only to be blocked by her big ol' maxi pad. It didn't even matter at this point. Comic relief was probably much needed in this situation. No telling where things could have gone had it been three weeks later and Secret's body was pretty much back to normal where she could do her usual things. A blooming friendship could have been jeopardized. Thank goodness they wouldn't have to find out. At least not tonight.

Chapter 10

"That's everything," Ray said as she carried the last of the grocery bags into Secret's apartment.

Secret was so glad to be back in the place she called home. It wasn't much, but it was hers. Even though she was still just a teenager, it made her feel all grown up. All of the furniture was the same old furniture she'd had before going to jail, but it just felt so brand new. Everything felt brand new. For once she wasn't thinking about Lucky, Detective Davis, or anything else. Just her and her baby.

"Thank you so much for stopping me at the store on the way to bringing me home," Secret told Ray.

"It was on the way. No problem," Ray said. "You gon' be all right here? You need anything else?"

"I think we're going to be good." Secret looked around her place, smiling. It was nothing even remotely close to Ray's place, but it was hers and it was home. Besides, once Dina got older where she could go to preschool, Secret planned on taking some college courses at the community college. No, it wasn't The Ohio State University and she would miss out on being a traditional college student living on the college campus, but right now she had to make the tallest and freshest glass of lemonade she could with the lemon life had given her.

"Well, I have to head into work. I'm working double shifts the next two days, which is rough considering Ivy will be back home in a couple days. I need to get the house ready for her and whatnot. She'll only be home for a few days before her band hits the road again. So I'll be pretty busy for the next week or so."

Secret listened to Ray go on and on. Once Ray stopped talking Secret said, "Why do I feel like you're breaking up with me?" She laughed, but inside that's how she felt. She felt as though Ray was running down why she wouldn't be able to communicate with Secret the next week or so. Out of sight out of mind. So after not talking for a week, the two would probably drift apart. Secret understood. Ray had just been doing her a favor. She never promised she'd be her best friend or even remain friends with her, and Secret was okay with that. Perhaps Ray had served her purpose in Secret's life. She hadn't promised her anything else.

"I'm not breaking up with you." Ray laughed. "Not that we were ever . . . you know."

"I know, I know," Secret said, waving her hand. "I didn't mean it like that. But anyway, I know you have a lot on your plate. You know where I live and I know your number. Speaking of numbers, I'm going to get my cell phone turned on as soon as I get a chance." Secret's cell phone had been given back to her when she was released from jail. It had been on her person when she got arrested. It was dead, of course, and when Ray had brought her to the apartment to check it out and grab a few of her things, she hadn't gotten the charger. She'd tried calling it to check messages from Ray's land line, but it wasn't in service.

"Well, when you get it on, be sure to give me the number."

"Most definitely," Secret said.

"No doubt," Ray replied.

"Yep." Now the two seemed to be trying to keep small talk going to avoid any awkward silence or to avoid having to say good-bye, one or the other.

Ray looked down at her watch. "Well, I guess I better go. I don't want to be late for work."

"No, we can't have that now can we?" Secret was looking down fiddling with her fingers.

Ray smiled. She looked over at Dina who was wide awake in her car seat on the couch. "I'm going to miss you," she said walking over to Dina.

"I'm going to miss you too." Secret looked up with a huge grin on her face, only to see Ray cooing at Dina. Secret's face flushed with embarrassment realizing Ray's sentiment hadn't been directed toward her. "Oh, I'm so sorry."

Ray had bent over and was rubbing the back of her fingers down Dina's chubby check while saying to Secret, "It's okay. I'm going to miss both you and Dina." She stood up straight and walked over to Secret, taking Secret's hands into hers. "Stay in touch, and I mean that."

Secret nodded. Ray released her hands and then went over and opened the door.

"Take care," Ray said.

"You too," Secret replied and then closed the door behind Ray. She stood there with her hands on her hips looking over at her baby. "Well, little one, it looks like it's just me and you." Secret walked over to the baby's car seat. She unsnapped the straps holding the baby in and lifted her out. "How's Mommy's Li'l Muffin?" A smile cracked on Secret's face when she realized Ray's little nickname had rubbed off on her. "Let's go get all these groceries put away, huh? Does that sound like a plan?" Secret rubbed her nose against her baby's, making the baby's eyes flicker open and closed. Secret laughed.

She went to pick up one of the grocery bags just as there was a knock on the door. Was Ray back already? Had she forgotten something?

Secret put the bag down and went to look out of the peephole. She sighed, her shoulders fell, and then she went and opened the door.

"Geesh, you didn't even give me time to get settled in, huh?" Secret rolled her eyes and then turned her back on her visitor.

"You've had three weeks to bond with the baby and all that good stuff," Detective Davis said, closing the door behind him. "Just think, if it hadn't been for me, you would have barely gotten three days with your baby." He reminded Secret of how striking a deal with him was more to her benefit than his.

"Yeah, yeah, yeah." Secret threw her hand over her shoulder as she went and sat down on the couch. She looked up to see the Detective just standing there. "Have a seat." She nodded to the chair by the door.

"Thank you." Detective Davis sat down and then got right down to business. "This weekend Lucky will be at some basketball tournament at a park. I hear he's got a lot of money on the line, so no doubt he'll be there. And you're just going to happen to show up there too."

Already Secret could feel her heart begin racing. Just the thought of seeing Lucky again gave her anxiety. She remained calm and listened.

"I'm not quite sure whether you should act like a bitch or play the naïve victim role. You're going to have to feel him out and see which would work best in your favor."

"How about I just be me?" Secret asked.

Detective Davis thought for a minute. He then shrugged. "Yeah, I guess that does make sense."

"You think?" Secret rolled her eyes in her head.

"Hmmm, I see jail has made you a little sassy."

"Pardon my rudeness, Detective, but you don't know me. How can you tell what a month of jail has done to me?"

"Remember." He winked. "I was watching you. Anyway, just be you. Try to forget that this is all a charade. Just go with the flow. Get him to trust you; then we'll go from there."

There was something about "we'll go from there" that didn't sit well with Secret. "What exactly do you mean by that?"

"Now, let's not get ahead of ourselves. I'll let you know what you need to know and when you need to know it." He paused for a moment. "So, you ready to do this?"

"It's not like I have a choice." Secret shrugged.

"I guess you are right about that." Detective Davis stood. "Well, that covers just about everything, for now anyway. Let me know if you have any questions. You have my number." Detective Davis had given Secret his business card the day he picked her up from jail. He turned to let himself out.

"As a matter of fact, Detective, I do have one question."

He paused and faced Secret.

"My apartment," Secret said. "It hadn't even been touched when I came back to it. From what I hear, a person suspected of being this big dope dealer usually gets their house turned upside down. Things considered to have been purchased with drug money are confiscated. None of that happened with me. You mind telling me why, Detective Davis?"

The detective just stood there, not even attempting to search for words. It was useless. Secret was a smart girl. How could she not have figured it out?

"The state never had any intentions of ever charging me, did they?" Secret asked. "That scenario would have never stood up in court. My first offense. You guys had been watching Lucky. You saw him bring that dope out of that house and place it in the trunk of my car. You probably have this evidence room like on television of pictures of him all over the walls. Pictures of him coming out the house with it, putting it . . ." Secret's words trailed off. She'd been a pawn in the police's game of chess with Lucky this entire time.

Never denying or confirming verbally, Detective Davis's silence gave Secret all the answers she needed as he exited her apartment. Secret wasn't a hateful person, but she couldn't help but feel anger and hatred toward Detective Davis.

How had she gotten herself into this mess? Although there were plenty of ways she could have gotten herself into it, there was only one way out. And she was determined to get out.

Besides, she couldn't turn back the hands of time, so how she'd gotten herself into this situation was no longer relevant. She had to figure out how she was going to get herself out of it . . . alive.

Chapter 11

Secret got off the bus about two blocks away from the park where the basketball tournament was taking place. Cars were parked along the streets within a half-mile radius from the park. As Secret strolled Dina along the sidewalk, she passed by cars parked in grass lots, partially blocking the driveway of residential areas and wherever else they could find a spot.

If all of these cars were any sign of how many people were in attendance at this outdoor basketball tournament, Secret couldn't imagine how she would find Lucky amid all these people. Perhaps she would get lucky and he would find her.

Once on the park grounds, looking around at all the people, Secret felt she'd have a better chance bumping into Lucky again at the free clinic, which was where she'd originally met him. She'd been there confirming her pregnancy and Lucky had claimed to be there with one of his boys. Secret didn't know whether to believe him. All she knew was that by the time she did have intercourse with him he was clean, because he hadn't given her anything.

Secret walked around and got as far as she could in an hour, fighting the crowd with Dina's stroller. The stroller was something Ray had purchased for her as a gift. The hospital had supplied the car seat/carrier through a program for mothers with low or no income.

Secret had fed Dina on the bus and the little one was sound asleep, but she didn't know how long that would last. Eventually Secret took a break at one of the vending trucks and purchased herself a hotdog. Finding a place to cop a squat was useless. It was way too crowded and weaving that stroller in and out of the crowd was a headache. Everyone was packed on the available bleachers like sardines. They were cheering, ranting, fussing, and cussing at the players. Secret didn't really want her baby all up in that anyway. Some folks looked to be so hot and bothered with their losing teams that a riot could very well break out. Secret was not about to get caught up in that. So she just stood next to the vending truck eating her hotdog, inhaling the scents of the various foods flowing from the vending trucks.

A fight had broken out on the court between two players. Sure people had bet money on these games, but the way these players were acting, one would have thought an NBA contract worth millions was on the line. All Secret could do was shake her head and ask herself what she was doing in the midst of this mess.

Halfway through her hotdog, Secret almost choked on it when her eyes landed on him. He was rooting, cheering, and pumping his fist while watching the game taking place on the court. The little bit of hotdog Secret had eaten almost came back up. She managed to tighten her throat and force it to stay down. She put her hand over her mouth as if that was reinforcement to keep it down.

Secret began to take in and let out quick deep breaths. She thought she would just about hyperventilate. Seeing him suddenly, like this, right here had caught her off guard. She hadn't been looking to spot him. She'd been looking to spot Lucky. And nothing could have prepared her for this moment of déjà vu.

Once again the same feeling that had come over her when she'd bumped into him outside of that Chinese restaurant had returned. It was him. It was the man she'd lost her virginity to. The stranger her father had set her up to have sex with for money. The man who had unknowingly fathered her baby. Now that he was right there in her view, she observed all of his features.

Secret unzipped the sun and bug shield attached to Dina's stroller. She peeked in at the still sleeping baby. She stared at her, then looked back up at him. The him whose name she didn't even know. She stared at him briefly and then looked back down at Dina. She exhaled. Dina looked nothing like him. She was a spitting image of Secret.

Thank you, Jesus, Secret said to herself before zipping the visor back up. She took a deep breath in and then exhaled. The last time she'd seen the man who had fathered her child it was when she'd gone looking for Lucky. Now that she was looking for Lucky again she'd seen him. Coincidence, or was it that just maybe this guy had some connection with Lucky? Secret got her answer when she looked up to see the guy high-fiving the person next to him. Secret allowed her eyes to wander to the owner of the hand and sure enough it was attached to Lucky. This time there was no forcing the content of Secret's stomach back down. She couldn't even make it back over to the trashcan before the vomit came up. She jumped back just in time for it to miss her shoes.

"Secret? Is that you? Are you okay?"

Secret couldn't immediately lift her head up to see who was speaking to her as she was still spitting the last of the vomit out of her mouth.

"Let me get you some water," she heard the same voice say.

Hunched over Secret could hear the person completing the transaction for the bottled water with the same vendor Secret had purchased the hotdog from, since she was still standing next to it.

"Here you go."

Secret saw a hand place a cold bottle of water to her lips. Secret took the water into her own hand and drank it. It was refreshing and just what she needed to not only settle her stomach, but to cool her off.

"Thank you," Secret said, finally able to look up and see who the Good Samaritan was in her life this time. "Katherine." There was no emotion one way or the other in the way Secret had said her half sister's name.

Once upon a time the two girls had been like Miss Celie and Nettie. As a little girl Secret would look forward to her father picking her up so that she could spend time with her siblings: Katherine and her two twin brothers. Unfortunately, when her sister and brother's mother found out their father Rolland was taking her kids to meet up with the child he'd had with another woman while married to her, she put an immediate stop to it. So Secret went years without having a relationship with her half siblings until several months ago when Secret ran into Katherine at a parking lot in a strip mall. It just happened to have been right after Secret had spotted her baby's biological father outside of the Chinese restaurant.

Reconnecting with her sister had been just what Secret needed at the time. She'd hoped the two could get close again, picking up where they'd left off as children. But the next time Secret would see her sister after that day was when she was driving off with Lucky in the passenger seat the day the police found the drugs in the car.

Secret was waiting in the back seat of the police car, still in disbelief she'd been arrested. Lucky was free to go, but was sitting on the ride he'd called to come pick him up. After about ten minutes both officers were still at the scene and Lucky still sat waiting for his ride. The officer with Secret in tow had called in the incident, requested a tow truck to tow her vehicle away, and had started filling out his report. The other officer was waiting for the tow truck to show up. The officer driving Secret put down the clipboard he'd been writing on the last few minutes and put his running car in drive. He rolled down the passenger-side window and then slowly rolled up beside his partner, who was waiting with his window down.

"The tow truck is about three minutes away. I'm going to go ahead and take her in." He nodded back toward a weeping Secret. Just then a royal blue Toyota crept up behind them and parked. Lucky shot up from off the curb and headed toward the vehicle.

"He's really leaving me," Secret said out loud, although it was just supposed to be a silent thought roaming through her head. Was this real? Was it really happening? Secret turned around as best she could to see where Lucky was going. She didn't have a full vision, but she saw him open the door of a car that was parked behind her. He got in and closed the door as if he didn't have a second thought about her. Secret turned back forward and tears just spilled from her eyes. As the car behind them slowly crept by in order to get back into traffic, Secret looked to her left. She'd wanted to lock eyes with Lucky. She wanted to look him dead in his eyes and try to read him. Was he this cold? Secret had no such luck as he was looking straight ahead with a stone face, like he couldn't bear to even look at Secret. Before the car could safely dip back into traffic though, Secret's eyes managed to lock on a sight she never expected to see: the driver. Katherine, aka Kat. Her sister. "Oh my God." Once again the thoughts in Secret's head had escaped through her mouth. Was this nightmare really happening? Had her man just practically left her for dead and driven off into the sunset with her sister? Was this some bad joke? If so, who was in on it? She needed answers.

With Katherine now standing in front of her, it looked as though Secret could finally get those answers she so desperately sought.

"Sister," Katherine said. She did have a tone behind her word. It was like she was asking Secret permission to be able to call her sister.

"Sister, huh?" Secret let out a sarcastic chuckle.

"Are you okay?" Katherine, who was usually the epitome of loud, hoodrat ghettoness, was very reserved.

"Am I okay? You drive off with my man, leaving your eight-months-pregnant sister in the back seat of a police car and now darn near two months later you ask am I okay?" Secret held her eyes wide open with her head tilted, waiting for Katherine to respond.

"I didn't know."

"You didn't know what? That Lucky was my man, that I was eight months pregnant, that I was your sister, what? Please tell me, Kat. Exactly what is it you didn't know?"

"I didn't know what was going on. I was so caught off guard. I didn't know the situation between you and Lucky, no more than you knew my situation with Lucky. We had just reconnected. We hadn't seen each other in years. How was I supposed to know?"

"Don't even try it, Katherine. You heard the way I talked about Lucky that day we hooked up again at the strip mall and then went to grab something to eat." Even though Lucky was no longer Secret's man, that past anger had resurfaced like it was today's news. Secret was saying all the things she would have said then.

"Yeah, I heard the way you talked about him, but it wasn't until that day you were arrested that I put two and two together and realized that Lucky had been the guy you were talking about. You never once said the name of the guy you were kicking it with, so how was I supposed to know that the man you claimed to be in love with was the same man who I had vowed to hate for the rest of my life and never say his name again?"

Secret opened her mouth to fire back at Katherine but then thought for a moment. Katherine might have had a point. She couldn't recall actually telling her Lucky's name, and surely if Katherine had mentioned his name an instant red flag would have gone up and Secret would have questioned it.

"I guess you're right," Secret admitted. But she wasn't letting her sister off the hook that easily. "But what about after you did put two and two together? You didn't come running to see about me. For all you knew I could have died in jail, both me and my baby."

Katherine cast her eyes downward. "I'm sorry, See-See," she said, calling Secret by the nickname she called her when they were little girls. "I had a warrant out for beating the ass of my so-called best friend. I found out she had been kicking it with Lucky for a while now."

Thank goodness Secret had already thrown up that hotdog. She'd probably have thrown it up anyway finding out that while Lucky had been with her, he'd been with a million other women at the same time. Perhaps she needed to go back to the free clinic for GP alone.

"So Lucky was seeing both you and your best friend while he was seeing me?" Secret didn't just want clarification. She was fishing.

"Secret, Lucky is a man whore. No telling who all he was seeing."

"So why did you even come pick him up that day if he was such a man whore and had been cheating with your best friend?"

Katherine opened her mouth but no words fell out. She thought for a moment and finally spoke. "I don't know, Secret. I've been fooling with Lucky for years. It's like he has this hold on me. He always said and did the right things, so I just kept going back to him." She shook her head. "I know, just stupid."

"So I take it you're with him now," Secret said.

"Oh hell no," Katherine was quick to say. "I'm here with my girl, Taneshia." Katherine let out a brief chuckle. "She's actually my best friend whose ass I had to beat. She just dropped the charges against me two days ago, so everything is good. We realized that our friendship wasn't worth losing over Lucky. Lucky is going to be Lucky. He is going to continue to play chicks and live the street life until the day he dies. The same way I had gotten caught up for years, so had Taneshia. I couldn't fault her for that. Besides, after what Lucky did to you . . ." Katherine paused and then continued. "If he can watch the woman pregnant with his own flesh and blood be carted off to jail for some dope he was holding, shitttttt, no telling what that nigga would do to me."

Secret was a little surprised to hear Katherine call Dina Lucky's flesh and blood. She was sure he would have told her the truth: that he wasn't the actual biological father. He was just claiming the baby for Secret's sake. Secret had shared with Lucky all the details of how her baby was conceived. Clearly he'd decided to keep that to himself.

"Speaking of the little one . . ." Katherine pointed to the stroller. "Is that the baby right there?"

Secret turned and smiled, then nodded proudly.

"Ooooh, I want to see auntie's baby." Katherine's attention immediately went to the stroller where she looked around for the opening. "How do you open this thing?" No sooner than she posed the question had she figured it out. She unzipped the hood of the stroller and peeked in at the baby.

Dina's eyes were open and she was looking around. The pink bow atop her head full of hair was twitching right along with her head.

"It's a girl. I have a niece," Katherine said. "And she's sooooooo beautiful." She looked up at Secret. "Girl, she looks just like you." She looked back down at the baby. "Thank God she doesn't look a thing like her daddy."

"You can say that again," Secret said under her breath.

Katherine made a fuss over Dina a little while longer before she zipped her back up. She stood up and looked at Secret. "I'm sorry, sis. I hope you will forgive me."

"There's really nothing to forgive you for. You didn't know the situation. I can't fault you for that."

"Then can I have a hug?"

"Of course," Secret said.

The two sisters went in for a hug.

"I was so glad to hear you got out," Katherine said as the sisters parted.

Secret looked a little puzzled. "How did you find out?"

"Girl, as soon as those charges got dropped against me and I cleared that situation up, I came straight to see about you. You my sister, girl. We blood. Even if I hadn't found out about Lucky and Taneshia, after what he did to you, he could forget about me running back to him ever again. I called him every dirty bastard in the book. I even got physical with him. That's when he told me he was fucking Taneshia, during our argument."

"Well, I'm sorry too." Secret just felt like she needed to apologize.

"For what? All you did was get mixed up with that loser."

"Yeah, but clearly he was your loser before he was mine."

Both women burst out laughing.

"Girl, I've been looking for yo' ass," some chick walked up and said to Katherine. She then looked to Secret and greeted her. "Hi."

"Hello," Secret replied, ending her laughter.

"Hey, Taneshia," Katherine said to the girl. "I just ran into my sister, Secret. The one I told you about."

"Oh yeah." Taneshia stuck her hand out. "Good to meet you."

"Good to meet you too," Secret replied, shaking her hand.

Taneshia looked to Katherine. "Girl, come on. I got these dudes watching our seats for us. You been gone forever. I didn't know what happened to you."

"I'm good," Katherine replied. "Just ran into my baby sis on my way coming back from the bathroom." Katherine looked to Secret. "We have to exchange numbers. I need to come see my niece and spoil her rotten."

"Sounds like a plan," Secret said.

The two sisters exchanged contact information, promising to stay in touch. Secret smiled as she watched Katherine walk away. It felt good to know that she wasn't alone, that she had someone who would have her back. Not only that, but this was a plus. Katherine said she'd been messing with Lucky for years. She could help her out in this little endeavor Detective Davis had Secret on. Share some inside information on Lucky. Speaking of such, Secret gasped, realizing that she'd gotten distracted from her purpose of being there: to connect with Lucky.

Secret quickly turned her attention back toward where she'd spotted the father of her child and Lucky. Neither man was in sight any longer.

"Damn it!" Secret said under her breath. She smacked the palm of her hand on her forehead. What the hell was she going to tell Detective Davis?

Chapter 12

"He was right there. What the fuck?" Detective Davis snapped. "Now we have to set something else up again."

"Do you mind keeping it down some? My daughter is upstairs sleeping," Secret told him.

Detective Davis stood pacing Secret's living room floor. "Now we have to figure out another time for you to just so happen to bump into him without it being obvious."

"Oh, and me showing up at a basketball tournament with a four-week-old baby wasn't obvious?" Secret threw her hand up. "Whatever. I ought to say the hell with this whole operation now," Secret said. "You've got nothing on me. With the right lawyer, I can get out of this mess without having to jump through all these hoops. After all, you're the smart one. You went to college to learn how to catch bad guys, right? What do you need me for?" Secret sucked her teeth. "Like I said, I could just wipe my hands of all this and—"

"I'm sure you could," Detective Davis replied, stopping his pacing and looking at Secret. "But in the meantime, while you're in jail fighting your case, there's always the issue of baby Dina." He nodded toward the stairs.

How could Secret have forgotten that quickly? Dina was the entire reason she'd agreed with this whole deal anyway. Going back to jail and leaving Dina out here to fend for herself would defeat her entire purpose. Secret had no other option but to see this thing through.

"So, if that will be all, I need to get out of here," Detective Davis said, walking over to the door. "There's a lot of bad guys out there I need to be catching, since that's what I went to college for." He shot Secret a smug look. "You have a good day." He went to leave and then turned back around. "Oh, yeah, I almost forgot." He dug into his pockets and pulled out a folded piece of paper. He extended it to Secret.

"What's this?" she asked, walking over and taking it out of his hand.

Detective Davis explained as she unfolded the paper. "It's to get your car out of police custody."

Secret wasn't expecting this. She had forgotten all about him telling her he was going to see about getting her car back. She figured with it being state property, it would be easier said than done. But Detective Davis must have been pretty high up there in rank. He was pulling all kinds of strings. "Thank you." Secret was relieved she wouldn't have to hitch a ride on the bus on a regular. Her last bus ride would be the one going to pick up her car. "Thanks for doing this for me." She relaxed her tone a little bit. Even though it was for his own selfish reasons, Detective Davis really was trying to look out for her.

"No, thank you." Detective Davis paused. "This will more than likely be our last time talking in person. We don't know whether Lucky saw you at the park, if he knows you're out. I can't take the chance of him coming around. I'll call you with details on where to go from here. I imagine here soon Lucky will start coming around again. And you never know; he just might be suspicious of you, watching you. All of this would be for naught if he was to find you out."

Secret nodded her understanding. There was a little hint of fear in her eyes. Even though Detective Davis was an asshole, she liked the idea of feeling as though he had her back. But now he would be way back.

"Don't worry," he said, noticing the look on Secret's face. "There are two other sets of eyes keeping a watch on things. It's all going to work out just fine, Secret. It's all going to be just fine. Just do what I tell you to do and trust me." On that note, Detective Davis exited Secret's apartment.

The sound of Dina waking up out of her sleep with a whine through the baby monitor prevented Secret from standing there wallowing in the miserable hand life had dealt her. She darted up the steps to go see about Dina, none the wiser that sooner rather than later, someone would be coming to see about her too.

"So I hear I got me a grandbaby?"

Those were the words Secret heard when she opened her front door.

"Ma." Secret was stunned. The last person she ever expected to see at her door was Yolanda, her estranged mother. So many things were going through Secret's mind. Was Yolanda friend or foe? Because the last time she'd been in her mother's presence, Yolanda's hands were around Secret's throat. Secondly, how did she even know where Secret lived?

"Shawndiece had given me your address back when you first moved here," Yolanda said after reading the surprised look on Secret's face. "I was being too bullheaded to reach out to you then."

"So why now? And why here? You could have reached out to me while I was sleeping on a one-inch mattress in jail."

Yolanda sucked in her lips and bit down on them. Secret wasn't sure if her mother was biting her tongue to keep from clocking Secret, or if she was feeling regretful.

"Look, the past is the past and ain't shit I can do about it. I come in peace. Heard you were out. Wanted to come see my grandbaby. Figured that even if you won't let me be a mother to you, you'll let me be her grandmother." She waited for Secret to reply.

"How did you find out I was out of jail?" Secret folded her arms and tapped her foot as she waited.

"Sissy told me she thought she saw you leaving the welfare building when she was coming out of her caseworker's office." Sissy was Yolanda's next-door neighbor.

Secret nodded. "Well, as you can see, yep, I'm out."

"She also said you had a baby with you," Yolanda said. "I take it who she saw was my grandbaby."

Secret nodded. There was silence. Neither woman was sure what to say or do next. Although she honestly didn't want Yolanda stepping a foot inside her house, neither did Secret want to stand there with the door open all day. After all, this was Secret's mother, the woman who had given birth to her. It just wasn't in Secret to slam the door in the face of the woman whose eyes she had.

"Do you want to come in and see her?" Secret offered. "She's right here." Secret opened the door so that the bouncer seat Dina was lying in was in full view.

"Can I?" Yolanda lifted her foot to step inside, but didn't allow it to land until Secret had given her the nod of approval. She headed straight over to Dina after Secret stepped to the side.

"Oh, my goodness. Looky here," Yolanda said, bending over and reaching her hand out to Dina. "A girl, and she looks exactly like you did when you were a baby. I kid you not." She looked up at Secret, smiled, then turned her attention back to Dina. "Look at gammaw's baby looking like her mommy," Yolanda cooed.

Secret didn't even realize she was standing there smiling. It really touched her to see Yolanda in such good spirits. The Yolanda who raised her was a cussing, fussing hell raiser to the tenth power. What in the world had happened to her in the past nine months or so since she'd last seen her?

"Can I hold her?" Yolanda asked.

This shocked Secret even more. Yolanda was anything but a baby person. One time one of their neighbors had an emergency with one child and needed someone to watch her eleven-month-old toddler. Secret had listened from her bedroom at Yolanda sending that woman away to ask someone else to help her out. "Sorry, I just don't do other people's kids, and especially babies," she'd told the woman.

Looked like that was no longer the case.

Although skeptical, in this case the child Yolanda wanted to hold was her own flesh and blood. Always the one to see the glass half full, Secret gave in. "Sure, you can," Secret told her. She closed the door. "Let me just help you get her out." Secret walked toward Dina and Yolanda.

"Child, I know how to take a baby out of a bouncy thingy," Yolanda snapped. "I mean, it's almost been twenty years since I've had to take care of a kid, but I think it's kind of like riding a bike, right?"

Secret shrugged. "I don't know, this is my first."

"Hmmm, I guess you do have a point there," Yolanda said. "How about we do it together?"

"Sure. Okay." Secret bent down and began to help Yolanda unstrap Dina from the bouncer. She kept stealing glances of her mother thinking the entire time, *who is this woman and what has she done with my mother?*

"There we go," Yolanda said, smiling, lifting Dina out of the bouncer and standing up with her. "Hey there, baby girl." She tapped her finger on Dina's nose. The baby blinked.

"Can't they go cross-eyed or something if you do that?" Secret asked.

"If that were the case, you'd be cross-eyed. I used to do that to you all the time." Yolanda kept her eyes on the baby, cooing and bouncing her in her arms.

Secret was so surprised at how well Yolanda was being with Dina. She'd never seen this side of her mother, not even when she won $5,000 on a scratch-off ticket. Even then she fussed and cussed about having to pay taxes on it.

"Not so hard, you might wobble her brain or something," Secret said to all the bouncing Yolanda was doing with Dina.

Yolanda stopped and glared at Secret. "You gon' let me hold my grandbaby or not? You act like I'm going to try to hurt her or something."

Secret crossed her arms, stood with her right leg planted straight and her left leg stuck out while raising an eyebrow. Everything about her body language screamed, "I wouldn't put it past you."

"You know what, fuck it, den. Take her." Yolanda shoved Dina into Secret's arms. "I was just trying to come over here and make amends, but forget it." Yolanda stormed over to the door mumbling under her breath. "I don't even know why I decided to do this."

Secret watched her mother, who was clearly hurt by the way Secret was coming at her. All these years Secret had watched Yolanda act mad, she couldn't help but wonder if what she perceived as mad was really sad. Perhaps all along her mother had been hurting inside and this had been her way of hiding it. Secret had been on the other end of being hurt enough times to know that it didn't feel good. The last thing she wanted to do was be the one to cause someone else hurt. "Wait, Ma, I'm sorry," Secret said as Yolanda went to open the door. "Please don't leave." Secret looked over to the couch and then extended her arm. "Please sit down."

Yolanda paused for a moment as if she had to think about whether she wanted to stay. Finally she gave in. "What the hell." She threw her hands up and walked over to the couch. "I'm here now." She flopped down.

"Can I get you something to drink?" Secret asked her mother. Yolanda was trying. The least Secret could do was give her some slack.

"You got any beer?" Yolanda asked.

Secret sucked her teeth. "Ma, you know I don't drink and I'm not old enough to buy alcohol even if I did."

"Well, I ain't know." Yolanda rolled her eyes.

"I have some pop, juice, bottled water," Secret offered.

"I'll take a bottled water."

Secret turned to go into the kitchen but then on second thought, walked over to her mother. "Here, you want to hold her for me?" She extended Dina toward Yolanda.

Yolanda hesitated. "You sure? I might break her or something," she said sarcastically.

"Ma, please."

Yolanda smiled and then took the baby into her arms. Secret could hear her cooing at the baby as she cleared the corner into the kitchen. A couple minutes later Secret returned with Yolanda's drink. She set it down on a coaster on the coffee table in front of Yolanda. She then took a seat over in the chair next to the door.

"So, how does it feel being a mother?" Yolanda asked Secret.

"Special," Secret replied. "It's a feeling I'll never take for granted. Hopefully it's a feeling that will always be with me so that no matter what, I'll always be reminded of how special it is to be a mother, therefore being the best mother that I can possibly be."

Not sure whether Secret was trying to throw a dig at her, she let it go. "Well, I'll warn you, you've got your hands full. Miller girls are something else."

"Hmmm, I don't know. I felt like I was a normal kid, thanks to Grandma."

Clearly, in Yolanda's opinion, that was a dig. "Look, I think I better go." She scooted to the edge of the couch with the baby. "I just wanted to stop by and see my grandbaby. That's all." She stood.

"But you haven't even drunk your water." Secret pointed to the bottle of water.

"I'll take it with me. It's hot out there."

Secret stood and took the baby out of Yolanda's arms. Yolanda picked up the water bottle and headed to the door.

"Well, you know where I live. If you ever need anything, need me to keep the baby while you work, go out, or do something, just let me know. Call me. My number ain't changed." Yolanda went to open the door, but it was locked.

Secret unlocked and opened the door for her mother. "Thank you for stopping by. I really do appreciate it." And Secret really did appreciate the effort her mother was making. Lord knows it took everything in that woman to be cordial for five minutes.

"All right, well like I said, call me if you need me. You still have my number don't you?" Yolanda asked Secret as she stood on the porch.

Secret nodded. Yolanda then walked to her car.

Secret closed the door and then said to herself, "Yeah, I got your number."

Chapter 13

"Do you really want to eat here?" Katherine asked Secret as they headed to the Chinese restaurant at the strip mall the two had reconnected at a few months ago.

"I figured this is where we reconnected. Why not?"

"So you have no idea this is Lucky's spot?" Katherine stopped at the door of the restaurant, throwing her hands on her hips.

"What do you mean? I never ate here with Lucky before." Secret wasn't lying. Lucky had never taken her here to eat before nor had he mentioned this place. It was Detective Davis who told Secret that she needed to come to the restaurant today to "just happen" to run into Lucky.

"Forget it." Katherine shooed her hand. "What are the odds we'd run into him here today anyway?" She opened the door and went inside.

"Yeah, what are the odds?" Secret said under her breath as she entered right behind Katherine.

The sisters walked up to the podium where a Chinese woman stood. "Two today?" the woman greeted them.

"Yes," Katherine replied.

The lady grabbed two menus. "Right this way." She led Katherine and Secret to a table in the middle of the small dining room. After the ladies sat down, the woman placed a menu in front of each of them. "Can I bring you drinks?"

"A Coke for me," Katherine said.

"Just water with lemon for me, thank you," Secret replied.

The woman bowed her head, smiled, then walked away.

"I know one thing," Secret said, "It sure does smell good in here."

"Don't get me to lying. They do have some good-ass food."

The two scanned the menu as the woman bought their drink orders.

"Do you know what you like or need more time?" the woman asked them.

"More time," the sisters said in unison, looking up at each other and laughing.

The woman left the two of them to observe the menu. Their heads were buried trying to decide which of the many delicious looking and sounding entrees they would order.

A couple minutes later the woman returned to take their food orders. Secret ordered General Tso's while Katherine, still undecided, continued skimming the menu.

"Ummmm, okay, I think I'll have the shrimp fried rice," Katherine finally chose. She scanned the menu one last time just to be sure. "Yeah, that's what I'll have." She closed her menu then looked up to hand it to the waitress.

With both menus in hand the waitress said, "Thank you. Your orders will be right out." She walked away, giving Katherine a clear view of the door.

"Well, I'll be damned." Katherine's mouth dropped open and she all of a sudden looked flushed.

Secret's back was to the door, so she had no idea what Katherine had seen that had her reacting this way. "What? What it is?" Secret said with concern.

"Well if it isn't Kat," Secret heard a male voice say behind her. She closed her eyes. She knew who that voice belonged to even without seeing his face. It was show time.

"If it isn't the Lucky dog himself," Katherine shot back. "Surprise seeing you here."

The voice was getting closer and closer to the table. Secret could feel the presence coming closer and closer as well until it felt like she was under the shadow of a giant.

"I can't say the same," Katherine said. She then looked over at Secret. "See, I told you we shouldn't have come to eat here."

For the first time, the gentleman who had been eye-balling Kat looked to see the person Kat was with. Secret looked up at him and the two locked eyes. Lucky stood frozen. Secret sat frozen.

Katherine rolled her tongue inside her jaw. "Mmm, hmmm. What's a matter, Lucky? Cat got yo' tongue?" She busted out laughing.

Neither Lucky nor Secret joined in on the laughter. The two remained staring at one another, waiting to see who would be the first to speak.

"Oh, yeah, how rude of me not to introduce you," Katherine jumped in. "Lucky, this is Secret, my sister. Secret, this is Lucky." Katherine let out a sinister chuckle. "Oh, but then again, you already know damn well who she is," Katherine snapped at Lucky. "She's your fucking baby momma, the one you left for dead in jail, you black son of a—"

"Katherine." Secret put her hand up to silence her sister.

Katherine's mouth hung open midsentence, following her sister's request.

"You're out?" Lucky said to Secret, not the least bit fazed by Katherine's mouth. After so many years of dealing with it, he was totally immune.

"Not 'where the fuck is my baby and is she alive,' no, you worried that she's out." Katherine couldn't help herself.

Once again Secret held her hand up to Katherine.

Katherine bit her lip and shook her head. "I'm sorry, girl, it's just that you are too nice. This mafucka needs to be wearing both our drinks."

Both Lucky and Secret ignored Katherine's rant as she continued to mumble under her breath.

"Looks that way, doesn't it?" Secret said to Lucky's statement about her being out of jail. "No thanks to you."

Lucky put his head down and brushed his nose off with his thumb. He looked back at Secret. "So, how did you get out?"

"Why? You still want her to be locked up serving time for your grimy ass?" Katherine clearly couldn't control her anger toward Lucky and by now the customers were getting agitated by her cursing rant. She saw the owner, a Chinese man, coming out of the back. Katherine recalled the man as the one who had thrown her out of the restaurant the time she'd gotten into it with Lucky in there before. "Look, I lost my appetite," Katherine told Secret. "I'm going to go wait outside in the car." Katherine had driven. She took her keys out of her purse as she got up from the chair.

"Hey, didn't I tell you no come back here?" the owner said once he spotted Katherine.

"I'm leaving, I'm leaving," Katherine said before he could attempt to throw her out again. Katherine said to Secret before she walked out the door, "I got my cell phone right here in my hand and I'm watching the door." She shot Lucky a look of death and then exited.

Lucky stood over Secret while she kept her eyes straight ahead. Lucky finally broke the lingering silence. "The baby." He pointed to Secret's empty womb.

"She's fine," Secret replied short and dry.

"She? So it's a girl?"

"Yes, she's with my mom."

"Your mom?" Lucky scrunched up his face. He knew about Secret's fight with her mom and the turbulent relationship they'd had. Secret's mother had never once come checking for Secret the entire time he had been with Secret so he was surprised to hear that she was back in Secret's life.

"Yep. She came to see about me when she heard I was out, trying to make amends. So I figured why not." Secret looked up at Lucky. "And I think everybody deserves a second chance."

Secret's last words clearly had Lucky feeling a little awkward as his eyes darted around, trying to look anywhere but at her. After a few seconds of silence, Lucky spoke. "So how did you get out?"

Secret looked him dead in his eyes and let out a har-rumph. "So Katherine was right. You're more worried with how I got out of jail than how the baby and I are doing."

"That's not true," Lucky was quick to say.

Just then the waitress came back over carrying the entrees Secret and Katherine had ordered. Noticing Katherine was gone, she looked back and forth from Secret to Lucky like "what to do?"

"Can you actually put them in carryout containers please?" Secret asked. "I'm going to take them to go."

The woman nodded and then walked away.

"I'm out on bond," were the words Detective Davis had told Secret to say, so that's what she'd said. "My public defender says I'm probably going to get off though. Some legal technicality, this being my first offense, I was pregnant, no history of any dealings with drugs. Blah blah blah." Secret waved her hand. "I don't know all that legal jargon; all I know is that I'm free now, free to be with my little girl."

"Well, you know if you need anything . . ."

"You'll come through for me like you have the last two months?"

Lucky washed his hand down his face. "You know I couldn't come up to that jail and see you." Now Lucky spoke almost in a whisper, leaning down toward Secret.

"Oh, and why not?"

"Come on, you know why."

"Actually, I don't. So why don't you tell me," Secret said. She matched his tone in a hard whisper. "Why did you let them take me to jail, Lucky? Why?" Secret fought back tears.

"Look, this isn't the time or the place to—"

"But you owe me!" Secret shouted, no longer able to contain her emotions.

"I know, I know." Lucky lowered his hands, signaling Secret to keep her voice down. "We'll talk, but not here." He thought for a moment. "You still have your apartment or are you staying with your moms?"

"I still have my own place, thank God." Secret rolled her eyes, having blinked away her tears before they could ever fall.

"How about I stop by and we talk? Not tonight. I have something to do, but in the morning. Would that be cool?"

Secret thought for a moment. "I don't know, Lucky. I mean you might show up with a duffle bag full of drugs and tell the cops it's mine."

"Hold that shit down," Lucky said.

"Like I held you down?" Secret reminded him.

He looked into her eyes. "Yeah, like you held me down."

The woman came back with two carryout bags for Secret.

"Thank you," Secret said.

"It's $21.87," the woman told her.

Secret went into her purse but Lucky stopped her. "I got this," he said to both Secret and the waitress. He looked at the waitress. "Put it on my tab."

The woman nodded and then walked away.

"Oh, so Katherine was right, you are a regular here. Got yourself a tab."

Lucky ignored her comment. "We'll talk tomorrow."

Secret took in a deep breath and then exhaled. She didn't say another word to Lucky. She placed both bags on one arm and her purse on the other. She cut her eyes at Lucky, got up from her chair, and brushed by him. The second she got out of the restaurant she let out a deep breath. "Oh my God," she said to herself. She placed her hand over her heart. She could feel it beating darn near out of her chest. She swallowed, juggled her purse and the bags, and went to the car.

Katherine was waiting in the driver's seat with the windows down listening to music.

"Is that Marvin Sapp?" Secret questioned the music blasting from the radio.

Katherine reached and turned it down. "Girl, yes. I needed Jesus after dealing with that rat bastard." She twisted her body around and looked at Secret as if she'd lost her mind. "And you need a little thug in you. Girl, had he left my ass for dead in jail, you would have been picking my acrylic nails out that son of a bitch's body like you was picking cotton."

Secret just shook her head and cracked a smile at Katherine. "Clearly you should be listening to the song 'I Need Just a Little More Jesus.'"

Katherine laughed. "Maybe you're right." She turned the music completely off. She looked down in Secret's lap at the carryout bags. "Good, you brought the food out. I'm starved." Katherine reached for one of the bags to check the content to see if it was hers.

"Oh, got your appetite back I see," Secret said.

The sisters figured out whose entree was whose and began to dig into their meals with the plastic wear the waitress had supplied.

"Mmm, this is good," Secret said after tasting the first bite of her delicious meal.

"Told you, girl. Chinese folks know how to cook up a cat."

"Uhhhhh," Secret said.

"Meow," Katherine joked just as she was about to take her second bite of food. She suddenly stopped before the forkful of food made it to her mouth. She scrunched her face up like she'd seen two flies humping on a mound of dog poop.

Secret was laughing at Katherine's cat imitation but it died down once she saw the serious look on Katherine's face. This was the second time this had happened in the last half hour.

What now? Secret thought, and then she said it out loud.

"I think I'm about to lose my appetite again." Katherine shook her head. "I can't stand that grimy scum bag. You think Lucky is a piece of shit; his boy Major put the S and the T in shit."

Secret turned to see a dude walking across the parking lot, looking as if he was headed for the Chinese restaurant. It was him again, her baby daddy. "You know him?" Secret asked.

"Yeah, don't you recognize him? That's Lucky's best friend, Major Pain."

"Oh, yeah, that is him isn't it?" Secret played along as if she knew who he was. Well she did know who he was, Dina's father, but she'd had no idea that he was Lucky's best friend. It hit her; the only two men she had ever slept with in her life just happened to be best friends.

"Don't he get on your fucking nerves?" Katherine rolled her eyes and then went back to eating her food.

"Well, you know, I don't really know him like that. I think I only saw him like once. Lucky never really had me around any of his people."

"Consider yourself lucky, no pun intended. You ain't missing nothing and you didn't miss nothing. They are both cut from the same cloth." Katherine looked to the restaurant even though Major Pain was long gone inside. "Was my self-esteem really that low that I felt the best I could do, the best I could ever do, was Lucky's sorry ass?"

Secret didn't reply.

Katherine looked over to Secret. "Oh, sis, I'm sorry. I keep forgetting he's your baby daddy."

The door kept opening where Secret could tell Katherine the truth, that Lucky wasn't really Dina's biological father. But then she might have to tell her who was, and she didn't really want to go there, not right now; maybe not ever. This game of cat and mouse was just beginning and she wasn't yet sure which direction things would go in.

Let Katherine tell it, for years Lucky had been her drug of choice and she the fiend. How did Secret know Katherine wouldn't fall back under Lucky's spell and get back with him, exposing any- and everything Secret shared with her? She didn't know. So for now she wouldn't show her hand to anybody, just play the cards Detective Davis dealt her.

"So what are you going to do about Lucky?" Katherine asked. "I mean, he is your baby's father. I know I want you to go *First 48* on his ass, but that's not who you are. You the type who practices that forgiveness shit. And I get that." Katherine pointed a stern finger at Secret. "But don't you go getting caught up romantically with his ass again. Coparent and leave it at that."

"Why?" Secret was quick to ask. "You still want him or something so you don't want me messing around with him?"

"Puhleeze with a capital P. You'll never catch me fucking around with him again. Don't believe me if you don't want to, but after what he did to you, that was it."

Secret nodded, but Katherine couldn't tell whether she believed what she was saying.

Katherine closed her food container up, bagged it, and placed it in the back seat. "See-See, I know we haven't been close in years, but you have to admit that when we were little we had a bond, yes?"

Secret nodded.

"I was so mad at my mother for so long for making it so that I couldn't see you anymore. You were my best friend. I loved you so much. You were always so nice, sweet, and kind." She chuckled. "Me and the twins, we used to tease you behind your back. We would say you sounded like a white girl."

Secret let out a light laugh.

"You were so happy and carefree. I didn't just want to be with you; I wanted to be you. You turned out good, sis. Graduated high school. Hell, I didn't get past tenth grade."

"Really?" Secret was surprised to hear this. She had no idea her sister hadn't graduated high school; then again, how would she have known?

"Really," Katherine confirmed. "So that day I saw you in the back of that police car," Katherine said, squeezing her eyes closed tightly, "instead of me imagining being you, I pictured you turning into me." Katherine opened her eyes and looked at Secret. The tears no longer had her eyelids to keep them locked in so they flowed freely. "Don't be me, Secret. You've still got a chance. Don't fuck with these streets or these street cats. I don't think you really know how big Lucky is in the game. Keep fucking with him and you will end up catching a case. God must have been watching over you this time, but don't think lightening is going to strike twice for yo' ass." Katherine quickly and roughly wiped the tears she'd just realized were streaming down her face. She was trying to be hard and school her sister. How effective would it be if she herself was sitting there like some crybaby?

Katherine sniffed a couple times. Secret closed her food back up and put it in the bag. She turned her body toward the door and stared out the window at the restaurant.

"You ready?" Katherine asked her.

Secret nodded.

Katherine started the car and drove off. "Wanna go pick the baby up?" Katherine asked Secret.

Again, Secret just nodded.

Katherine headed in the direction to Yolanda's house, where they'd dropped Dina off on the way to the Chinese restaurant.

Katherine turned the music back on to fill some of the silence in the car. After about a minute or two, she turned it back off. "I'm sorry if you felt like I was getting on you back there. I'm not trying to be your momma or anything like that."

"I know," Secret said. "I just have so much on my mind. Seeing Lucky stirred up so much in me."

"Like I said, I know how it is. I've been there and done that with Lucky."

"I know, I know already. You fucked my baby daddy!" Secret snapped, tired of being reminded that she and her sister had both slept with the same guy and she'd slept with best friends. "You don't have to keep drilling that fact into my mind. Trust me, it's forever embedded."

"Secret, do you think that's the worst shit anybody has ever done? Please. You have no idea how tricks get down out here." She looked at Secret quickly and then put her eyes back on the road. "Not saying you're a trick or anything. But it ain't no joke trying to survive and eat out here sometimes. You got single mothers doing all and anything they can to feed their babies. I kept fucking with Lucky knowing he was fucking everything that moved, but he fit a need and filled a void." Katherine didn't continue. She focused on the road.

Secret, curious as to what those two things were, said, "And what was that?"

"Attention from a man, that was the void. Shit, it wasn't like Daddy was around to let me know I was special, that I was important, that I meant something."

"And Lucky made you feel that way?"

"Didn't he make you feel that way?"

Secret swallowed without answering. She looked down. Yes, he'd made her feel all those ways, but she couldn't force herself to say it. She felt like such a fool. She really thought she meant something to Lucky. She'd actually believed she was special. But his actions had spoken to her loud and clear. She hadn't meant any more to him than she had to her own mother and father.

"As far as needs," Katherine continued, "well, that's an easy one." She turned onto the street where Yolanda's apartment complex was. "Ol' Lucky knows how to take care of his own. That's for sure." She tapped the steering wheel. "Where do you think I got this car?"

Secret looked around the vehicle. "He didn't try to take it back when you broke things off with him?"

"He used to try to all the time at first. But we broke up and got back together so much, he knew it was useless," Katherine said. "Besides, it's actually in my name. After about the third time he took it, I called the police and reported it stolen." Katherine pulled up into the apartment complex, then looked at Secret with a sinister grin. "He wasn't trying to fuck with the police."

"I bet," Secret said. "So you're really done with him this time. You think he realizes that? Especially now that he's seen us together. Maybe since he knows for sure this time that you two are done he will try to take the car."

Katherine thought for a moment as she pulled in front of Yolanda's place and parked. "Well, he certainly can't do shit with it since it's in my name. But I can see that foul-ass nigga setting it on fire, stripping it down for parts or something. Anything else than to have my fine ass riding around in it." Katherine smiled. "But, naw. He's over our situation I'm sure, or he'll be over it soon. I heard he's fucking with some other chick right now. Some girl named Shaun, Shaunna, or something like that. And you know how dudes are with new pussy. He'll be wrapped up in that for a minute until he comes up for air."

Secret shook her head. "I don't even know how he ever even had time for me. He was with me, you, your best friend, and God knows who else."

"It doesn't even matter; your only concern now is Dina and making sure that nigga takes care of her. Mafucker wanna take care of bitches? Take care of your own goddamn daughter. How about that?" Katherine looked over at Secret who was looking at her like she was crazy.

They both burst out laughing.

"Sis, you are crazy. You be going in," Secret said. "I swear you remind me of Shawndiece." Mentioning her best friend's name reminded Secret that after picking up Dina, she wanted to drive over to Shawndiece's mother's house to see if she could get in touch with her. She put her hand on the door handle and opened the door.

"Yeah, that's it!" Katherine snapped her finger. "Shawndiece. That's the name of the chick Lucky is fucking with."

Chapter 14

Secret's hand trembled as she gripped the steering wheel of her car. Dina sat in the back in her car seat doing a little bit of fussing. When Katherine had dropped her off at her mother's house to pick Dina up, the little one had been sound asleep. She was cranky after being awoken in order to get situated into her car seat.

Yolanda had invited Secret to stay and hang out until Dina woke up, but Secret couldn't even think straight after Katherine telling her that Lucky's new girl was named Shawndiece. What were the odds that Lucky's Shawndiece wasn't the same Shawndiece Secret had been best friends with for years? In Secret's heart she wanted it to be all just one big awful coincidence. No way would her girl stab her in the back like that.

Secret had already been sitting outside of Shawndiece's mother's house for almost five minutes. All kinds of thoughts were running around in her head. She wondered if Shawndiece was inside. If she was, how would she act toward Secret if she was in fact seeing Lucky? How would Secret react to the fact that her best friend was sleeping with the enemy?

She hadn't spoken to Shawndiece since that day she came to the jail to visit Secret. The same thoughts as before and then some began swarming through Secret's head. Her imagination ran wild as she pictured that for the past couple months Shawndiece had been hugged up with Lucky, too ashamed to face Secret, which was the reason why she never came back to visit her.

"No, no, no," Secret said, shaking her head. She let out one more loud, "No!" and slammed her open hand on the steering wheel. Dina began fussing even louder. "Oh, I'm sorry, Mommy's baby," Secret said turning her body toward the back seat. She fiddled around to find the pacifier that was tucked next to Dina down in the car seat. She plugged it into Dina's mouth, which calmed the baby down.

Secret turned back around and faced the steering wheel. She looked up at Shawndiece's mother's house, still gathering the nerve to go up to the door. If Shawndiece was there, what would Secret say to her? Would she just come right out and ask her if she was with Lucky? Just asking the question alone could change the dynamics of their relationship, regardless of what the answer was. If Shawndiece was kicking it with Lucky, that would be the ultimate betrayal and Secret would never have two words to say to Shawndiece. If Shawndiece really wasn't messing around with Lucky, she could get so offended by Secret accusing her of it that it ruined their friendship anyway.

Secret looked back at Dina. She was sucking on her binky fighting going back to sleep. Secret didn't want to take her out of the car seat and start her up fussing again. She decided to simply roll the windows down and run up to the house real quick. She didn't plan on going into the house, just on the porch. She wasn't going to let her baby out of her sight.

Secret got out of the car and walked up onto the porch feeling like with each step her legs were going to buckle right up under her. She finally arrived at the door after what felt like the longest trek ever. She looked into her car at her baby half asleep and then knocked on the door. She waited a few seconds and after not getting an answer she knocked again. Still no answer. She exhaled a gust of wind and then turned back around and headed to her car.

Once she was off the porch she heard the clicking of the door. She stopped and turned back around and watched as the door opened.

"Secret, baby, is that you?" Shawndiece's mother said, sounding surprised.

"Hey, Miss Franklin," Secret said once she saw Shawndiece's mother standing in the doorway.

Miss Franklin stepped out of the house and onto the porch. "Girl, I thought you was locked up for selling drugs. I couldn't believe it. I always thought you was different. I guess hanging around that daughter of mine finally rubbed off on you huh?" She laughed.

Secret would have joined in on the joke, but she wasn't in a laughing mood right now. "Is Shawndiece around?" Secret asked, not addressing anything her best friend's mother had said.

"No, she hardly stays here anymore since she done snagged her a so-called baller." She put the word "baller" in quotation marks with her fingers. "I hope she don't think that just because she ain't been here that much this month she ain't got to pay me no rent. Shit, I can't go stay at one of my dude's house then tell the mortgage company I ain't paying 'cause I ain't been here that much. She tried to pull that shit last month." Miss Franklin pointed a finger at Secret. "And you tell her that if you see her." She rolled her eyes. "Hey, you ain't pregnant no more. You done had the baby?"

"Yes," Secret answered and then nodded to her car. "She's out here in the car."

"Girl, you left your baby in that hot-ass car? You lucky don't no white people live around here. They'd call the police on you in a minute. Them some tattling folks. Clearly snitches get stitches don't apply to them." She pulled her shirt up over her bra strap that was showing. "Let me see that baby of yours." She walked off the porch and met up with Secret. The two of them approached the car together.

"There she is," Secret said, pointing at the open back window.

The two women stood outside the car peeking at Dina.

"Well look at that pretty princess," Miss Franklin said. She turned and looked at Secret over her shoulder. "Looks just like you." She turned her attention back to Dina. "Did she get her daddy's anything?"

Secret just smiled. Her mind was still on getting in touch with her best friend. "So you don't know where Shawndiece is staying?"

"Nope. And she got her cell phone number changed, again. You know she changes it every five minutes." She snickered.

"I know. I tried to call it when I got my phone but it was no longer in service." Secret had actually tried to call Shawndiece a couple of times. Even though the first time she'd called she'd gotten a recorded message about the phone not being in service, Secret tried again a few days later thinking that maybe it had just been temporarily off for nonpayment. Miss Franklin confirming Shawndiece could no longer be reached at that number put a damper on Secret's attempts to connect with her best friend.

Miss Franklin stood up straight and faced Secret. "I figure this time she got it changed so I couldn't call her up and harass her about my rent money." She laughed. "That daughter of mine, I don't know where I went wrong. Anyways, let me get back into this house and check on my food I got on the stove." She put her hand on Secret's shoulder. "You want something to eat, baby?"

"No, I'm good, but thank you."

"All right. You take care of that baby of yours, and bring her back by when she's big enough for me to stuff her with some real food." She chuckled and headed up the steps. "I'll tell Shawn you're looking for her. She'll be happy to hear her best friend is home."

Miss Franklin disappeared back into the house while Secret said under her breath, "I'm sure she will."

Secret could hardly see Lucky's face when she looked through the peephole. She could see, though, a big pink teddy bear with a purple bow around its neck, and an oversized baby bottle filled with all types of baby accessories. He juggled diapers, shopping bags from department stores, and what looked like a walker.

Secret moved away from the peephole and straightened her outfit. It was a denim Capri romper with the Juicy Couture flip-flops she'd purchased on one of her last shopping outings prior to getting locked up, compliments of Lucky. She looked over at Dina who was lying down on top of a blanket-type play mat. She then turned and opened the door.

Secret swung the door open. She didn't even greet Lucky. She just stood there with her shoulder-length hair, straightened, tucked behind her ears. She usually wore her hair up in a ponytail or a bun, so this was one of the first times Lucky had seen her literally just let her hair down.

Although he didn't compliment her, Secret could tell by the look in his eyes that he liked what he saw. His mouth had hung open three seconds too long before any words had even come out of it.

"Come in." Secret stepped to the side while Lucky felt his way into the doorway, because he sure couldn't see where he was going. He tripped.

"Watch it," Secret said, grabbing his arm to help him balance. She immediately pulled back as if she'd touched something hot and had been burned.

Lucky stood there as if a volt of electricity had flowed through his body. Was it possible that even though Secret desperately didn't want to feel anything for Lucky, a physical attraction was, indeed, still there?

Once Lucky was able to find his voice he said, "I bought the baby some stuff. I didn't know what you needed. I put the receipt in one of the bags, so you can take back whatever you don't need and just get what you do need."

"You didn't have to do that, but I guess guilt can get the best of a person," Secret shot back. Inside, she was grateful for the items, but she wasn't about to let Lucky off that easy by showing him a single ounce of gratitude. "You can set everything right there." Secret pointed to the landing of the stairs.

Lucky set everything down. He then rubbed the palms of his hands down his pants as if they were sweaty. He looked over at Dina. "She's a cutie." He walked over to where the baby was lying down. "Man, she looks just like you." He laughed. "She's like a little lady."

"Thank you," Secret said dryly. She watched Lucky stare at the baby a little longer. "Can I get you something to drink?"

"Oh, no, I'm good," Lucky said.

"Something to eat," Secret offered. "I made a casserole."

"Tuna with the peas, cheese, and onion?" Lucky asked. Secret nodded.

That had been one of Lucky's favorite dishes that Secret made. Had Secret remembered that and made it especially for him? Was it her way of saying she forgave him? Lucky didn't want to make any assumptions, but he wasn't about to pass up the delicious dish either. He rarely got a home-cooked meal, always in the streets on the run eating fast food.

"I'll definitely take some of that," Lucky said.

"All right. I'll fix you a plate." Secret disappeared into the kitchen for about five minutes and then returned with a plate of the casserole along with a can of pop. "Here you go." She set it down on the dining room table.

As Lucky walked over to eat Dina started fussing.

"Okay, missy. You hungry too? Mommy's got you." She picked up Dina and carried her into the kitchen with her. She prepared her a bottle and then returned to the living room. She sat down on the couch and fed Dina a bottle while Lucky sat at the table and ate.

"I didn't know what kind of milk she drank or I would have bought her some of that, too," Lucky said with a mouthful of food.

"It's cool." Secret looked over to the pile of items sitting on the steps. "It looks like you've done plenty."

There was the sound of Lucky's fork hitting the plate and him chewing. Secret looked down at Dina while she fed her. A couple minutes later Lucky was laying the fork across his plate and pushing it to the center of the table.

"Damn, that was good. I forgot how good you could cook." He stood up, rubbing his belly.

"You forgot about me altogether," Secret said.

Lucky exhaled. He knew the inevitable was coming. "Yeah, about that . . ." He walked over and sat down on the living room chair.

"Lucky, just tell me why. How could you?" Secret's voice trembled.

"I really don't want to go into details, just know that I am truly, one hundred percent sorry. I mean, that day I . . . I just froze. I was scared. It was a setup, I could just feel it. And I honestly believe that no matter what we said, they were taking us both to jail that day. I know for a fact that had we said it was my dope, whether it was or it wasn't, they were going to put us both away. You might not believe me, but I figured I'd have a better chance of getting you out than you would getting me out. But if we were both locked up, then we both would have been screwed."

"Really, and just when did you plan on getting me out?"

"I had to fall back, lay low a little. But I had every intention of hiring you the best attorney in the city once you went to trial." Lucky leaned in and rested his arms on his knees. "You have to believe me, Secret. There's no way I would have just thrown you away like that."

"I want to believe you, Lucky, but how can I? Why should I?"

"Because if I didn't wanna fuck with you, I would have long been not had nothing to do with you. I wouldn't have waited until that day to say the hell with this girl. No, I would have said that the day you told me about how the baby you was pregnant with wasn't mine even though you had pretended it was. How you only got with me in the first place was to try to run game on me. But, baby, that day in the hotel when you confessed it all to me and shared with me how you really ended up liking me and didn't want to hurt me, I trusted you. I stayed with you regardless. So now, I guess, I'm just asking for a little reciprocity here."

Secret thought for a minute. Lucky had a point. Who was to say that what he had done to her was any worse than what she had done to him? Secret shook off her thoughts. She was getting too much into her feelings. Regardless of how she really felt about Lucky one way or the other, she had a job to do, and that was get Lucky to trust her. If pretending to trust him was what it would take, then so be it.

"I guess you have a point," Secret said, looking into Lucky's eyes.

"So what does that mean?" Lucky asked.

"It means that I'd be being a hypocrite if I didn't give you a second chance, considering you gave me one."

"So exactly what does giving me a second chance mean?"

Secret shrugged. "I don't know. What do you want it to mean?"

"Well, I know it's not like we can pick right back up where we left off," Lucky said. "But we had a plan." He eyeballed Dina. "I mean, I was supposed to be her daddy, sign the birth certificate."

"I already filled out the information for the birth certificate," Secret told him. "I did it while I was in the hospital."

"So, I know many niggas, after getting a paternity test, who went back and added their names to the baby's birth certificate."

Secret shook her head. "I really don't think all that is necessary now. It was a nice little fairytale, but now, it is what it is."

"And what is it?"

"I don't know, you tell me. Before I got handcuffed and taken to jail, you were my man. I was having a baby we were going to raise as ours." Secret let out a harrumph. She removed the bottle from Dina's mouth and placed her over her shoulder. "But then I saw my sister come scoop you up and the two of you ride off into the sunset like fucking Bonnie and Clyde." Secret began to pat Dina's back.

A shocked look appeared on Lucky's face. Lucky wasn't used to Secret cursing. Had a month in jail changed her that much?

Secret had to ask herself the same question. Never one to get all gangsta and ghetto, Secret managed to stay pretty level-headed most of the time. But being falsely accused of a crime and thrown in jail can definitely change a person.

"Kat," Lucky said, then shook his head. "Kat was my homegirl. I been down with Kat since forever."

"Yes, I know," Secret said. "She told me everything."

Lucky paused. "So you two are sisters, huh?" he asked. "I mean what were the chances that my homegirl from back in the day and my woman were sisters?"

"Every man's fantasy come true, huh?" Secret asked as the baby burped. "Good girl." She kissed her on the cheek and then continued to feed her the remainder of the bottle.

"More like a nightmare in my case," Lucky said. "Again, you have to believe me on this, but I had cut off things with Kat permanently long before that day we got pulled over by the cops. It's just that when I needed a ride, she's the first person I thought of. She and I got into it big time not too long before that. Then we got into it again once I explained to her my situation with you—"

"And her best friend," Secret added.

"Damn, Kat did tell you everything, huh?" Lucky said.

"We're sisters. That's what sisters do, tell each other everything." Secret looked down at Dina who had milk dripping out the corners of her mouth. She was falling asleep and had stopped sucking and swallowing the milk. Secret placed her back on her shoulder and began patting her pack.

"Meeting you and you just happening to be Kat's sister was a fluke. I'm not that grimy nigga who would be playing two sisters like that."

"I believe you, Lucky. Really I do." Secret stood. "But you are grimy enough to be playing two best friends, huh?" Secret stood.

"Man, Taneshia was just a gold-digging stank. And if she was really Kat's best friend, she wouldn't have been fucking with me."

Secret laughed and then headed up the steps.

"What's so funny? Where you going."

Secret stopped midway up the steps. "I'm going to lay the baby in her crib and what's so funny is you."

"Me, how am I funny?"

"You know darn well that Taneshia is not the best friend I'm talking about."

Lucky looked puzzled.

"Let me put Dina to bed and then I'll be back down so we can talk about the best friend I was referring to. My best friend, Shawndiece."

Chapter 15

Secret loved walking away leaving Lucky feeling like a deer caught in headlights. When she said Shawndiece's name, Secret practically had all the answers she needed. Lucky was probably downstairs choking on the canary's feathers, because he surely looked like the cat who'd just eaten it.

Secret laid Dina in the bed and then went to the bathroom. She didn't have to use it. She just wanted Lucky to sit down there sweating. Too anxious to hear what Lucky had to say for himself, Secret couldn't stall any longer. She made her way back downstairs. She walked right past Lucky and over to the dinner table. She grabbed Lucky's plate and empty can from the table. She could feel Lucky watching her every step.

She went into the kitchen and scraped the plate, placed it in the dishwasher, rinsed her hands and then moseyed back onto the couch in the living room. She sat with her arms spread eagle on the couch and her legs crossed. She then stared at Lucky and said, "Well?"

"Well what?"

"We really aren't about to play this game are we?" Secret said. "Shawndiece. The streets are talking and they say she's your new girl."

"And since when do you listen to the streets?" Lucky asked.

"Never mind all that. I want to hear it from the horse's mouth."

"Do you really think I would be kicking it with your best friend?"

"Did Kat really think you would be kicking it with hers?"

Lucky stood up. "My situation with Kat is not like my situation with you. You are differ—"

"I know, I'm different," Secret snapped. "Yeah, you've told me that before and it looked like being different wound up not working in my favor. If I was the typical hoodrat street-smart bitch, I would have played your ass, but instead I got played and almost ended up giving birth to my daughter in a jail cell!" Secret began to cry. "And now I find out while I was locked up, you was off lollygagging with my best friend."

"I have not been lollygagging with your best friend."

"So you aren't with Shawndiece?" Secret wiped her tears away, upset that she was crying in front of this man. She'd wanted so badly to play hardcore, but this Shawndiece thing hurt.

"I'm not with ya girl, not like that. Not like the way you thinking."

"Then how, Lucky? Because it's funny how my best friend went MIA right along with your ass!" Secret was on a roll with the expletives.

"Just calm down, please," Lucky pleaded. "Look, I see Shawn, but it's not for what you think."

"Shawn," Secret said, snapping her neck back. "Oh, so you know her like that now? It's not Shawndiece; it's Shawn. Wow!"

"I really don't want to get into Shawn . . . Shawndiece's and my relationship, but—"

"Relationship? Okay, so it is like that." Secret just shook her head.

"I'm not screwing your girl if that's what you're thinking."

"Then what else could you and Shawndiece possibly be doing? And why hasn't she told me about it herself?"

"Basically your girl just works for me now, that's it. Ain't no funny business going on or nothing like that."

Secret paused, giving Lucky the side eye. "Works for you? Wha . . . what do you mean?" Secret had an idea of just what Lucky might have meant by that, but no way would Shawndiece get involved with something like that, with someone like him. But then again, she had. Yeah, her best friend might have made a career out of hustling dudes for their money, but never would she be one to get hustled by a dude. And after what Lucky had done to Secret, clearly Shawndiece had to realize he was a no-good hustler out for self.

"Like I said," Lucky stated, "I really don't think it's my place to get all into that with you. I will tell you though that after you got locked up, your girl came at me clownin'. I had been laying low so I don't even know how she caught up with my ass." He laughed and shook his head as if reminiscing. "But she found me nonetheless. Came charging my ass. Didn't even care she had about four gun barrels pointing at her ass. She came storming over to me, kicking off her stilettoes, taking off her earrings, and putting her hair in a ponytail." Lucky started imitating her. "'You got my girl locked up. I'ma fuck you up.'" He laughed again.

Secret almost laughed just picturing Shawndiece going in on Lucky on her behalf. Secret was starting to feel a little better about the situation. She knew her girl wouldn't play her like that by sleeping with Lucky. But Secret didn't let her hopes get up too high. It might not have been a romantic relationship, but clearly there was some type of relationship going on. Secret sat back and continued listening to Lucky just so she could find out exactly what it was.

"Long story short, she went on and on about how she put her last on your books and couldn't pay her mom's rent, blah blah blah. I kind of broke down to her why I did what I did. I told her like I told you: I was going to get you out, I just needed to lay low and work on some things." Lucky paused as if he really didn't want to tell Secret the rest.

"Then what?" Secret pressed, forcing Lucky to continue.

"Basically, I told her how I needed a little help getting shit back in order, and well, she offered to help, if it meant getting you out."

Secret walked over to Lucky. "And just what kind of help are we talking about here, Lucky? What you got my girl caught up in?"

"First off, I ain't got your girl caught up in nothing. She offered. Nobody put a gun to her head." He thought for a minute. "I mean, yeah, she had four guns on her, but nobody was twisting her arm to put in work."

"Put in work?" Secret questioned.

"Come on, Secret. I know when it comes to the streets you ain't on all that, but you ain't completely dumb to the situation and my line of work."

"Your line of work?" Secret questioned. "You're an entrepreneur. You run your own business. Right? Isn't that what you told me?"

Lucky cut in before Secret could continue. "Secret, please. You knew what time it was, and if you didn't, your girl damn sure did. You never asked exactly what I did to make my paper and I never told you. But come on yo, you never asked for a reason. And that's a good thing, because the fact that you didn't know anything is probably why your ass is out of jail right now."

"You're wrong, I'm out of jail right now because—" Secret had to cut her own self off from talking. Anger would have her saying the wrong thing and ruining everything, possibly landing her back in jail. "I'm out of jail right now due to luck, not Lucky. The police fucked up, and clearly so did I by getting involved with someone like you."

Lucky stood and got in Secret's face. "You can play that dumb and naïve girl role as much as you want to, but I refuse to believe you were blind to the world you were living in. I kept you in the dark on a lot of shit, but you wasn't blind, so quit acting like you are some martyr and I'm in this by myself. You different from me, but not better, Secret. Remember why you start fucking with me in the first place."

That was the second time Lucky had to put Secret in her place. Secret wasn't used to seeing this side of Lucky. As a matter of fact, the months that they were together, she couldn't even recall if they ever even had a single argument. Secret was coming to the conclusion that Lucky had been hiding a side to him that she didn't know about and didn't want to know about.

She had to admit, though, that there had been some truth in what Lucky was saying. Secret had buried her head in the sand when it came to Lucky. He'd managed to create a little world that had only included the two of them. She'd never met any of his people and the only person she'd ever introduced him to was Shawndiece. Secret had liked it that way. Lucky was a street cat and that wasn't unbeknownst to Secret. She wasn't street, though, so she had absolutely no desire in being a part of that side of Lucky. It had paid off as far as her being able to have peace of mind. But it hadn't paid off as far as Major Pain and Kat. She would have at least known about their role in Lucky's life if she hadn't been kept in the dark, or simply never turned the lights on.

"I don't want to argue and fight with you, Secret," Lucky told her. "That's never who we were. That's what made you so special. That's what made us so special." He took Secret's hands into his. "You are special to me, Secret. That's why I never even had you around the bullshit. And the one time I did . . ." He shook his head. "I fucked up. I've fucked up a lot in life. But I've always managed to fix my fuckups." He pulled Secret in close to him. "Let me fix this. Will you let me fix this?"

At first Secret just looked off in thought. She hadn't practiced what she would say to Lucky. What she wouldn't say to Lucky. Therefore, she had no idea exactly what to say. But she knew that whatever it was, it had to be believable.

She was a forgiving person. But the verdict was still out on whether her heart concurred with what her mouth was about to say. Secret's eyes met Lucky's. "I will. Like I said. Everybody deserves a second chance."

Lucky placed a soft kiss on Secret's forehead.

"Just don't fuck up again."

Lucky smiled. "I won't, I promise." He gave her one more kiss on the forehead, then released her hands.

"Oh, and one more thing," Secret said.

"Yeah."

"Tell my best friend to call me."

Chapter 16

"How was your first day of work?" Yolanda asked Secret as she walked into Yolanda's place.

"Good," Secret replied.

"I'm happy for you. Got you a little job, taking care of your baby," Yolanda said. "In spite of everything, you making it happen."

"Well you know, I am a Miller woman. We do whatever it takes to survive and take care of our own, right?" There was a hint of sarcasm in Secret's voice.

"Humph, you ain't got to tell me. I learned from the best. Your grandmother wasn't no joke, that's for sure."

"So I've been told." Secret was short. She could tell that her mother was extending an olive branch, but just like with Lucky, Secret did not want to make it that easy for her. All the hell Yolanda had put Secret through, Secret felt entitled to put her through a little something something.

There was a moment of awkward silence. "Well, like I said"—Yolanda sat down on the couch—"I'm happy to see you got some fight in you. You was so soft and dainty, prim and proper when you was little. I used to tell myself, 'Lord, this child ain't gon' never survive on these streets.'" She shook her head. "So I had to make you tough. Just like my mother made me." She looked at Secret.

If Secret wasn't mistaken, she'd say the look she now saw in her mother's eyes was one of regret. She waited to see if the words that followed would mirror the look.

"From a kid's eyes, I know you probably thought I was the biggest bitch of a mother you ever met," Yolanda said.

Secret didn't deny it.

"But I had to be. I had to make sure that if anything ever happened to me, you would be able to hold your own. I had to make you tough. I was hard on you for a reason, Secret."

"Growing up I always thought that reason was because you hated me."

"Girl, no." Yolanda shooed her hand. "If anything I hated myself for even bringing you into this fucked-up world. That's my only regret in life."

A solemn expression instantly popped up on Secret's face. Realizing how the words she'd said had just come out, Yolanda spoke.

"I don't mean that I regret having you. No, no, it's not that at all. I regret that I brought you into this life the way I did. Young, dumb, stupid, and chose another woman's husband as your daddy. What was I thinking? What made me think it was okay to bring a child into a situation like that?"

If Secret could recall correctly, this was really the first mother-daughter conversation she'd ever had with Yolanda. The only time Yolanda had ever talked to her was when she was calling her every kind of bitch and whore in the book or cussing her out at the top of her lungs. Perhaps it had something to do with the fact that now that Secret was a mother herself, Yolanda saw her as an adult and could have a grownup conversation with her. Secret didn't know what it was or what had changed, but she liked it. Still, she wasn't going to get all mushy and express that to Yolanda. She wanted Yolanda to extend that olive branch until her arm fell off. Maybe then Secret would feel as if they were even.

"Well, we can't live the rest of our lives with regrets," Secret said. "It will just hold us back."

"You right, and I don't know about you, but I'm tired of being held back. I want to move on, if you know what I mean."

Secret nodded.

"You tired? Did they work you to death today? Did you learn everything okay?"

"It's just ringing up and bagging groceries. Doesn't take a college education to do, that's for sure," Secret replied with a sigh.

While in the grocery store a few days ago Secret had noticed a HIRING sign hanging up. As she stood in line staring at the sign it dawned on her that she couldn't sit and live off of welfare forever. What kind of example would that be setting for Dina? Even if Secret felt that she'd never move away from Flint, she'd at least be able to tell her daughter that she tried. Plus, she did not want to be at Uncle Sam's mercy receiving a welfare check and food stamps for the rest of her life. She needed to have her own. Minimum wage at the local grocer wasn't much, but it was hers.

She filled out the application, did a phone interview, and was hired on the spot. They'd wanted her to start that very next day, but she had to figure out her childcare situation. Luckily Yolanda would be on vacation from her own job for the next week, so she would be able to keep Dina at least for the next few days. Secret had called her case worker about assistance with childcare. She'd gone in that same day to fill out the paperwork and was expecting any day now the letter in the mail telling her what percentage of the childcare the government would pay. She'd also received a list of childcare providers to look into. She had several home visits scheduled to go check a few of them out. Everything looked to be falling into place. Not being a procrastinator was paying off for Secret.

"Well, uh, you know, at least a job at the grocery store is something," Yolanda said in a fidgety voice, then changed the subject. "Let me go get the baby. She's in your old bedroom." Yolanda walked off to the back bedroom down the hall. She returned a few seconds later with Dina in her arms. "Look who's here to get her baby." Yolanda rubbed her nose against Dina's and the baby cooed.

The sound and sight of her little one put a smile on Secret's face. She extended her arms to take Dina. She began planting kisses all over her baby girl's face once she had her in her arms.

Yolanda stared at the sight before her for a moment before she spoke. "Aren't you glad you didn't kill her? And you can thank me for that."

Secret stopped immediately and looked up at her mother. "Excuse me?"

"Aren't you glad you didn't get an abortion, you know, like you'd planned on doing at first?"

Secret felt a rush of embarrassment and even humiliation. Even though Dina had no idea what was being said, it pained Secret that she had, in fact, thought of aborting the baby. She could only imagine how that would make her daughter feel if she ever found that out.

Suddenly a sense of selfishness came over Secret as well. She'd had dreams of going off to college, which was one of the main reasons why she had planned on getting an abortion once she found out she was pregnant; that and the fact she had no relationship with the baby's father and didn't think she'd ever see him again for as long as she lived. In being honest with herself, Secret could truly admit that had she gotten that scholarship and been accepted to OSU, Dina would not be in her arms today.

Determined not to be like her mother and end up a bitter woman in Flint for the rest of her life, Secret was going to get a college education and make something of herself and she wasn't going to let anything interfere with that, not even her unborn baby. But the day her mother gave her the news that she hadn't received the scholarship, Secret felt she had nothing to live for, nothing to lose, and nothing to gain, so why not just have the baby? She was destined to end up like the women in her family one way or the other.

Yolanda was bitter and broke working at a subpar job. Secret's grandmother had managed to make a come up, living in a nice suburb. But let Yolanda tell it, she had to sink her claws into and marry a white man to make that happen. Had Secret inherited the many traits of the Miller women? She looked into her baby's eyes. And would she pass them on to her daughter.

"I'm glad Dina is here," was Secret's response to her mother's query. Secret began looking around. "Are all her things together?"

"Most of them, yeah. Let me go get the rest of her stuff." Yolanda went back into the bedroom. She exited moments later with a couple of items. She went and placed them into Dina's diaper bag that was sitting on the couch. She gathered a couple more items and then stuffed them into the bag as well. "I think that's everything." She swept the room with her eyes. "It ain't like she won't be right back tomorrow. If you left anything you can get it then."

Secret got Dina together and then walked to the door. Seeing that Secret's hands were full, Yolanda hurried over to open the door for her.

"Thanks, Mom," Secret said.

"You're welcome," Yolanda replied.

"I mean for everything. I appreciate you watching Dina for me."

"That's my grandbaby," Yolanda said proudly.

Secret smiled. It was still hard for her to believe this was her mother talking. But then again, there was something special about Dina. She could soften the heart of Satan himself, so it shouldn't have been a surprise to Secret that she could chip away at Yolanda's cold heart. This made Secret reflect, again, on what Yolanda had asked her about being glad she hadn't aborted her baby. Perhaps Dina was just what was needed to actually bring Secret and her mother together again. God surely worked in mysterious ways, but Secret would soon find out that so did the devil.

Chapter 17

"Damn, damn, damn," Secret said as she scoured her living room looking for her car keys. She'd already overslept this morning and had to hurry up and get Dina over to her mother's so that she could make it to work by eleven o'clock. Dina had been cranky and restless last night. By the time Secret got her settled and to sleep, her alarm was going off. She thought she'd just hit the snooze button, but she'd actually turned the alarm off. She happened to roll over and see that the clock read ten-thirty. She had jumped out of the bed so quickly that she got a headache. Her heart was beating out of her chest as she'd stumbled to the bathroom.

She didn't even have time to change Dina out of her pajamas. She'd placed her outfit for the day in her diaper bag. Yolanda would just have to bathe her and get her cleaned up.

Secret looked up at the living room clock that read ten forty-five. She wanted to cry. It was only her second day of work. She could not be late, but it looked as though she would be. If she didn't find her keys in the next five minutes, she'd have to ask Yolanda to come to her house and give her a ride. Her mother was already keeping Dina for her; she hated to have to ask her to be a chauffeur as well. That might have been the breaking point for Yolanda and bring out the beast in her. Things were going well between them. Secret didn't want to push her luck.

"Yes!" Secret shouted upon finding her keys tucked in Dina's diaper bag. She must have accidentally placed them in there when throwing things haphazardly into the diaper bag.

She placed the diaper bag on her arm, grabbed her purse, then snatched up little Dina who had been watching her mommy run around the apartment like a chicken with her head cut off. "All right, baby girl, let's go."

Secret did one last sweep of the room and then opened the front door. She gasped immediately at the figure standing on her doorstep.

"I heard you were looking for me."

Secret didn't know whether to throw her arms around her best friend or slam the door in her face. She had mixed emotions for sure. But this was her best friend since the age of ten. She had to give her the benefit of the doubt. She'd heard Lucky's version of things. She owed it to Shawndiece to hear hers.

"Oh yeah, and where did you hear that from?" Secret asked.

"A mutual friend."

"Friend, huh?" Secret said, raising an eyebrow.

"I wanted to talk." Shawndiece lifted up a McDonald's bag. "I brought breakfast." She looked at Secret's arm full of items. "But it looks like this isn't a good time." She looked at Dina. "Oh, is that my li'l goddaughter? She is so beautiful."

"I've been worried about you," Secret told Shawndiece. "I didn't hear from you anymore after you visited me in jail.

"Yeah, well, I've been kind of busy."

"So I hear."

Shawndiece looked downward. "We need to talk. We have some catching up to do."

"Definitely, but right now I have to get the baby to Yolanda's so I can make it to work."

"Yolanda?" Shawndiece snapped her neck back. "As in your momma Yolanda?"

"The one and only," Secret confirmed.

"So you two made up, huh?" Shawndiece had a smile on her face.

"Yes, and I guess I have you to thank for it. She said you gave her my address. She stopped by once she heard I was out."

"Good for her. I didn't think she'd do it, especially since I called her a sorry excuse for a mother when I gave it to her."

Secret laughed. "Why doesn't that surprise me?"

"You know me."

"Yeah, I thought I did." Secret's laughter stopped. "I have to go, but my break is at four. I'm working over at the grocery store on Fenton Road." Secret thought for a minute. "On second thought, I'm probably going to have to work through my break since I'm going to be late. But I'm off at eight."

"That works," Shawndiece said. "I'll see you then."

"Cool, see you then." Secret stared at Shawndiece for a minute. The next thing she knew Shawndiece pulled her in for a hug. The two friends embraced. Both unknowingly closed their eyes to fight back tears. These two had a bond that ran deep. They'd been joined at the hip since day one of meeting one another. And even though at this very moment the two were so close, they felt so far apart. Something had changed, and at eight o'clock tonight, Secret hoped she'd find out just what it was.

"Secret, it's seven-thirty. You're good to go," the store manager said to Secret as she rang up a customer's groceries.

Secret looked at the time on the register. "But I don't get off until eight."

"According to the time clock you didn't take a break today."

"I was a half hour late this morning, so I worked through my break."

"You were scheduled to come in at noon. You clocked in at eleven-thirty. You're still over like a half hour."

"Really?" Secret was confused as she continued to scan grocery items.

"Yeah, and you'll wanna watch that," the manager warned. "You don't want to go over your forty-hour workweek. That will push you into overtime pay. That comes out of the store budget."

"Yes, sir. I'm sorry," Secret apologized.

"I'll send Ramona to come relieve you."

"Thank you." Secret apologized again.

A couple minutes later Secret was finished ringing up the customer and her coworker took over. Secret was about to leave but then realized that she was supposed to be meeting Shawndiece at the store at eight. She hadn't gotten Shawndiece's new cell phone number so she couldn't call her and tell her she wouldn't be there. Secret didn't know what she was thinking by not having Shawndiece meet her back at the house in the first place. Secret decided she would get a little grocery shopping in to kill time.

Secret strolled her cart through the aisles of the store picking up little odds and ends. She was comparing the price of a store brand box of cereal to that of a name brand when she heard someone say her name.

"Secret Miller. My star student."

Secret turned to see a blond-haired older woman standing in the aisle behind a cart of her own.

"Mrs. Langston." Secret was so surprised to see her high school guidance counselor, but apparently not as surprised as her guidance counselor according to the look of shock on her semi-wrinkled face.

"Secret? What are you doing here?" Mrs. Langston asked as she abandoned her cart and walked over to embrace Secret. "How are you doing?"

"I'm good, Mrs. Langston," Secret replied. She put her head down. Such a rush of shame and embarrassment fell upon Secret and she began to fidget around with some items in her cart.

Thoughts of Mrs. Langston, one of the only other people to ever believe in her, about to watch Secret whip out her food stamp card made Secret feel bad. After all this woman had done to guide Secret down the road of success during her high school years, this was the way Secret repaid her for all of her time: by becoming a welfare, teenage, single mother. That was what the rest of the world had expected of Secret all along, but not Mrs. Langston. Never Mrs. Langston. But that's exactly what she'd become. Secret could barely look the woman in the face.

"How are you?" Secret figured she'd at least ask that and then get as far away from the woman as she could. "Are you still counseling over at the high school?"

"Yes, well no. Yes and no." Mrs. Langston giggled. "I'm still counseling, but at a different high school. One in which I can see the fruit of my labor." Mrs. Langston leaned in to whisper to Secret. "You know not all of your peers were like you, Secret. They'd be content with living in Flint for the rest of their lives doing nothing." She pulled away and began to speak at a regular tone. "But you were different, so determined. That's why when I received a copy of that letter from the scholarship committee that you'd received the full ride, I wasn't even surprised. I was happy for you, yes, but not surprised at all. If anyone deserved that scholarship, it was . . ."

Mrs. Langston's lips were still moving, but Secret could not hear a word that was coming out of her mouth. Even when she had been able to interpret her high school counselor's words clearly, had she actually heard her correctly? Oblivious to the fact that she was interrupting Mrs. Langston going on and on about the different caliber in students from the ones at Secret's old high school to the one she worked at now, Secret spoke.

"You said the scholarship committee sent you a letter?" Secret asked.

"Well, uh, yes. They'd CCed me on the letter since I had submitted it on your behalf," Mrs. Langston said, then moved right back to the subject matter Secret had ripped her from. "You know some of your classmates didn't even want to put forth the effort to fill out a scholarship application, but the kids I work with now, like yourself, are willing to do whatever it takes to get a higher education."

Mrs. Langston followed Secret's stare into her cart where she'd been fiddling in the entire conversation. She suddenly snapped her finger. "Oh, shoot. I forgot milk. I'm so glad I just noticed it in your cart." Mrs. Langston put her hand on Secret's shoulder. "It was so good bumping into you while you're back in town." She pointed into Secret's cart. "Getting snacks for your dorm, eh?" She playfully elbowed Secret. "Beware of that freshman twenty, or whatever they call it."

Secret knew what Mrs. Langston was referring to. There was a myth that when kids went off to college for that first year they gained fifteen pounds because of the poor eating habits they engaged in and the lack of healthy foods on the college campuses.

Mrs. Langston gave Secret the once-over. "Although it looks like you might already be five in the hole." She winked. "But you still look fabulous."

Secret looked down at herself realizing she was heavier since the last time Mrs. Langston had seen her. But she had a good reason and opened her mouth to tell her old high school counselor just that. "Oh, that's because I just had a . . ." Secret's words fell off. No way was she about to tell this woman she'd had a baby. She wasn't ashamed of Dina nor did she want to deny her, but she refused to be privy to the look of disappointment she knew would take over Mrs. Langston's face. "Never mind." Secret shooed her hand. "I guess I am a little thicker."

"Well, as long as you're feeding that brain that's all that matters." She looked at Secret with such admiration in her eyes. "I'm so proud of you. You made it. You worked hard for four years for a free ride to college and did it." Mrs. Langston's eyes began to water. "I know I can't take credit for it of course, but I'd like to think that my guidance had a little something to do with it."

"It did, Mrs. Langston. It did." It was harder now than ever for Secret to focus on the conversation with Mrs. Langston. She was still stuck on the fact that she'd said she'd received a letter from the scholarship committee granting her the scholarship to OSU. Mrs. Langston thought that Secret had made it. That she was off living the college life. She didn't want her to think any differently.

"I wish you nothing but the best in life, Secret," Mrs. Langston said. "I know you are going to get everything out of life that you've always dreamed of. Take care," were Mrs. Langston's final parting words before going back to her cart and rolling off.

Secret watched as Mrs. Langston hustled her cart down the aisle in pursuit of her forgotten milk. "There . . . there has to be some mistake," Secret said softly, to no one in particular. "My mother said the letter said . . ." Secret couldn't even get the words out she was full of emotions.

Devastation, disbelief, hurt, anger, confusion. She didn't know how to feel. She was mad. She didn't know who to be mad at. Somewhere someone was confused. Was it Mrs. Langston or was it her mother?

There was only one other way to find out.

Chapter 18

"Mrs. Langston?" Secret said, out of breath after abandoning her cart and racing to the dairy section to find Mrs. Langston.

Mrs. Langston turned around stunned. "Oh, Secret. Yes, dear, what is it?"

"The letter. You said you got a copy of the scholarship letter."

"Yes." Confusion laced Mrs. Langston's smile.

"I was wondering if I could have a copy of it. I'd really like to have it as a keepsake. I, uh, lost mine. Probably with all the packing and the moving to the dorm, you know. It would really mean so much to me if you could give me a copy of that letter."

"Oh, of course," Mrs. Langston said. "I still have it. I, too, wanted it as a keepsake. When I retire someday I'm going to go through all my letters and see how many of my students made it big. I know you're going to be one of them." She smiled. "Just give me your address and I'll mail it to you."

Secret quickly dug down in her purse and pulled out a piece of mail she had along with a pen. She wrote her address down on the envelope and then ripped the piece off and gave it to her former high school counselor.

Mrs. Langston looked at the paper. A puzzled expression came across her face. "This is a Flint address."

"Yeah, well uh . . ." Secret stammered for words.

"Oh, yeah, I know it's hard keeping up with mail when you're dealing with dorms and roommates. Students use their parents' mailing address all the time. Don't you worry; I'll make sure I get the copy mailed out to you."

"Thank you so much, Mrs. Langston. The sooner the better and I really do appreciate it."

"No problem, Secret. Take care."

Secret nodded then headed back up the aisle to the exit door. Her mind was a million miles away from the cart full of groceries she was leaving behind and the fact that in ten more minutes she was supposed to be meeting Shawndiece.

She made her way to her car just in time for the dam to break. She could no longer contain her mixed emotions. Secret gripped the steering wheel as tears poured from her eyes. Had either Mrs. Langston or her mother made a mistake? Had there been some sort of crazy mix-up on the scholarship committee's part?

If anything, Secret felt her mother would have had deliberate intentions, lying to Secret just to keep her from her dreams. But was Yolanda really that hateful where she would rip all that Secret had worked for right from underneath her? Secret didn't know.

"But what I do know," Secret said to herself, "is if that bitch stole my life, I'll kill her."

By the time Secret made it to Yolanda's door and was banging on it like she was the police, her emotions had gotten the best of her. She couldn't even remember if she'd shut the car off, closed the door, or even how she'd managed to get to the apartment safely. She'd been crying and her emotions had boiled over.

"What's wrong?" Yolanda said as she snatched the door open and stuck her head out. She was looking over each of Secret's shoulders. "Is a dog chasing you? You gotta pee or something? You knocking like it's a matter of life and death."

Secret brushed past her mother. "It is." She stood inside the door with her arms folded across her chest. "Why are you doing this for real?"

Yolanda had a look on her face that Secret couldn't quite make out. Either she was feeling confused or feeling busted. "Doing what, Secret?"

"Why did you all of a sudden feel a need to patch things up with me? Was it guilt?"

"Guilt? I have no idea what you are talking about." Yolanda went to walk away while uttering, "Let me get this baby ready for you."

"No!" By the time Secret realized she'd jumped in her mother's path, it was too late. So she stood her ground. "I want answers, Mom."

Yolanda stood in front of Secret taking in deep breaths as if she was trying to keep her cool. "Look, girl, watch yourself. Don't take my kindness for weakness." She went on to walk around Secret.

Secret spun around to see that her mother's back was to her while she walked over to the playpen that Dina was lying in. Yolanda had bought it for her grandbaby.

"Did you lie about the scholarship?" Secret just came out and asked, stopping her mother in her tracks.

"Pardon me?" Yolanda replied without even turning around to face Secret.

Secret cleared her throat and willed herself to keep the courage to continue the conversation with her mother. "Did you lie to me about the scholarship? That day we got into it and you kicked me out, you told me that the letter from the scholarship board had come in the mail and they'd denied me the scholarship. Was that true?"

There was too long of a pause, in Secret's mind, for it not to be true. Finally her mother slowly turned around and faced her.

"And so what if I did?"

There it was. There was the tone Secret recognized. There was the look in her mother's eyes she recognized. The real Yolanda was back. This sudden shift in demeanor startled Secret to the point where she took a step backward. She was stunned to the point where she didn't even reply to her mother's question. So Yolanda repeated herself, taking a step toward Secret.

"I said, 'And so what if I did?'"

"Well, I, uhh . . ." Secret hadn't thought about that one. She'd been so hell bent on finding out whether her mother had sabotaged her out of going off to college that she hadn't even considered what she'd do once finding out the answer.

"You walking up in here like Billy Bad, like you da baddest bitch. Banging on my goddamn door like you ain't got no fucking sense." Oh, Yolanda was back in full force. "So I lied about the scholarship letter. So what? You shouldn't have been walking around this bitch like you was better than everybody else. Like you was the smartest motherfucker to ever walk the planet. Fuck that." Yolanda rolled her eyes and stood her ground as if she was just as right as the day was long. She stood there practically daring Secret to do something about it.

Secret was absolutely fuming on the inside. Her head was throbbing and her heart was hurting. Her eyes were watering and her bottom lip was trembling. If she had to compare the feeling of Lucky watching her go to jail and the feeling of knowing her mother destroyed her chances of going to college, she didn't know which one hurt the worst. Both had changed her life completely, had put her on a path that couldn't have possibly altered her life for the better in any way. At least that's how Secret saw it in this actual moment.

"I don't even know what to say to you right now," Secret said.

"You can start with a thank you."

"Thank you?" Secret said shocked. "For what?"

"Prior to me telling you that you didn't get that scholarship you were going to get an abortion and go head off to Ohio. If that had happened, this baby wouldn't be here." She pointed to Dina.

Secret's eyes traveled over to Dina as she recalled the exact thoughts that had run through her mind after finding out she hadn't received the scholarship.

"Why can't I keep this baby?" she asked herself. The main reason why she was even considering aborting the baby in the first place was so that she could live her dream of going to college and making a better life for herself. But Yolanda was right: no money no college. She hated to admit it, but as Secret stood in the mirror she wondered if perhaps her mother was right about everything. Secret's destiny appeared to be sewn up in a bag. A life in Flint just like her mother's and every other chick on the block was the life she would live. There was no going up against destiny. The more Secret thought about things, the more she began to lean toward giving birth versus taking a life. After only a few more minutes, Secret's mind was completely changed and completely made up. "Oh, well, baby. Looks like it's just going to be you and me," Secret said to her unborn child.

And even now it would still just be Secret and her baby. She would have loved for the three generations of Miller females to have a relationship, but that wasn't going to happen. She was in a position where she was forced to forgive Lucky, but when it came to her mother, it was 100 percent up to Secret. She looked at the evil, relentless, coldhearted woman who stood before her. No way could she forgive her. Not today, not tomorrow, not forever. A leopard never changes its spots, only its location. Once a bitch always a bitch.

All Secret could do was storm past her mother and go get Dina.

"Whatever," Yolanda said. "Take her. Take all her stuff and don't even think about showing up with her at my doorstep tomorrow for me to watch her while you go to work."

Secret ignored her mother as she gathered up her baby and all her belongings. She even went to the kitchen and made sure there wasn't a single bottle or can of milk. If Dina grew up and wanted a relationship with her grandmother, so be it, but as long as Secret had a say, she would keep her daughter as far away from Queen Bitch as she could. Otherwise she might risk the chance of having to raise Princess Bitch.

With Dina and all of her belongings in hand, Secret was at the front door. When she went to open it, Yolanda jumped in her way.

"Wait a minute, hold up. We can't do this again," Yolanda said, reconsidering. "I'm sorry. You can bring her back tomorrow. She's my grandbaby. Got nothing to do with what's going on between me and you."

"She has everything to do with what's going on between me and you," Secret begged to differ. "I got lucky. I didn't turn out like you, and I know you don't want to believe it, but I owe that to Grandma. And I know you say Grandma wasn't who I thought she was. Clearly from the time she raised you from the time I got older she changed for the better. So it's my prayer that the same will happen with you. Now excuse me, but I'm taking my daughter and getting the hell out of here." Secret snatched open the door and hauled it on out of her mother's house, vowing it would be the last time, for real this time, that she ever stepped foot in it.

As Secret made her way to the car Yolanda was furiously shouting out insults. "Take your bastard-ass baby,"

Yolanda shouted. "I was just trying to help you. I tried to be nice to your ass, but I should have known that all the money in the world wasn't worth it."

Secret steadily put everything in the car and buckled Dina in as Yolanda finished her rampage. Just as Secret opened the driver door to get in Yolanda shouted out one last thing.

"That detective can offer me all the money in the world. Hell, he can have back what he gave me. I'm done fucking with your stuck-up ass. You didn't get an abortion, but I should have." Yolanda walked back into her house and slammed her door.

Secret stood paralyzed. Typically when a person is paralyzed, they can't feel anything, but she was full of pain. She could feel every knife reentering every wound, and fingernails pulling off unhealed scabs. Her body was throbbing. Her head was throbbing. Her heart was aching.

Whatever little voice that was inside of her telling her not to let her mother in so quickly had been on point. Her mother wasn't trying to make things right. Her mother had only reached out to her because apparently she'd been paid to.

With tears streaming down her face, Secret hopped into her car. She needed to find out if there was anyone else who had been paid to reenter her life.

Chapter 19

"My own mother! You paid my own mother to be a part of my life?" Secret screamed to Detective Davis through her cell phone as she drove away from her mother's apartment complex. "Who else have you paid?"

"Nobody, Secret, I promise," Detective Davis assured her. "I know how you must feel, but believe me—"

"And why should I believe you? How do I know I'm not the one being played here? For all I know this could be a set up to throw my black ass back into jail." Secret didn't know who or what to believe now.

"I promise you, your mother is the only person we reached out to. And that's only because I knew you'd need someone to keep an eye on the baby for you." Detective Davis continued, "If it makes you feel any better, she didn't ask for the money; we offered it, you know, to sweeten the deal."

"Yeah, but she took it," Secret said. "You had to pay my mother to spend time with me and my baby like some trick. I can't believe this."

"Look, I'm sorry, Secret, but this isn't about you. I like you and you are a sweet girl. I'm sorry you got caught up in all this, but the thing is, you're in it now and there's only one way out."

Secret hung up in Detective Davis's ear before he could say another word. She wiped the tears from her eyes as she continued to drive. She looked in the rearview mirror at Dina in her car seat.

"You are the only one Mommy can trust now, Dina. And I promise you'll always be able to trust me. Mommy is never going to let anything happen to you. Ever."

Secret cleared her tears away and made her way home. By the time she walked into her front door she was all cried out. Like her mother had said, she was moving on. She had tougher skin than she thought. Not many girls would have been able to so easily get over the fact that their mother wished they'd been aborted and was only playing a part in their life because she was getting paid to. She had a daughter to worry about now. No way was she going to give Yolanda another second of her time.

Secret inhaled and then exhaled. She allowed her mother's awful and evil words to play inside her head. This go-around they truly had no effect. They didn't make Secret angry. They didn't hurt her. Finally turned out Yolanda had done something right after all. She had taught Secret to be tough. Yolanda was who she was. She was never going to change, not even if she got paid to. And Secret realized there wasn't a damn thing she could do about it. For the next few moments she mourned the death of the mother she had always dreamed of but would never have. All cried out about the situation, Secret was more than ready to move on.

With Secret no longer having Yolanda as a caregiver for Dina, thank God her childcare assistance from the state kicked in, and right on time. Secret found a nice older woman who only lived about five minutes from the store to care for Dina. The woman's, Miss Good's, spirit reminded Secret so much of her own grandmother's, who she missed dearly. Yolanda had been removed from Secret's life, but Miss Good was certainly filling in the void as a grandmother for Dina. Miss Good had only been caring for Dina a couple of days, but her warm and inviting ways made Secret feel as if she'd known this woman all her life. She was just what the doctor ordered.

"She's just the sweetest little chunky button ever." Miss Good cooed over Dina as Secret fastened her up in her bucket seat.

Baby Dina just smiled and kicked as the older woman talked to her. She would even look at Secret and smile as if to say, "You see the nice woman, Mommy?" It comforted Secret's heart knowing that her baby got the same type of vibe from Miss Good as she did.

"I fed her before we left," Secret told Miss Good.

"What did you feed her?" Miss Good asked.

"Milk."

"Milk?" Miss Good scrunched her face up. "You mean you gave her something to drink then. You feed people food. Milk ain't food."

Secret chuckled. "She's just a baby," she told the caregiver.

"And babies are little people, and little people need to eat!" Miss Good was emphatic.

Secret just shook her head and smiled. "Her bottles are in her bag."

Miss Good brushed Secret out of the way and started talking to Dina. "Don't you worry. Momma Good's got something good for you. They don't call me Miss Good for nothing." She then shot Secret a look, daring her to even fix her mouth into talking Miss Good out of giving Dina anything solid.

Worry covered Secret's face, as the doctors had said Dina couldn't have solid foods until she was six months.

"What's that look for?" Miss Good asked Secret, throwing her hands on her hips. "Child, I been taking care of kids longer than you been born. I know what I'm doing. I ain't gon' give her nothing but a little bit of baby cereal."

Secret felt a bit more relieved and it showed as some of the tension left her face.

"Maybe a little grits and scrambled eggs," Miss Good mumbled.

"Miss Good," Secret said, tilting her head to the side.

"Child, I'm just playing with you. Carry yourself on to work." Miss Good shooed her hand.

Secret kissed Dina one last time and then headed to the door. Before walking out she pointed to Miss Good and said, "No mashed potatoes either. I know how your generation thinks it's okay to give babies mashed potatoes and gravy just because it's soft. Then y'all wonder why there is child diabetes and high blood pressure."

"Get on out of here already," Miss Good ordered playfully.

Secret laughed and went to her car. Ten minutes later she was already clocked in at work and working the cash register.

While Secret checked out customers in the grocery store line for the next couple hours, her mind was 100 percent focused on the job and not worried about the safety of her child. Secret didn't know how she was going to feel leaving her baby with a complete stranger. But Miss Good didn't feel like a strange at all. That was a priceless piece of mind for a working mother.

"Have a great day and thank you for shopping with us," Secret said to her customer who she'd just finished waiting on. She immediately let the next spiel fall out of her mouth while straightening up a few plastic bags. "Did you find everything okay?"

"Absolutely," she heard a voice say.

Secret looked up from the bags only to find herself staring right into Lucky's eyes. "Lucky, what are you doing here? And how—"

"I came here to see you of course. Oh, and pick up this loaf of bread." Lucky held up a loaf of bread he'd just randomly picked up to have an excuse to go through Secret's line.

"Boy, please. In all the time I've known you I've never seen you make a sandwich. You don't need that bread." Secret looked over her shoulder and saw that she had two customers standing behind Lucky. She turned her attention back to Lucky. "Let me take care of the rest of these customers in line and then I'll get off the register."

"Cool." Lucky went to walk out of the line.

Secret playfully snatched the bread from him, shook her head, smiled, then set it down in the basket of items that needed to be returned to the shelves.

Lucky smiled and went off to the side and waited.

Secret turned off her light so that customers would see her lane was closed and wouldn't get in it. She rang up her last customer, grabbed the basket of returns, and signaled Lucky to follow her.

"So how did you know where to find me?" After the incident with Detective Davis and her mother, Secret was leery of the entire situation now.

"Your girl," Lucky said.

Secret thought for a moment, at first thinking it was Kat. Besides Kat and Yolanda, Secret hadn't really told anyone else where she worked. But Lucky didn't know Yolanda and why would Kat be talking to him.

"Shawndiece," Lucky said after watching Secret rack her brain.

"Oh, yeah." Secret nodded.

"She said she was supposed to come up here and holler at you, so that y'all could talk, but you played her."

"I didn't play her. I had a situation." Bumping into Mrs. Langston and finding out about the whole scholarship thing had trumped meeting up with Shawndiece. "I had a family emergency and had to leave."

"Was it the baby? Is everything okay? Anything you need from me?"

Secret's heart began to patter. She had to take deep breaths. Hearing the sincerity in Lucky's voice, him wanting to be at her beck and call, him wanting to rescue her, made her feel so good and wanted. It reminded her of how things used to be between them, how things were supposed to be. Lucky had saved her from the streets, literally. He'd been there to protect her and supply her with all her needs without her ever even having to ask. That was every girl's dream come true, at least the dream of all the girls Secret knew. She'd heard enough conversations in the girls' bathroom at school to know what their motives and aspirations were when it came to men. And Secret had achieved such without even having to work for it.

The same went for Shawndiece when it came to guys. Secret had seen her run through men like it wasn't nothing. Anybody she gave herself to had to be giving her something in return. She hoped eventually she would hit the jackpot and end up with one dude who would cater to all her needs so she could just have to worry with one lame. At least those were her words. But to date it hadn't happened, which was why Secret kind of understood how Shawndiece could have gotten caught up with the dope game. It was quick, fast, and easy money; sometimes good money.

There was a time, though, where Secret felt Shawndiece was jealous of the fact that the first baller Secret had gotten with was the jackpot, while Shawndiece had been trying to rope one in ever since her cherry got popped. But in so many words Shawndiece had used Biggie Smalls' words on her: "I made you . . ." So why would Shawndiece play her?

Secret could honestly say that throughout her entire friendship with Shawndiece, Shawndiece never asked for or ever wanted a thing from Secret. The only thing Shawndiece had ever wanted for her was to survive. She made sure she taught Secret everything she knew in order to be able to survive.

Secret hated that Shawndiece thought Secret was trying to play her the other day by not waiting for her to show up at the store. That hadn't been the case at all, but Secret could wholeheartedly understand how Shawndiece might have thought that.

"Nothing was wrong with the baby. Everything is good. I don't need anything. I'm going to have to get with Shawn though and let her know what was up."

"Well, I'm glad everything is good with you," Lucky said.

Secret began to restock some canned goods out of the basket. "So you said you came by to see me. For what?"

"I hadn't heard from you since that day I came to your place."

Secret gave him the once over. "I haven't heard from you either," she shot back and then continued restocking.

"I kind of figured the ball was in your court though. I wanted to respect your feelings about the situation."

"Look, like I said, everybody deserves a second chance. You explained yourself about the matter, I kind of get it. I'm out of jail. I have a beautiful, healthy baby girl. No harm no foul." Secret shrugged and kept focused on her work.

Lucky stared at Secret in awe. "Girl, where did you come from? I know I've said it a million times, but I can't help it because it's true. You are not like other chicks from here. And I can't even believe you are related to Kat. You are nothing like her." Lucky laughed. "If this had been her, she would have went ham on me and probably tried to . . ." Lucky's words trailed off once he noticed the sour expression on Secret's face.

"You really gonna compare me to my sister right now? Really?"

"Oh, my bad," Lucky said.

Secret let a smile slip through. "I'm just messing with you. I get that situation, too."

Lucky watched Secret struggle to place something on the top shelf. She couldn't quite reach it. "Here, let me help you." Lucky went and stood behind Secret.

The heat from his body was warming her. She could smell his soft daytime cologne. Places in her body started to get moist.

Even once Lucky had removed the item from Secret's hand and placed it on the shelf, he stood behind her a few seconds, inhaling the smell of her hair. "Suave Professionals."

"Huh?" Secret turned around, her front side now against Lucky's.

"Suave Professionals. I remember that is the kind of shampoo you use. Remember that time I washed your hair in the shower?"

Secret smiled. "Yeah. I was pregnant and getting too fat and tired to do it myself."

"Let me do it again." Lucky said it in a whisper with his lips practically pressed up against Secret's. "Damn, I missed you so much. I didn't know what I was going to do without you."

"I'm sure you found plenty of women to fill the void," Secret said.

"With your watchdog, cock blocking–ass best friend around? Shitttttt."

Secret couldn't help but laugh. That was Shawndiece for you. Secret stopped laughing. She stopped smiling. She didn't want to be all up in this dude's face hee hee hawing, not for real and hardly for fake. But she couldn't help herself. She couldn't shake the feelings rising up inside of her, some old and some new. This was something she hadn't thought about when agreeing to rekindle a relationship with Lucky. She thought for sure all the hate would drown out the little bit of love that still might have been lingering around.

Lucky touched her cheek. Secret quickly turned away.

"What's wrong?" Lucky asked.

"I can't right now," Secret said as she pushed Lucky from in front of her and went in search of the aisles she needed to be in to put the remaining items in the basket in.

"Wait! Secret wait!" Lucky rushed behind her and grabbed her arm.

"Hey, is everything okay here?" the store manager came around the corner and asked. He looked down to see Lucky gripping Secret's arm. "Hey, young man. Get off of her."

"Dude, I'm having a conversation with my girl," Lucky told the store manager while Secret was trying to loosen her arm from him. He kept a tight grip on it though.

"Well, this looks like more than a conversation to me. You are being physical. If you don't take your hands off of her right now, I'm calling the police."

Lucky released Secret and stormed over to the manager, pointing his finger and getting all up in his face. "Man, I said I'm just talking to my girl here." Spittle was flying out of Lucky's mouth.

"That's it. I'm calling the cops now." The store manager went storming back up the aisle.

Lucky looked at Secret in a panic. His eyes pleaded with her to do something. She knew that look all too well. She'd had the very same look in her eyes that day of her arrest. She'd pleaded with Lucky but he did nothing. Payback was a bitch.

Secret watched as the store manager pulled out his cell phone. She then looked back to Lucky and his pleading puppy dog eyes. She took a step toward her manager. "Wait, Mr. Farmer. Please, no need to call the police," Secret told him just as he was about to dial 911.

Mr. Farmer looked to Lucky and then back to Secret. "I understand domestic violence. My mother protected my father for years. You don't have to be afraid. I'll be a witness and—"

"Mr. Farmer, no, it's not like that. He's my baby's father. He was sharing something very important with me about the baby. He was touching me more so out of passion versus being violent. I'd never allow a man to put his hands on me. Ever."

Mr. Farmer stared at Secret a few more moments trying to read her face. He wanted to make sure she was telling the truth and just wasn't afraid of the repercussions from her abuser if the police were called.

For assurance Secret said, "And after hearing about your mother, you can best believe I'll never let a man put his hands on me. I'm so sorry your mother went through that, and that you had to experience that. I won't allow that to happen to myself or my child." Secret rubbed her manager's shoulder. "But thank you so much for caring enough to want to protect me." She was still speaking to her manager but looked to Lucky when she said, "No one has ever protected me like that before." She looked back to her manager who 100 percent believed everything Secret was saying.

Mr. Farmer looked to Lucky. "Hey, I'm sorry about that, man. It just looked like—"

Lucky cut him off. "Don't worry about it. Like my girl here said"—he pointed to Secret—"thank you for looking out for her. It's good to know that if something did happen to her, there is a good person like you around to take care of her."

The pride building up in Mr. Farmer was obvious by the way his shoulders lifted and he held his head up high. "I just did what any decent person would do. That's all." He looked to Secret. "Secret, we need you on register four." He then walked away.

Once Mr. Farmer was gone Lucky walked over to Secret. He touched her on her elbow. "Thank you so much." He exhaled. "You didn't have to do that for me. I don't even know why you did considering . . ." His words trailed off as he shook his head.

Secret finished his thoughts. "Especially since you didn't do the same for me when you had a chance?"

Lucky nodded. "That would have been a golden opportunity to pay me back."

"I don't need to pay you back, Lucky. 'Vengeance is mine thus sayeth the Lord.'"

Lucky had a confused look on his face. "What's that supposed to mean?"

"According to my grandmother, it means God can get you back way better than I ever could." Secret pulled her arm away from Lucky and walked away while throwing over her shoulder, "And by the way, I'm not your girl."

Lucky watched Secret walk away while mumbling under his breath, "Not yet anyway."

Chapter 20

"Ray, oh my goodness! What are you doing here?" Secret said after slinging open her door.

Ray looked Secret up and down. Secret was dressed in a nice flowing off-the-shoulder chiffon top. She wore white leggings underneath and some studded flip-flops. Her hair was in flat twist straight back and she wore some silver dripping earrings. "Looks like you were expecting company, just not me." Ray looked over Secret's shoulder and into her apartment. She could see where the dining room table was set. There was even a candle in the middle of the table.

Secret followed Ray's eyes to the table. "Oh, that. Yeah, well." Secret turned to face Ray. "But, uh, you can come in." Secret stepped to the side.

"You sure? I don't want to interrupt your evening."

"You came all this way. At least come in and say hi. Besides that, I've missed you."

Ray stepped into the apartment. "I can tell." There was a hint of sarcasm behind Ray's tone.

Secret immediately felt convicted for having not even bothered to pick up the phone and call Ray these past weeks. After all, if it had not been for Ray stepping in to save the day, Secret could very well still be in jail. And it wasn't because Secret hadn't appreciated everything that Ray had done for her that had kept her from calling up Ray. It just felt so awkward.

It was no secret that there was some type of attraction between the two women. They'd shared a kiss at Ray's home. Not just some little "Secret kissed a girl and she liked it" peck. It had been a deep, passionate kiss that had sent chills through Secret's body. Had she not recently given birth to Dina at the time, Lord only knows what might have happened between the two that night. Never ever having felt that way about a female before, those feelings she was having toward Ray scared her. So it was safe to say that fear was the main reason why Secret hadn't reached out to Ray.

Ray stepped inside and Secret closed and locked the door behind them. Ray sniffed the aroma wavering throughout the room. "Mmmm. Smells good in here."

"Yes, I just finished cooking dinner," Secret said. Feeling as though it would be rude to have Ray over smelling all that delicious food and not offering her any, she made a suggestion. "I'd love it if you'd do me a favor. Come and taste some of what I cooked and tell me what you think."

Ray stuck her hands down in her pockets. "Nahh, from the times you cooked while staying at my place, I'm sure it's just fine," she complimented her. "Where's Dina?" She looked around. She saw a couple of Dina's toys and her baby swing, but the baby was nowhere in sight.

"She's down for the evening. Well at least for the next few hours. That child doesn't hardly sleep through the night."

"Yeah, that must be tough, getting up in the middle of the night."

"I really don't mind. Her little face puts a smile on mine every time."

"I imagine. She has a face just like yours."

Secret blushed at Ray's compliment. "Anyway, come." Secret waved Ray into the kitchen. "Taste this food for me."

Ray followed Secret into the kitchen and watched her take pans out of the oven and lids off pots on the stove. Secret retrieved a spoon and fork from the kitchen drawer and fed Ray samples of all the different foods she'd prepared.

"Girl, you are the young, black Martha Stewart," Ray teased.

"So I take it you approve?" Secret asked.

"Absolutely."

"Then I'll have to have you over and cook like this for you sometime."

"I'd really like that, Secret."

The two just stood there smiling in silence. Finally Secret figured she should speak on whatever this thing was, or wasn't, between the two of them.

"Look," both women began at the same time. Then they both laughed. "You go ahead." Again the two women spoke at the same time.

"I just wanted to say that I hope I haven't made you uncomfortable in any way." Ray finally got her words out.

"Uncomfortable." Secret feigned dumb. "Why would I be uncomfortable around you?"

"Come on, Secret. Let's not play games. We're better than that." Ray took Secret's hands into hers. "You're a sweet girl. Nice and beautiful. I just want to clarify that in no way did I want anything from you in return for helping you out. So I hope with that kiss and getting my little feel on I didn't make you, you know, feel like you couldn't be around me."

Secret shook her head. "No, no, it's not that at all. I'm a big girl. Trust me, every decision I make, I make on my own. Good or bad. Besides, I'm the one who kissed you first. Remember?"

"I hear you," Ray said. "So was it good?" She looked into Secret's eyes.

"Huh, what?"

"The kiss, was it—"

"Oh, it was good, real good," Secret expressed.

Ray smiled. "I was going to ask was it a good decision to kiss me."

Secret felt embarrassed. "Oh, oh, my bad, I thought—"

"It's okay. I'm glad the kiss was good. I'm flattered."

Secret looked down at her hands that were still nestled inside of Ray's. Ray looked down.

"Oh, I'm sorry." Ray let go of Secret's hands. "I didn't mean to—"

"It's okay. Please, I didn't mean anything by, you know." Secret took Ray's hands into hers. She didn't want Ray to think she had looked down at her hands as a sign for her to not touch her. She liked Ray's touch.

Ray took her thumbs and rubbed the back of Secret's hands. "So soft."

"Thank you," Secret said. She could feel Ray tugging on her hands, pulling her into her. Secret didn't resist. She found herself nose to nose with Ray.

Ray leaned in slowly and brushed her lips up against Secret's. She then placed a kiss on them. On the second kiss, she could feel Secret participating. Slowly Ray slid her tongue into Secret's mouth. Secret began to inhale and exhale as she became hot and bothered. Ray pulled her hands away from Secret and placed them around her small waist. She pulled Secret into her then allowed her hands to cup Secret's ass.

She massaged Secret's butt cheeks as she deep throated her with a passionate kiss. Looking into Secret's eyes Ray took her hand and brought it around to Secret's private spot and began massaging her through her white pants.

"Ahhh," Secret moaned.

Ray suddenly stopped. "What am I doing?" She went to pull away but Secret pulled her back close.

"You're making me feel good, that's what you're doing," Secret said. "Please don't stop. I like it." Secret pulled Ray up against her and began kissing her.

Ray gave in and allowed her hands to begin roaming Secret's body. She cupped Secret's breast through the chiffon shirt. She then placed her hand under the shirt, cupping her breast through her bra. Once again Ray allowed her hand to massage Secret's privates. Ray could feel the warmth coming from Secret.

"Damn, you're so hot," Ray panted. Ray kneeled down and removed Secret's flip-flops. She then stood up in Secret's face, staring in her eyes as she slipped Secret's pants and panties down her thighs. She bent down again and slid them off of each of Secret's feet. She then lifted Secret's right foot up to her mouth and began massaging each pink-painted toe with her tongue.

The feeling practically drove Secret out of her mind. She grabbed the counter with one hand and the refrigerator handle with the other in order to balance. Ray was making her weak.

Ray ran her tongue across each toe, placing each one in her mouth, popping it out with a thud sound. She used her tongue to trace in-between Secret's toes. Next she placed kisses all up Secret's legs and thighs until her face was right at Secret's triangle. Ray used her mouth to nuzzle and part Secret's vagina lips.

"Oh my goodness," Secret moaned.

Ray began licking Secret's clit like it was a lollypop. She sucked the clit and could feel Secret almost lose her balance. Ray sucked and licked like the last supper was between Secret's legs. With her hands pulling Secret into her face by her butt cheeks, she toyed and teased Secret's clit.

"Oh, oh, oh," Secret began to holler until the sound of the doorbell interrupted everything. "Oh, shit," Secret said, coming out of the trance Ray's tongue had her in. "That's my company." Secret frantically began to put her clothing back on.

Ray watched at first, trying to get in where she could fit in to help Secret. "Here." Ray handed Secret her flip-flops.

"Thank you," Secret said, taking the shoes and putting them on her feet. She looked around the kitchen while patting her hair down. Everything looked and felt okay, so she headed to the front door. The doorbell rang one more time before she could get to it. "I'm coming," Secret called out in a hard whisper, not wanting to wake Dina up. Before opening the door, she gave herself one last pat down. She cleared her throat and then opened the door. "Lucky," she greeted him upon seeing him standing on her doorstep.

He looked Secret up and down, admiring her outfit and her post-baby body in the outfit. "I'm lucky as hell. I get to have dinner with your fine ass."

Just then the door opened farther and for the first time Lucky spotted Ray. The smile that had been on his face faded.

Noticing the look on Lucky's face, Secret turned her neck to look at Ray. "Oh, Ray, yeah. Ray, this is Lucky. Lucky, this is my friend Ray. She just stopped by to say hey. She was just heading out."

Ray came around, basically trading spots with Secret and extended her hand to Lucky. "Nice to meet you, Lucky."

Lucky stared at Ray's face while extending his hand. "You look so familiar," Lucky said, shaking Ray's hand.

"I work in the ER at Genesee Hospital. Ever been shot or stabbed? Perhaps I've stitched you up before," Ray said.

"I have a couple soldier wounds. Maybe so."

Not 100 percent certain, but Secret felt as though there was some tension in the air between Lucky and Ray. It could have been all in her head considering she was in the middle of getting eaten out by Ray when her date for the evening, Lucky, knocked on the door. A little awkward standing between the girl who just ate you and the guy who you're about to feed.

"Well, uh, Ray, I'm so glad you stopped by," Secret told her. "It was good seeing you. I'll call you. We'll have to do lunch or something."

"Yeah, that sounds good, considering I didn't get to finish eating, so I'm still a little hungry." She rubbed her stomach while winking at Secret.

Secret began blushing and her cheeks turned a fiery red. Her mouth dropped open. She could feel Lucky staring at her. She looked to him and he had a proverbial question mark on his face. He wanted to know what was really going on.

"Uh, yeah," Secret began to stammer to Lucky. "I, you know, had Ray taste the meal I prepared for you. I wanted to get her opinion." There was silence. Secret didn't know if Lucky was buying her story. "Right, Ray?" she turned to Ray and said, her eyes begging for backup.

Ray paused for a minute, watching her friend squirm. She then replied, "Yep, that's right."

Secret and Ray stood there staring at each other. Lucky stood staring at them, his eyes going back and forth from one to the other.

"Well, Ray, how was it?" Lucky decided to ask.

Still staring into Secret's eyes Ray replied, "How was what?"

"What you tasted," Lucky said.

"Oh, that," Ray said, snapping out of her trance. "It was delicious." She licked her lips.

Secret pictured Ray's tongue rubbing across her clit. She twitched her legs a little and a moan escaped.

Both Ray and Lucky looked to Secret. Embarrassed Secret said, "Sorry. I'm just a little faint. Had to work all day, get Dina down for bed, and cook. I haven't even eaten myself, so perhaps we should go on inside and eat." Secret took Lucky's hand into hers.

"Yeah, perhaps we should," he agreed.

That was clearly Ray's hint to leave, but it took her a couple of seconds to get the hint. She then cleared her throat.

"Oh, yeah, well let me let you two go ahead and enjoy your meal." Ray gave Secret a hug. "You take care." She then pulled away and looked to Lucky. "It was nice meeting you. Enjoy your meal. Save me some." She winked and then left.

Secret thought she was going to faint and only prayed that Ray's subliminal messages to her had gone over Lucky's head. She closed the door, locked it, and then turned to see Lucky standing there staring at her.

"What?" Secret asked.

Lucky shook his head. "I know ol' girl from somewhere."

Secret shrugged. "Like she said, maybe you have seen her in the ER or something."

"Yeah, maybe," Lucky agreed, still pondering where he might know Ray from.

"I know." Secret snapped her finger. "You might have seen her that night at the gas station when you came to pick me up after my mom put me out. She's the one who let me use her phone to call you. She was still there when you came to pick me up."

Lucky twisted his lips while in thought. "Maybe. Must mean she was really worried about you if she waited there with you for me to show up." Lucky let out a harrumph.

"Your store manager, Ray . . . You got a lot of people who just happen to be in the right place at the right time showing up to rescue you, huh?"

Secret thought about Lucky's comment for a moment. "Hmmm, I guess I do. And you were one of those people as well," Secret concurred. "Anyway, dinner is ready. Let's eat."

Secret headed into the kitchen and fixed her and Lucky's plates. She set them down on the dining room table. Lucky was sitting over on the couch watching television.

"Your feast awaits you," Secret said to Lucky.

Lucky picked up the remote, turned the television off, and then went and joined Secret at the table. "Damn, you showed out," Lucky said. "Roast, mac and cheese, greens, corn muffins, sweet potatoes. Is it Thanksgiving already? This is better than me taking you out to dinner."

Lucky had called Secret a couple days ago and invited her out to dinner. Secret hadn't called him since their little tiff in the grocery store, so he'd decided to make the first move. Secret declined. She didn't really want to take Dina out in the evening to her babysitter. It was bad enough Dina was away from her all day while she worked. The last thing Secret wanted to do was dump her off back to the babysitter's that evening.

Knowing she had to start moving things along with her and Lucky's connection, Secret didn't want to pass up the opportunity to spend time with him, so she opted to cook dinner for him at her place instead. He'd gladly accepted, so now here the two sat breaking bread together.

"This looks good as hell," Lucky said about the spread on the table.

"Let's hope you think it tastes as good as it looks." Secret said grace and the two began to dig in.

"Ray was right," Lucky said. "This is delicious."

"Thank you," Secret said not sensing any type of sarcasm from Lucky at the mention of Ray's name.

The two finished off their meals and sat at the table full and satisfied.

"You want dessert?" Secret asked Lucky.

"What you made dessert too? What is it?"

"It's a cherry pie, but I cheated. It's from the frozen section at my store."

Lucky laughed.

"But it's still good," Secret said.

Lucky looked Secret up and down. "Mmmm, I bet it is still good." He licked his lips.

Secret wriggled in her seat a little bit, blushing.

"You look good tonight."

"Thank you." Secret smiled.

"You can't even tell you just had a baby."

"Well, the baby is four months old, so technically I didn't just have a baby."

"Yeah, but chick's kids be twelve and they still be talking about they carrying baby weight."

Secret laughed.

"I'm serious." Lucky laughed as well. "But you do look good though, ma."

"Thank you," Secret said.

"The food tasted as good as it looked, so I'm wondering if the same goes for you."

"Huh? What?" Secret said in a coy manner.

Lucky got up from the table and walked over to Secret. "Girl, let's stop playing games. Clearly we still have a connection."

"And what makes you so sure of that?" Secret asked.

"I wouldn't be here right now if we didn't."

"You think?" Secret asked.

"I know. If I don't know anything else about you, I know you don't play games. It ain't in you. You keep it one hunnid, which is what always turned me on about you. And as you can see, I'm turned on now." Lucky's eyes roamed down to his manhood that was practically bulging out of his pants.

Secret caught herself staring at it, reminiscing on how good Lucky used to make her feel. *No, no, no,* she scolded herself. *This assignment does not have to include sex.*

Sure she had to form a relationship with Lucky, but Detective Davis never said it had to be sexual. Secret's mind was telling her no, but her body was damn sure telling her yes.

Lucky extended his hand. Still torn in her own thoughts, Secret just stared at it for a minute.

Seeing the contemplation written all over her face Lucky said, "I'll never hurt you again, Secret. Anything I do from this point on will only make you feel good. I promise you it won't hurt."

Secret couldn't resist one second longer. It had been so long since she'd been made to feel good. Lucky didn't deserve her. He didn't deserve her body. She knew that deep inside. Not after the way he'd played her. But for just once in her life Secret wanted to be selfish. She wanted to make this all about her and her needs. Yeah, Lucky might get his off as well, but she was damn sure going to get hers.

Chapter 21

Secret slowly placed her hand into Lucky's. He smiled and pulled her up to him. He slowly led her up to her bedroom, closing the door behind them.

Secret lay across the bed as Lucky slowly began to undress her. He removed her flip-flops first, then slid her panties and pants down. It felt like déjà vu. Not too long ago it was Ray who had been doing this exact same thing to Secret.

Ironically, Lucky had finished off the meal Secret had started with Ray. Now Lucky was about to finish off what Ray had started with Secret.

"Damn, you wet as hell down there," Lucky said, staring down at Secret as he began to undo his pants. "I can see the juices flowing already."

There was no telling whether it was freshly squeezed juice, or the juices Ray had already gotten to flow earlier. Nonetheless, the wetness drenched Lucky's fingers when he began plunging them inside Secret.

She crooned and grooved her hips as Lucky played inside her sugar walls. He got harder by the moment watching her lie there with her eyes closed taking in his fingers.

"Damn, I got to get in that pussy," he said, taking his hands and spreading Secret's legs apart. The two were naked from the bottom down, still had on their shirts. They were both so heated that there was no more time for foreplay or for removing the remainder of their clothing.

Lucky placed the tip of his penis inside Secret. He was confused when she pulled away from him. "What?" he asked.

"Hello, condom."

"You serious right now?"

"I just had a baby. My stuff if like fertilized ground right now. I'm liable to have twins if I get pregnant," Secret argued.

"Please just the tip. Please, Secret." Lucky began to kiss Secret. "Please." He managed to use his hand to maneuver his penis back to Secret's wet pussy lips. "Please, baby, please." He kissed Secret and pumped the tip of himself in and out of Secret.

"Lucky, no," she moaned loving the way just that tip of Lucky felt inside of her.

"Come on, you know this shit feels good. You know you miss this dick," Lucky coaxed as he slipped more and more of himself inside her.

At first Secret subconsciously began to throw her hips back and forth, taking more and more of Lucky in and loving every inch of it. But then upon him thrusting his entire vessel in her, her eyes opened wide. Not just her two eyes, but her mind's eye. What was she thinking? As bad as she wouldn't mind experiencing an orgasm right about now, no way should it be with Lucky. She forced herself to replay in her mind him allowing her to be handcuffed and thrown into the back of a police car while eight months pregnant. He drove off and left both her and her baby for dead. No way was he about to bust one off up in her.

"No, we can't," Secret said as Lucky thrust in and out of her.

He was so caught up in the feeling of being inside of her, he continued his strokes. His ears were tuned in to the sound of him dipping in and out of Secret's wetness. "I'm 'bout to come," Lucky moaned.

Finally Secret placed her hands on his chest and in one powerful thrust, pushed him off of her.

"Secret, what the fuck," Lucky said right on the verge of coming. He grabbed himself and began to jack off as cum squirted on Secret. "Fuck," he said, throwing his head back, his eyes rolling to the back of his head as he continued to jack off.

Secret jumped out of the way, got up, and ran into the bathroom. She placed her hands on the sink and just stood there breathing heavily. Her eyes caught the stains on her shirt from Lucky's fluid. She gagged. She felt so dirty, so nasty. She put her hands behind her head and attempted to unzip the shirt's zipper that went from her neck slightly down her back. She got it somewhat but then it got stuck. She struggled and fought with it until she ended up ripping the shirt off.

Tears flowed down her eyes as she turned on the shower water. She didn't even wait for the water to warm up. She stood in the shower and allowed the cold pellets to hit her skin. She felt the same way she felt after having sex for the first time with that stranger, who she now knew to be Major Pain.

Secret grabbed the soap and began washing up. She had a mental pep talk with herself at the same time. She was not going to beat herself up about this. She was going to go back out there, apologize to Lucky, and get her head back in the game. After all, this was just a game.

Secret came out of the bathroom with a towel wrapped around her. She stopped and peeked in on Dina to make sure she was still sleeping sound. She then walked into her bedroom where she found Lucky sitting on the edge of her bed, his elbows on his knees and his hands resting in his head. She pushed the bedroom door closed behind her and it creaked. Surely he'd heard her enter the room and could feel her presence, but still, he never looked up.

After letting out a deep breath, Secret went and sat next to Lucky. She just sat there twisting her lips for a second, trying to think of what to say. Finally Lucky slightly turned his head, still buried in his hands and looked at her with one eye.

"What's up?" Lucky asked.

"You," Secret replied.

He looked down between his legs. "Not anymore."

"Yeah, about that."

"Naw, it's all good, ma. You don't have to explain nothing to me. That's your body. No means no, right?"

Secret couldn't tell if he was being serious or a smart ass. She didn't reply.

"Well, let me go get cleaned up and get out of here." Lucky stood. "Can I use your bathroom?"

Secret looked up at him. "Lucky, you don't have to ask me if you can use my bathroom. You're not some stranger."

"Oh, for real? 'Cause I couldn't tell just a minute ago. You pushed me away like I was a stranger."

"I'm sorry about that. I was tripping," Secret said.

"Tripping or teasing?"

"You know I'm not that girl."

"Really I don't, because you let a nigga get all up in there and then cut him off right when he 'bout to nut." Lucky rolled his eyes and a look of embarrassment covered his face. "Man, you know how long it's been since I had to jack off? Then to do it in front of a female." He shook his head.

"You mean on a female." Secret was hoping her little comment softened Lucky up.

He looked at her and cracked a smile. "Yeah, that shit was kind of nice."

Secret laughed. "You so nasty." Lucky laughed a little too and then both their laughter died down. "I'm sorry I freaked out like that. It's just that it's been awhile. And having Dina was rough. I can't imagine getting pregnant and have to go through all that by myself again."

Lucky cut her off. "But you wouldn't be by yourself. I'm here."

"But how can I trust that, Lucky? My mom threw me away. My dad didn't want me. You threw me away and my best friend has obviously already learned the street code of money over bitches because she's not around. I can't set myself up for that again. It's sad, but a baby who can't even walk or talk is all I trust wholeheartedly right now."

Lucky took in her words. "I feel you on that."

"Do you really?" Secret asked. "You get where I'm coming from?"

"Yeah." Lucky exhaled. "I still don't know why you ain't let a nigga come up in there though. I was only like this much from coming." He used his index finger and thumb to express how close he was.

Secret laughed and stood up. "Yeah, I was too. But at least you got yours." And Secret wasn't joking when it came to that. For the second time tonight she'd been on the verge of coming with no such luck.

Lucky brushed a loose piece of hair down on top of Secret's head. "You really are special."

"And you really make me feel special."

The two stared into each other's eyes.

"Let me go get cleaned up before I find myself jacking off again," Lucky said. He turned to walk away.

Secret grabbed his hand. "Can I go with you?"

Lucky looked at her with squinted eyes. "What? You serious?"

"I just want to be where you are right now. That's all," she told him. "I need you, Lucky. I want things to be right with us again no matter how long it takes. I just hope you're willing to wait."

After staring at Secret for a moment, Lucky nodded and pulled Secret into the bathroom with him. While Lucky showered, Secret sat outside the shower talking to Lucky, catching up.

He pressed his luck when he stuck his head out of the shower and asked, "Will you wash my back for me?"

Secret smiled mischievously but obliged. While Lucky finished up in the bathroom, Secret went downstairs and fixed them each a slice of pie with whipped cream. When Lucky exited the bathroom she was coming up the steps with dessert in hand.

"For me?" Lucky asked.

"All for you," Secret replied, then nodded for him to go to her bedroom.

Lucky sat down on Secret's bed. She sat next to him and placed their dessert on her nightstand table. Taking a forkful of pie, she placed it at Lucky's mouth.

"Open wide," Secret ordered him.

Lucky eyeballed Secret in a playful suspicious way. He did as he was told and opened wide. He inhaled the dessert. "Mmmmm."

"Is it good to you?" Secret asked seductively.

Lucky bust out laughing. He covered his mouth so that he wouldn't spit out his food.

"What is so funny?" Secret didn't know whether to be offended. She wasn't sure if Lucky was laughing at her trying to be seductive.

"You are what's funny," Lucky replied. "I mean, why you teasing a brother? What's really going on?"

"I didn't mean to tease you. I wanted it just as much as you did. But, Lucky, I'm not about to get pregnant again. It's hard enough to take care of Dina. I can't imagine trying to take care of two kids." Secret looked down sadly.

Lucky began to feel sorry for Secret and her struggle. He knew so many mothers trying to raise their children alone. He saw some of the ends they would go to in order to feed their children. He was no stranger to that. He thought back to the Secret he'd met that day at the clinic. She was so sweet and special, and different. He hated to see her now a statistic. But it happened to the best of them.

"I told you that if ever you need anything—" Lucky started until Secret cut him off.

Secret placed her index finger on Lucky's lips to silence him. "Shhh. I don't want to talk about all that now." She set the pie down then looked into Lucky's eyes. She leaned in and began kissing him.

At first Lucky just allowed her to kiss him, then he participated in the kiss. The next thing he knew, Secret's hand was cupping his manhood.

"Oh no." He'd pulled out of the kiss and pushed her hand off of him. "You ain't about to get me all worked up again. I done already had to jack off once." Lucky went to get up.

Secret quickly jumped in front of him and pushed him back down. "Oh, you won't have to jack off."

The next thing Lucky knew, it wasn't just Secret's hand stroking his penis, but her mouth was wrapped around it.

"Damn, girl," he moaned as he fell back on the bed and allowed her to please him orally.

Secret sucked, stroked, licked, played with his balls; she did everything she could think of to make him feel good and to get him to hurry up and come. Since he'd already come once, she knew it was going to take him longer to come a second time. But she had to do what she had to do. She did not want Lucky leaving her home unsatisfied with an excuse not to return. She couldn't risk him thinking she was just playing games with him and decide not to come around anymore. It wasn't a chance she was trying to take. She didn't know how serious Detective Davis was about throwing her back in jail and putting Dina into the system if she didn't fulfill her end of the bargain. She'd taken risks with her own life in the past. But she refused to take risks when it came to her daughter's. So if this is what she had to do, then so be it.

"Mmmm," Secret moaned as her mouth bobbed up and down on Lucky's manhood while she massaged his balls. The faster she did it, the louder he moaned.

"I'm 'bout to come. I'm 'bout to . . ." Lucky arched up and began to climax.

Secret had quickly removed her mouth and cupped her hands around Lucky's jerking penis. She stroked his entire vessel with both hands, allowing him to shoot off in her hands. She cupped his fluids in her hand, and once he'd rested his body back down on her bed, she knew he was finished coming. She stood up and went into the bathroom and washed her hands. She turned the water off and before drying them, she looked at herself in the mirror.

She threw her hand over her mouth, suffocating the cry she really wanted to let out. She looked down into the sink as the last drop of water scurried down the drain. This became a symbolic moment for Secret. The last drop of water had flowed and was gone, as it should be when it came to her tears. It was time for her to grow up, to stop crying like a baby and do whatever the fuck she had to do in order to protect her baby. It was time to take off the diaper and put on the big girl panties. Period, point blank. There wasn't going to be too much more of this dick sucking and carrying on. And she wasn't going to feel bad about the fact that she'd just done it.

"A girl's gotta do what a girl's gotta do."

Those had been Shawndiece's words. Well now they were Secret's and at the moment she vowed she would take them to heart.

This time there was no shame there. No guilt. It was like she wasn't even looking at herself anymore. This was a different girl from the helpless single mom caught up in a situation she'd wished she'd never gotten herself into. This was a single mom willing to do whatever she had to do to survive and fix the situations she'd gotten herself into. She'd made a lot of bad choices for all the wrong reasons. And deep in her soul she knew she was still making bad choices. But this time it was for all the right reasons.

She finished drying her hands off and then made her way back into her bedroom. Lucky was lying in her bed sound asleep. Secret shook her head and watched him sleep for a moment. Then finally she went and climbed in bed and lay down next to him. She watched his chest rise up and down thinking, *we really could have had something had you never shown me who you really were. Had you never thrown me away just like everybody else.* Secret lay down on her back with her arms folded looking up at the ceiling. Lucky snoring turned her attention back to him.

He'd started off as her prey and now here he was her prey again.

He'd been fed, he'd bust a nut, he'd gotten a back wash, dessert, a blow job, and now he was lying there snoring on her bed.

Secret turned her body to face Lucky and then cuddled up under his arm. She felt him tuck her even closer by putting his arm around her and then pulling her in. She had him right where she wanted him. The real games were about to begin.

Chapter 22

"Aww, baby, please don't leave," Secret purred in a whiney voice as Lucky got dressed. She lay in her bed naked with nothing covering her but a sheet.

"Girl, I've been up under you all week," Lucky said, buttoning up his shirt, and that was no lie. Ever since their dinner date Lucky and Secret had been inseparable, just like before when they'd first gotten together. Lucky used to turn his cell phone off and everything when he was up under Secret. Today she'd called off work, but still took Dina to Miss Good's anyway just so she and Lucky could be alone.

"Don't you like being up under me?" Secret asked.

"Yeah, girl, you know I do. But I got business to handle."

Secret climbed up out of the bed and stood behind Lucky. She wrapped her arms around him. "Then let me go with you."

Lucky shook his head and wagged a finger. "Oh, no, especially not after the last time you was with me when I had to put in a little work."

"Yeah, but I get everything now. I know what's going on."

Lucky turned around to face her. "Oh, you do? And just what is going on?"

"You are one of the biggest hustlers in the state of Michigan, that's what," Secret said in a know-it-all tone.

"You telling me or are you asking me?" Lucky said.

Secret shrugged. "I don't know. Kind of both." Secret got serious and went and flopped back down on the bed. "Before, I can honestly say I didn't ask too many questions about what you did for a living because I didn't care. I loved you and I didn't want anything changing how I felt about you. I also didn't want to know because I didn't want to be a part of anything that wasn't on the up and up. But as we both know, I learned things the hard way. Things might have been different if I had been clued in on some things, you know."

Lucky sat on the bed next to Secret. "I didn't want to drag you into my situation."

"You didn't have to. The police did a fine job of that."

Lucky put his hand on top of Secret's.

"I just think I would have respected you more if everything had come from you and not the police."

"So the police talked to you about me?" Lucky asked.

"Yeah, a little bit."

"What did they say?"

Secret looked into Lucky's eyes. "Does it matter what they said? Do you trust everything the police say?"

"Hell no."

"Exactly. They just wanted to make an arrest and I was scared to death. Those bastards were probably just telling me anything, which is why I half believed the half I did hear. I didn't want them telling me things about you. I felt anything about you I deserved to hear it from you. Don't you agree?" Secret asked. "Don't you think that I at least deserved that? Deserve that now? The last thing I want to do is get caught up in some bullshit. I have Dina here in my house—"

"You can stop right there." Lucky put his hand up. "I ain't never and ain't gon' ever bring that shit to your place."

"Just my car?" Secret said, shooting Lucky in the heart.

He sucked his teeth and went to get up.

Secret pulled him back down. "No, I'm sorry. I didn't mean it like that. But things did go down the way they did. I did time and have a record. I work for you as far as they are concerned anyway, so I was thinking . . ." Secret's words trailed off.

"You were thinking what?"

"If they already thinking it anyway, why make liars out of them?"

Lucky shook his head and held up his hand like he didn't even want to hear it.

"Seriously," Secret continued. "You know, if we're going to be together, then we're going to be together. I don't want to be in the dark again when it comes to you." Secret began rubbing Lucky's neck. "You know I have your back. I've proved that. But if a bitch is going to be going down for some shit, don't you think I should get a little bit more out of it than just a nice handbag here and there?"

Lucky looked at Secret and stared at her for a moment. "So what are you trying to say?"

"I want in. Just like Shawndiece."

Lucky burst out laughing. After a moment he realized that he was the only one laughing. Secret sat with a straight face.

Lucky's face got serious as well. "You dead shit serious, ain't you?"

"Why not? I'm living here in this shithole apartment on government assistance working at a grocery store. I have another mouth to feed now. Back then it was just me so I didn't care as much, but I have a baby girl to look after now. I didn't make it out of this town, but, Lucky, I have to make sure she does." Secret's eyes began to water.

"I hear you, ma, and I feel you. But you're talking out of emotions now. You have no idea how life is on these streets."

Secret got up on her knees anxiously. "Then teach me."

Lucky read her face. "You're serious, aren't you?" Secret's eyes watered. "Baby girl, come here." Lucky pulled Secret onto his lap. "I got you. I'm going to take care of you. As quiet as it's kept, I'm indebted to you. You kept my black ass out of jail. You took one for the team, so as soft as you are"—he touched her cheek—"I know you'll go hard. And I trust you more than any other broad I've ever fucked with."

"That all sounds good, so why do I hear a 'but' coming?" Secret asked. "You said it yourself: I took one for the team. Is it fair that I took one for a team I'm not even officially a part of?"

Secret was making hella sense. "You're right in everything you are saying," Lucky said.

"Here comes that 'but.'" Secret sighed.

"All I've ever wanted to do was protect you from the streets, not put you in the streets."

"You're not putting me in the streets. This is my choice." Secret climbed off of Lucky's lap and sat on the bed with her knees against her chest. "I've been thinking about all this for a minute now. And to keep it real with you, it was something I was going to do with or without you. But I'd much rather do it with you."

"Trust me, ma, you wasn't gon' do it without me." Lucky chuckled. "Ya boy got the city on lock. So whoever you thought you were gonna get put on by, trust me, nine times out of ten, they work for me anyhow."

"Maybe so. It's some dude Kat was telling me could put me on. Some dude named Pain, or something like that." Secret pretended as though she was trying to recall the name of Lucky's best friend. But she knew exactly what his name was. She just had to play her hand right.

"Major Pain?" Lucky shot up off the bed. "Kat trying to hook you up with him, huh?" His nostrils began to flare.

"Yeah, she said he could hook me up. Help me earn a little extra money on the side." Secret was lying through her pretty pouty lips, but it was okay. Lucky and Kat would never talk so he would never know Kat hadn't said two words about hooking her up with Major Pain.

From the outside looking in, it was truly difficult to tell who was playing who, or if the game was over and this was now real life.

"Why do I feel like you're Denzel and this is *Training Day?*" Secret said as she sat next to Lucky in his Escalade. She'd finally convinced him that she could handle being in the game with him. She even ran down the guilt trip of him letting her best friend make some paper but not her. Eventually Lucky's hand was forced to give Secret a try at the game to keep her from thinking he had something going on with Shawndiece. He told her before he started giving her a little work, which meant transporting dope and making re-up runs, he would let her spend the week watching how he operated. Today was her first ride-along situation. They had just left the shooting range where for the last two hours he'd given Secret her first lesson on how to handle a gun. Now he told her they were on their way to what he would only refer to as The Spot.

"*Training Day.*" Lucky laughed. "You crazy."

"Yeah, I must be." Secret looked out the window as Lucky drove through some very suspect neighborhoods. Every other house looked to be boarded up or burnt down. There were various characters just hanging out. A porch full of young, black men wearing the same color shirts and/or bandannas. Women with half their butt hanging out of the bottom of their shorts and everything but their nipples hanging out of their tops. An old man or woman pushing a shopping cart that looked to have their entire life possessions in that basket roamed aimlessly on the streets. There were paper thin folks walking around scratching an itch or looking for a scratch for their itch.

The apartment Secret had grown up in with her mother hadn't been in the best neighborhood, but clearly it hadn't been in the worst.

"Never made it over to this neck of the woods before, huh?" Lucky asked Secret after watching her stare at her surroundings as if they were foreign.

She shook her head.

"This is why I never brought you around this shit. It ain't you. Yeah, you might have been born and raised in Flint, but you don't know nothing about the real nitty gritty, this hood life." Lucky looked around. "This right here is my home field."

Once upon a time, when her and Lucky first got serious, Secret wondered if Lucky had been ashamed of her, if maybe that was why he'd never taken her to his home, taken her out to meet his friends or anything. If this was his home field, she now realized how blessed she had been that he hadn't. She would have thought him to be anything but a baller. Secret never did understand why dudes were in the dope game claiming and appearing to have all this money, but still lived in the hood. It just didn't make sense to her.

"The hood is where the money at," Shawndiece had once told her. "That's where they make that paper."

That answer had never made much sense to Secret either. But she was confident she was about to understand sooner rather than later.

"You scared?" Lucky asked her. "Change your mind yet about wanting a piece of the action?"

"Nope," Secret said with confidence.

"Damn, who knew?" Lucky shook his head.

"Knew what?" Secret asked.

"That underneath all that book smart, innocent girly girl stuff you were a soldier."

Secret turned and looked back out the window. "Yeah, who knew?"

Chapter 23

"Yo, Lucky, my main man, what's up?" said one of Lucky's workers after he and Secret entered a warehouse.

The outside signage had read LUCKY'S GARAGE. The way Lucky had kept referring to the place as The Spot as if it was top secret confused Secret as they'd walked straight up into the place. The door wasn't locked and there were no big dudes with guns wanting a password for them to enter or questioning who had sent them.

Secret shrugged her expectations off. Perhaps she'd watched one too many gangster movies. Secret looked around the makeshift auto repair shop. There were old beat-up cars outside in the lot as well as a couple in the shop with hoods opened, but nobody really seemed to be working on any cars.

While Lucky greeted his comrade, Secret spotted a tool shelf. All the tools looked to be new and shiny as if they'd never been touched. There was a large, shiny red toolbox that glistened. Everything looked to be kept up to par.

"And who do we have here?" the worker asked. He rubbed his hands together looking back and forth from Secret to Lucky. His eyes questioned Lucky as to why this new face was around and if it was okay to talk in front of her, or if he needed to filter the conversation.

"Oh, this here is my girl," Lucky said. He put his arm around Secret and pulled her in. He nodded to the guy. "This is Fonda. He works the front door. You know, makes sure we're open for business from nine to five, just like our business hours are listed." Lucky winked.

"Yep, and if anybody tries to get in outside of business hours, I got that tool for them." Fonda tapped the shiny red toolbox.

It didn't take a rocket scientist to realize that nine times out of ten he kept a gun hidden in the toolbox.

"So this is your girl, huh?" Fonda snickered and shot Lucky a "yeah, right," look.

"Yeah, my girl," Lucky confirmed with a stone face and stern voice. It wiped the snicker and smile right off of Fonda's face. "Her name is Secret."

"Hello," Secret said with a nod.

The worker nodded back. He looked Secret up and down. "And just how long have you been keeping this Secret? And more importantly, does Secret know how to keep secrets?"

Lucky shot dude a look and then said, "Come here for a minute."

Fonda gave Secret the side eye and then followed Lucky into an office that had a huge glass window. Lucky closed the door behind them then Secret immediately saw Lucky snatch dude up by the neck and slam him against the glass.

"Motherfucker," Secret could hear Lucky shout through the glass. It was muffled considering they were in the office, but she could still make out the words he was saying. "You questioning me in front of my bitch, because, nigga, I will—"

Fonda put his hands up in defense. "No, no, man, it ain't nothing like that. I just wanted to make sure—"

"Nigga, you ain't gotta make sure shit. All you have to do is make me my muthafuckin' money and get paid in the process. Ya heard?"

"Yeah, man. It's all good. My bad."

Lucky released him and then straightened up dude's shirt for him. "You trust me, Fonda?" Lucky asked.

"Yeah, man, you already know."

"Then you trust the people I roll with, right?"

"Yeah."

"I've made a couple of bad judgment calls in my day, but haven't you known me to handle muthafuckas?"

Fonda nodded.

"Right," Lucky said. "And ain't shit changed about me."

"All right, I hear you, man."

"Good. Then we won't ever have to have this conversation again, right?" Lucky said.

"Right."

"My nigga." Lucky put his hand on Fonda's shoulder and gave him a pat. He then walked him over to the door and opened it. "After you."

Fonda walked ahead of Lucky. The next thing Secret knew, Fonda was hitting the floor and she could see Lucky's foot landing back on the ground from kicking Fonda to the ground.

Secret threw her hand over her mouth. She felt so bad for the guy who had been caught off guard and had hit the ground face first. When he lifted his head up blood was seeping from his mouth. He spit out a tooth and used his hand to wipe the blood away as he sat up on the ground trying to catch his bearings.

Secret had never seen this side of Lucky before. He'd just cold-bloodedly kicked this guy to the ground and then had practically stepped over him like a piece of trash on the sidewalk.

"Now don't make me have to put my foot in your ass again, literally," Lucky said to Fonda as he approached Secret and offered her his elbow.

Secret, still a little shocked, hesitated and then looped her arm through Lucky's. He then escorted Secret by the arm down a hallway. Before walking away Secret had looked over her shoulder at the guy on the ground. He looked up at her, still wiping his mouth. The two locked eyes.

Secret's eyes were filled with pity for the guy. His eyes were filled with warning. This gave Secret pause.

"You all right?" Lucky asked Secret.

She turned her attention to the path ahead of them. Shaking off the scene that had just played out in front of her she replied, "Yes, I'm good." Her voice was uneven.

Sensing she was feeling a certain kind of way about what had just gone down, Lucky stopped in front of a door and took Secret's hands into his. She flinched when he first raised his hands to touch hers.

"Baby, come on," Lucky said, confused and offended Secret would act as if he was going to put his hands on her in a harmful way. "Why you all jumpy?"

Secret looked down.

"That back there." Lucky nodded toward the room they'd just left. "That wasn't nothing. Just always have to let these cats know who the boss is. Otherwise they might try to try a nigga. I'm a nice dude, you know that. But niggas try to take my kindness for weakness. I can't have that. You know what I'm saying?"

Secret knew she had to quickly man up in order to be believable. Lucky had to think she really wanted to be a part of this life, his life. She'd have to recall and apply all the street smarts her best friend had showed and told her over the years. She knew eventually they'd all come in handy.

"Oh, I get it one hundred percent," Secret said. "I just thought he deserved worse for questioning you like that." Secret leaned into Lucky and looked up at him. "In front of your girl and all." She gave him the sexiest look she could muster up over the fear she was suppressing.

He grinned, licked his lips, then looked up smiling. "How you gon' get a nigga all hard before we go in here?" This time he nodded to the door in front of them.

Secret smiled and followed suit by licking her lips. "Ummmm, we can go out to the car and take care of this." She cupped his manhood. "Or certainly there's some dirty little closet with cleaning supplies that we can go into and get our quickie on, like they do in movies."

"Where did this girl come from?" he said to Secret, closing his eyes and taking in the good feeling of the intimate massage Secret was giving his private parts through his pants.

"She's been in here, locked up inside trying to get out," Secret replied.

"I see when they let you out of jail, they freed your alter ego as well."

"You can say that," Secret agreed. "So what do you say?" She squeezed his nuts playfully.

Lucky shooed her hand away and laughed. "Girl, stop playing. We can't mix business with pleasure."

"Oh, yeah, tell Jay-Z and Beyoncé that." Secret crossed her arms like a pouty child.

"Girl, come on in here." Lucky untucked his shirt out of his pants to cover up his hard on.

"I can't believe you're going to let that hard, stiff one go to waste." Secret sucked her teeth and shook her head. "Oh, well. You're the boss." She extended her hand to the door. "After you, boss."

Lucky walked past Secret and in front of the door. She smacked him on the behind.

"I'm 'bout to fire your ass before you even get started," he said playfully.

Secret raised her hands in defense. "All right already. I'm going to be a good girl now. I promise." She pouted her lips then crossed her heart.

"Damn, you so cute. I love you." He looked up to the heavens. "God, how did I fall in love with an angel like her?" He shook his head and turned to open the door.

Floored and stunned by his words, Secret just stood frozen. He'd never expressed his being in love with her ever in their entire relationship. His actions had shown that he definitely had loved her, but in love with her? Secret didn't even really know how to feel about the words that had just been shot by Cupid. Now the question was would the arrow hit its intended mark and change the game?

Chapter 24

"Secret, what the . . ." Shawndiece's words trailed off as she stood there staring at her best friend in the doorway. She'd greeted Lucky when she saw him come in. Secret had cleared the corner a few seconds after him, to Shawndiece's surprise.

Secret hadn't seen her best friend in a grip, not since the day they were supposed to meet up at the grocery store. What she really wanted to do was to run over and give her friend a huge hug. Secret was feeling so emotional, like the real her was trapped inside of this bad ass she was portraying. Only Shawndiece would understand and know what a struggle it was for her. But this wasn't the time. This wasn't the place. With at least six other people in the room, all dudes, Secret definitely had to keep up the façade.

"Hey, Shawn," Secret said dryly. "Sup?" She gave a head nod.

Shawndiece snapped her neck back. "Sup?" Shawndiece twisted up her face. "Since when don't you speak proper English?"

Lucky interrupted. "Hey, everybody. What's up?"

"Ain't nothin'," one guy said.

The others responded verbally in one way or another as Lucky walked over and greeted them with a pound, dap, or five and slide.

Shawndiece walked over to Secret and was all in her ear while the fellas greeted one another. "What the hell you doing here? This spot is off-limits with the exception for workers. No girlfriends, boyfriends, cousins, baby mommas, or whatever. Lucky don't budge on that rule. He don't even . . ." Shawndiece's words trailed off as the reason why Secret was there began to set in. "Wait a minute, you're not thinking about—"

Lucky cut Shawndiece off when he walked over and threw his arm around Secret. "Everybody, this is Secret," Lucky introduced her. "I've known her for over a year. Y'all know I like secret weapons right?" He looked down at Secret and kissed her on the forehead. "Well, this is one of 'em." He winked at his crew.

"Yo, Secret, what's up?" a couple greeted her.

"Hey," Secret replied with a smile. She loved the way they were all showing her respect.

"Secret, damn, you sure do look familiar," said Major Pain as he came up the rear of all the crew members. Secret hadn't spotted him at first, thanks to Shawndiece immediately stealing her attention.

"So do you," Secret played along, staring Major Pain right in the face. She was secretly taking a mental picture of all his features. Dina looked nothing like him. Nothing. A smile spread across Secret's lips.

"Trust me, I can guarantee you two don't know each other," Lucky interrupted. He then went to introduce Secret to another member of the crew. "Yo, this is my man TJ."

"Wasup, Secret?" TJ said with a head nod.

"Yeah, Secret, what's up?" Shawndiece snapped. The displeasure in her tone did not go unnoticed as all eyes landed on her, including Lucky's.

"Is there a problem?" Lucky asked Shawndiece with bass in his voice.

Shawndiece quickly straightened up her attitude.

"I thought you of all people would be happy to see your girl join the team," Lucky said.

"I . . . I am. I'm just so surprised to see her is all. We were supposed to connect and . . ." Shawndiece's words trailed off. She had never been one to be fake, so it was very hard for her to play this role. She grabbed Secret by the arm. "Come on, girl. I'm so excited. Let's go catch up." Shawndiece led Secret to the door by her arm.

"Don't be long," Lucky said to Secret. "It's still training day."

Secret smiled and then walked out of the door with Shawndiece. That smile was flushed clear off her face when Shawndiece's nice little grip turned into her yanking Secret by the arm and pulling her into her face.

"Have you fucking lost your mind?" Shawndiece spat in a hard whisper, spittle splashing on Secret's face.

Secret snatched her arm away. "No, but clearly you have." Secret rubbed her arm that was still throbbing somewhat from the grip Shawndiece had on it.

"I'm sorry, it's just that . . ." Shawndiece shook her head. "I can't let you do this, Secret."

"Do what, the exact same thing you're doing? What, you think you're the only one who can make money? I'm supposed to just live and raise my child on welfare for the rest of my life?"

"No, but not like this, Secret. You're better than this. You're better than me. I was doomed to this lifestyle, but not you. You never wanted any part of this while I, on the other hand, gravitated to it. This is my shit. This is my life. What can I say? I love thug niggas and I love the thug life, but you . . ." She pointed Secret up and down. "You ain't built for this. Niggas trying to fuck you, rob you, rape you, and make you feel like shit just 'cause they see you as a helpless female."

"I don't see you getting raped and robbed," Secret shot back.

"That's 'cause mafuckas know better. I can hold my own, but you . . ." She sucked her teeth. "You ain't hardly 'bout this life. And there ain't no way I'm gon' be able to concentrate on making money if I'm worried about your ass."

"Then don't worry about me. After all, did you forget you are the one who taught me about hood life? What? Are you doubting your skills now?" Secret folded her arms as if she was challenging Shawndiece.

"I taught you how to recognize game, not be a player in it."

"Not true, because you are the one who taught me how to handle a dude like Lucky in the first place."

"I taught you how to handle a dude like Lucky in the sheets, not in the streets."

"Same difference," Secret begged to differ.

Shawndiece shook her head. "Really it's not. Trust me, you're gonna see a totally different side of your little boyfriend."

Secret already knew that much to be true. But what she didn't know was that she hadn't seen nothing yet.

"Y'all two bosom buddies done playing catch up yet?" Lucky asked as he stuck his head out the door and into the hallway where Secret and Shawndiece stood.

"Yep, we're finished out here," Secret said and then walked over to Lucky.

"For now we are," Shawndiece said.

"Come on then. There are some things I wanna go over with you with the crew," Lucky said to Secret. "Then we have one more stop to make."

"Where to?" Secret asked.

"You'll see." Lucky looked to Shawndiece knowingly while still addressing Secret. "You'll see."

***

"Take off your clothes."

"Excuse me?" Secret said to Lucky as they stood on the back porch of a house. The porch was closed in with shades drawn.

After going over a so-called "business plan" back at the garage, Lucky had driven Secret to a more upscale neighborhood. They'd driven up a private alley to the back of what looked to be about a 3,500-square foot home. Lucky had used a key to get them in the black security fence they had to go through in order to get to the back porch.

As they walked up the walkway, Secret had noticed security cameras on the house. She looked around and saw a dog house with a huge dog bowl in front of it. Lucky had noticed her pause at the sight of the dog house.

"Don't worry. There's no dog. We keep a big dog bowl of water on the front porch too. It's more like a deterrence. Punk-ass niggas don't wanna take the chance of being eaten alive by a dog while trying to break in. And if they do, we got somethin' for that ass inside."

A chill went through Secret. This was the second time a gun had been alluded to. Secret wondered if Lucky had ever killed anybody and if he'd eventually expect her to kill. That was something she just would not do, so hopefully she'd be able to get Detective Davis exactly what he wanted and soon. Murder would be where she drew the line.

After getting past the fear of the invisible dog, Secret had now found herself standing on the porch being told by Lucky to take her clothes off.

"You're joking right?" Secret chuckled.

Keeping a straight face Lucky asked, "Do I look like I'm joking?"

A chill went through Secret's body. Lucky looked to be transforming right before her eyes. He had just spoken to her like he was speaking to someone on the streets. It was such a hard tone, and that look in his eyes . . . She couldn't explain it, but it made her uncomfortable.

Fear rose up inside Secret as Shawndiece's words replayed in her head. *"Trust me, you're gonna see a totally different side of your little boyfriend."*

Secret had seen what he'd done to Fonda; how in a matter of seconds he'd gone from this happy-go-lucky dude to kicking his friend down to the ground. Perhaps that's where Secret was making her mistake, by thinking that was Lucky's friend. When it came to business and money, maybe Lucky saw everyone as an enemy so that's how he treated them. Secret didn't want to take the chance of ending up face down with her teeth knocked out.

Slowly, with a trembling hand, she removed her shoes. Next her socks. She looked at Lucky dead in the eyes as she took her pants off. She then lifted her shirt over her head and paused.

"All your clothes," Lucky said. "Bra and panties."

Secret was crying inside but kept on a brave face. Perhaps this was just a test, Lucky trying to figure out how good she was at taking orders. After all, she'd rather be ordered to take her clothes off than to kill somebody. On another note, this very well could have been Lucky's house and he had something sexy and romantic waiting for her inside. Keeping that thought at the forefront of her mind, she removed every stitch of clothing she had on.

"Now go find an empty drawer and place your stuff in there." Lucky pointed toward the wicker patio furniture table that was surrounded by four matching chairs. The table looked to have drawer compartments on each side.

Secret scooped up her clothing and walked over to the table. The first drawer she pulled out had a terry cloth hot pink romper in it with a pair of flip-flops. She closed it and opened the one next to it. It had a pair of jeans,

T-shirt, bra, and canvas tennis shoes in it. It was apparent that Lucky didn't have something planned exclusively for Secret. From what Secret could tell, there were at least two more buck-naked women inside that house. With several other drawers that could be full of female's clothing, no telling how many more could be inside as well.

After finding an empty drawer, Secret placed her belongings inside it. She was moving at a snail's pace. Her nerves were truly getting the best of her. She stood up straight and turned around to face Lucky. She stood there as naked as a baby when it's born. Looking into Lucky's eyes, she had a hint of seductiveness behind her own. Perhaps that would calm the raging beast. He seemed to have looked right through her though.

"Come on." He waved his hand for Secret to follow him. "Let's go."

Any other time had Secret been standing in front of him with her birthday suit on, he would have complimented her, tried to feel on her, suck a titty or something. He was acting like a naked girl standing in front of him outside on a porch was an everyday thing.

Secret looked back at the table with drawers full of women's clothing.

Perhaps it was an everyday thing.

Secret walked over to Lucky while he opened a security box and started punching in codes. The heavy metal door cocked open. Lucky stepped inside and Secret followed behind him just as she'd done back at the garage.

"Oh shit!" Secret stopped in her tracks, stunned, and grabbed her heart.

Lucky hadn't been fazed by or had even spoken to the four men, two on each side of the door, who stood wearing all black with protective gear and heavy artillery. He'd just moseyed on inside like he was coming home from a hard day's work, headed for the shower, used to and therefore oblivious to his surroundings.

Secret, on the other hand, had to tighten her private area and slightly twist her legs to keep the piss from running down them. That's just how much this scene had frightened her and caught her off guard.

Lucky turned and looked her. "Girl, come on in here. They ain't thinking about you. They see this every day." He shooed his hand and continued walking.

He must have thought Secret was trying to hide her privates from the men instead of keeping her bladder from emptying right there on the floor. Secret gathered her composure and continued following Lucky.

They went through a kitchen and then down a short flight of steps into what was more like a lower-level den than a basement. There Secret saw four pool tables with two women on each longer horizontal side and one woman at each vertical side. There was all kinds of drugs on the tables.

"Daddy's home," shouted a naked thick half black, a quarter Asian and a quarter of some other nationality girl. She was as short as Lil' Kim with breasts a stripper would pay for. They jiggled up and down as she bounced over to Lucky and kissed him on the cheek.

"What's up, mommy?" Lucky asked her, a smile spreading on his lips.

"Mmmm, let me guess." She looked down at his private area and licked her lips.

"Sorry, Quasi, I can't play house with you today," Lucky told her. He eyeballed Secret.

"Oh, I see you brought another foster kid home to add to the family," Quasi said after she turned quickly and looked at Secret. She then looked back to Lucky, her two pigtails swinging and swishing.

It didn't go unnoticed by Secret that this Quasi chick hadn't even given Secret the once-over. No side eye and no up and down look with her nose twisted up in the air. This was an indication that she felt Secret was absolutely no threat to her at all. A jealous woman would have looked the other woman up and down to see what she was working with, to see what kind of competition she was up against; kind of like how Secret was giving Quasi the once-over on the low low.

"You know how I am about familia." Lucky grinned.

"Well, good. We can use her, considering Shawn has graduated." Now Quasi showed a hint of jealousy in the way she was looking at Lucky after mentioning Shawn, which more than likely she was referring to Shawndiece.

"We've already talked about this a million times," Lucky said in a playful, scolding tone.

"I know, I know," Quasi whined. "You need mommy to take care of the house and makes sure the kids are well behaved doing what they are supposed to do."

Lucky kissed Quasi on the lips. "Can't nobody run this shit like you."

"You better fuckin' believe that shit," Quasi said with confidence. "It's just that I wouldn't mind being on the outside ridin' with choo. You know I can handle that type of shit."

"Yeah, but if it ain't broke, I ain't gon' fix it."

"I hear you, I hear you." She waved Lucky off and rolled her eyes. She then walked off, summoning Secret to follow her. "Come on, young'un," Quasi said to Secret. "It's training day."

Secret looked at Lucky. He shrugged at the use of Quasi's words that mirrored Secret's earlier that day.

"And take good care of her," Lucky called out to Quasi. He then looked to Secret and winked. "She's special."

"Aren't they all just special?" Quasi threw over her shoulder sarcastically.

Secret didn't budge. She just looked at Lucky with questioning eyes.

"Go on." He nodded toward Quasi who'd stopped and put her hands on her hips after realizing Secret wasn't behind her. "I'll be back to get you later."

Quasi walked back over and stood between Lucky and Secret. "What?"

"Nothing, she's good," Lucky answered. "Like I said, just take good care of her."

"I got choo, Daddy," Quasi said to Lucky.

"I know you do." Lucky play spanked her on the ass and then exited back up the stairs.

Just two seconds ago the girl had been smiling huge at Lucky, but now her face was all twisted up at Secret. "Come on. Let's do this."

"Lucky?" Secret called out with a trembling voice.

He stopped on the staircase and looked back at her.

Secret looked at Lucky. She wondered if he could see her heart beating out of her chest. She wanted so badly to just tell him never mind; that she didn't want to do this anymore, that she'd made a mistake. But she had no idea how he would react. Right now he wasn't treating her like a princess. He was treating her like a worker. Clearly he had no problem at all separating business from pleasure. On another note, if Secret pulled out, would it ruin her chances of fulfilling her obligation to Detective Davis? But she'd had enough information, didn't she? She knew where his main crew hung out. She knew where his drug supply was at. Wouldn't her word be good enough for them to bust into the place and raid it?

But what if Lucky wasn't there when they raided it? What if they couldn't connect him to the home? After all, she had no idea whose house that was or whose name it was in.

Secret's head began throbbing at all the thoughts going through her head. Thank God Lucky couldn't read her mind; otherwise, if he was a killer, he would have probably put a bullet right through her head.

"What is it, Secret?" Lucky spoke to Secret as if she was a child getting on his nerves.

"See you later." She waved innocently.

He turned and walked up the steps; no smile, no return wave, no nothing.

"You can work next to Nikita," Quasi told Secret as she went and stood next to a naked girl at one of the pool tables. Quasi said to Nikita, "Show her the basics and then I'll come over and school her in a minute."

Nikita nodded and Quasi walked away.

Secret looked the dang near six foot tall, paper-thin woman up and down. The girl gave her a stare right back. Secret tried her best to keep on a poker face, but she was scared. One could see it. One could smell it.

As Secret gave her new coworker the once-over, she almost gagged when she noticed the tampon string hanging from between Nikita's legs.

The girl noticed Secret looking between her legs. "What? I'm not supposed to work when it's that time of the month? Do you think a stripper lets her menstrual cycle stop her from making money? I sure the fuck ain't about to. Now bring your scary ass on so I can show you how this shit is done."

For the next two hours, Secret had no sense of time. It felt like she'd been in that dungeon like atmosphere for days. After all, there were no clocks hanging up anywhere so she had no sense of time. It was dim, just a sixty-watt bulb hanging over each pool table.

Nikita had run down to Secret the different types of drugs and pills, how to count, scoop, and measure them. "The cooks work third shift, so we ain't got to worry about that," Nikita had told Secret.

Secret wasn't 100 percent certain, but she was sure the cooks Nikita was referring to weren't chefs, and they weren't showing up to cook a dinner so that everyone could sit down at the dinner table like one big happy family. She reckoned it was coke they were going to cook.

Quasi eventually pulled Secret into her office, which was nothing but a little table with a monitor that surveyed each pool table. From the angle of the camera, it looked as though it was probably planted somewhere in the lighting base of the single bulb over each pool table.

Quasi never left that room. If she had to go to the bathroom, or even if one of the girls had to, they did it right there in one of the four red chitterling buckets that were lined up against the wall.

Secret stood at Quasi's desk, as the queen bee herself sat at the only chair in the room. She listened to Quasi tell her all the rules she had to abide by.

"No stealing, no poppin' pills, no . . ."

Quasi's words faded out. Secret knew that no matter what, she was never coming back to this place again.

Fuck the rules. Secret kept a straight face as Quasi went on for about twenty minutes straight. It sounded as though she might have been reading a script, but everything she was rambling off had been memorized.

"How'd she do?"

Lucky's booming voice over Secret's shoulder brought her out of her daze. Secret turned around to see Lucky walking toward her. He was like the messiah himself, there to save her from hell.

Secret felt as though she could breathe for the first time in hours.

"She did good," Quasi replied to Lucky. "What can I say? You know how to pick 'em."

"And you know how to raise 'em."

"Touché," Quasi said with a smile.

Lucky looked to Secret. "You ready?"

Was he being funny by asking her that? Didn't she look ready enough?

Secret wanted to jump up and down and shout, "Yes, yes, I'm ready. Daddy, please get me out of here," like the child he was treating her as. But instead she just nodded.

Quasi rose up out of her seat. There was a box sitting on the floor behind her little desk, that didn't have any drawers. She reached into it, pulled something out, and started walking toward the steps. "All right, let's go," she said as she began to place rubber gloves on her hands.

Lucky walked Secret over to the steps and then stopped. Quasi was standing there with her fingers gloved and spread out like she was about to perform surgery in the ER. Secret looked to Lucky, then looked to Quasi, then back to Lucky again. Somebody needed to tell her what the hell was going on.

Before Secret could even ask, Quasi spoke.

"Open your mouth."

Still looking at Lucky with questioning eyes, Secret slowly opened her mouth. Lucky pulled out his cell phone and started texting while Quasi looked around and fingered the inside of Secret's mouth.

Once Quasi was finished searching Secret's mouth, she lifted each breast and ran her finger underneath them. Next she ran her fingers through Secret's hair. "Don't waste your money on a fancy hairdo if you coming here to work," Quasi told Secret. "Notice all the other girls have their hair pulled back in ponytails."

Secret looked over her shoulder at the women. She hadn't paid much attention before to the fact that each one of them actually did have their hair in a ponytail.

"And don't do pigtails," she warned Secret with a glare. "That's momma's style." Quasi used her palms to bounce the bottom of her pigtails. She looked in and behind Secret's ears and up her nose. She then stood there looking at Secret with her hands still raised.

"What the fuck you just standing there for?" Quasi asked Secret. "Bend it over."

"Huh? What?" Secret asked.

Quasi sucked her teeth and then walked behind Secret. She placed her hand in the middle of Secret's back and pushed her over.

She placed her hand between Secret's legs on her inner thighs, then pushed them apart. Secret's hands hit the ground so that she could balance and catch herself from falling.

"Ummm, you know I like this part," Quasi said as she inserted a finger into Secret's vagina.

Secret squeezed her eyes tightly and folded her lips in. Lucky just stood there half reading a text, looking up every few words to watch Quasi finger Secret.

Quasi licked her lips and winked at Lucky as she crooned her body to the movement of her finger inside of Secret.

Lucky smiled and shook his head. "Girl, you ain't right."

Quasi pulled her finger out of Secret, but before Secret could rise up, Quasi was already fingering her anal area.

All of Secret's blood had drained to her head. She felt as if her dome was going to explode. Violated wasn't the word to describe how Secret felt at that moment. She was in rage that Lucky was standing there texting, allowing this to happen to her. Was this all part of some sick test he was putting her through? Was he trying to see how strong she was? If she would break?

"All done," Quasi said. She spanked Secret on the ass while saying, "You can get up now, *mami*."

Secret stood up erect. She allowed her blood to circulate through her body for a moment. She didn't want to rush, taking a step and get lightheaded. Just as she was about to move, the door at the top of the steps opened.

"Coming through. Delivery!" a male voice shouted as he carried a box. "The ice cream man has arrived."

Behind him was another gentleman carrying a box. One of the guys who had been suited up at the front door followed them, gun drawn.

Lucky pulled Secret out of their way. Lucky nodded at each guy. Once they were at the bottom of the steps, Lucky put his phone in his pocket and escorted Secret up the steps. Secret followed in silence. Lucky didn't say a word either. He led her to the back porch where Secret retrieved her things and then got dressed.

There was still silence as Lucky walked Secret back to his Escalade truck. Once they were comfortably seated in the vehicle, Lucky started it up. He then looked over to Secret who was sitting stone-faced staring straight ahead. Lucky grabbed her by her chin and turned her face toward him. He looked into her eyes and smiled.

Now that was the Lucky Secret knew. She no longer saw that heartless man she'd been accompanied by just a few minutes ago.

Lucky leaned in and kissed Secret on the lips. "Let's go get something to eat." He then pulled off.

Secret was stunned at how easily Lucky had been able to separate personal from business. It really was as if he'd had an on and off switch. It was almost inhuman. Well, Secret wasn't programmed like that. She didn't come with an on and off switch. She couldn't control her emotions so calculating. But for now she would have to do her best at pretending she could. Hopefully long enough as to where soon it would be lights out for Lucky and his entire drug trade forever.

Chapter 25

The next day Secret was glad she was on the schedule to work at the grocery store. That was her excuse for getting out of day two of her training with Lucky.

"Why don't you just go ahead and put your two-week notice in now?" Lucky told her. "You about to be making money hand over fist here in a minute."

"Well at this second I'm not and I have a baby to take care of," Secret had told Lucky as they spoke over the phone.

"You know I got li'l mamma," Lucky told her, "and whatever you need." Lucky had given Secret a wad of cash the day he'd dropped her off after her ride along with him. She figured that was for a day's work of pay though. So she'd more so earned it rather than him giving her something for nothing, which was what he was insinuating.

"If I wanted to depend on you my entire life, then why would I even bother with all this in the first place?" Secret had told Lucky. "Duhhh."

He chuckled into the phone receiver. "You independent women crack me up. But I ain't mad at ya. Do ya thang, ma."

"I am, and that's exactly what I'm about to do now. So I need to let you go so I can get to work."

"Cool. I'll talk to you later."

Secret ended the call and let out a huge sigh of relief. She'd managed to get out of hanging with Lucky today, but Lord only knew what tomorrow would bring.

***

"It's been two days; when we hooking up again to . . . you know?" Lucky asked Secret as she washed dishes and he held Dina.

Watching Dina smile and coo at Lucky stung Secret's heart. She did not want her poor child to think for one minute this man was her father. And to just think that once upon a time that was exactly who Secret wanted Lucky to be. But now, now that she was able to see who Lucky really was, the mere sight of him repulsed her, let alone when he touched her. When she had to let him touch her. Slowly but surely though, Secret was able to psych herself out. She was able to tell herself that this was all just business. She was doing a job for the state. It was nothing personal. Funny how just a couple days ago she couldn't understand how Lucky had so easily been able to turn his emotions on and off, yet here she was in the midst of mastering the same skill.

Secret finished up the dishes. Lucky watched television while Secret bathed and put Dina to bed. She eventually joined Lucky on the living room couch.

"A woman's work is never done," Secret said, flopping on the couch and exhaling.

"You the one hell bent on being superwoman," Lucky told her.

"Not because I want to, but because I have to," Secret offered.

"I hear you." Lucky grabbed the remote and flicked the channel. "So, what's up with tomorrow? Or have you had a change of heart?"

"I'm good. I have to work though."

Lucky sucked his teeth. "There you go."

"No, for real, I do," Secret said. "But I'm on the early shift. I'll be off by three, and then I'm all yours."

"Cool. Quasi misses you," Lucky joked.

"Ugghh, Quasi," Secret said with disdain and then moved away from Lucky.

Lucky laughed. "Oh, you don't like Quasi?"

"Can't you show me some other tricks of the trade besides that? I don't want to be condemned to the basement of some house." Secret crossed her arms in a pout. "Plus, I know that Quasi chick is feeling you," Secret said, playing the jealous role. "I can hardly focus on what I'm supposed to be doing for side eyeing her. Something tells me it's only a matter of time before she and I clash."

"Aww," Lucky said teasingly, "A couple hours in the dungeon got you all bent out of shape and feeling bold." Lucky went to kiss Secret on the cheek.

Secret pulled away.

"Oh, it's like that?"

"Just show me some other stuff," Secret said.

"Shawndiece started in the dungeon."

"I'm not Shawndiece." Secret turned to face Lucky. "You said I was special. Special chicks don't get treated like the next trick." She squinted her eyes at him. "Are you trying to treat me like the next chick?"

"Never that." Lucky shook his head. "But when it comes to business—"

"When it comes to business I still expect to be treated special. 'Spite popular opinion, I'm ultimately going to be the queen bitch around here, so you might want to give your girl Quasi the memo." Secret rolled her eyes.

"Damn that hard side of you turns me on," Lucky said, grabbing his manhood.

"Then is it settled? I mean, I know eventually I'm going to have to do what I have to do, but I don't want to be a one-trick pony like Quasi. I want to know everything there is to know."

"Everything?" Lucky questioned.

Secret turned her body toward Lucky and seductively said, "Everything."

After about another ten minutes of persuasion and a nice, long blow job, Lucky gave in. After Secret got off work at three o'clock tomorrow, he agreed to show her something new. The dungeon was permanently off the list of things to do.

At three-thirty on the nose Secret heard Lucky blowing for her outside of her apartment. She said a silent prayer that God would watch over her, grabbed her purse, then bounced outside to Lucky's truck.

"Hey, beautiful," Lucky said as he stood waiting for her with the passenger side door open.

"Hi," Secret said, getting in the car.

"Damn," Lucky said as Secret bounced right up into the passenger seat then looked at him to close the door. "A nigga don't even get a kiss? You don't want me to treat you like a regular chick, but yet you just played me like a regular nigga."

Secret laughed. "My bad. Let me try this again." Secret got out of the truck, ran back up her walkway then came back down. This time when she got to the truck, she grabbed Lucky behind his neck, pulled him down to her face, and stuck her tongue down his throat. After a wild, passionate kiss she pulled away, looking him in his eyes and said, "Hi."

Lucky laughed and shook his head at her. "Girl, get your crazy ass in that car."

Secret smiled and hopped back into the car.

Lucky closed the door and then climbed into the driver seat. He took her to a couple of the trap houses where he checked in on things and even collected money.

"I don't usually do this type of thing," Lucky had told Secret after they exited the house. "I got other soldiers who handle this type of thing. I just wanted to show you everything per your request."

They got back into the vehicle and went to another spot. This one being one that Secret was very familiar with. It was the one she'd taken Lucky to that day to get the duffle bag full of drugs out of. The duffle bag full of drugs that would ultimately land her in jail.

They walked up to the house and Lucky knocked. "Yo, it's Lucky," he called through the door. A few seconds later a young guy with a mouth full of bling answered the door.

"Wasup, my main man Lucky?" the young guy greeted him.

"I can't call it, young blood," Lucky replied, giving the boy some dap. Lucky entered the house.

Secret noticed that this was the first time Lucky had actually grabbed her hand and led her inside. With her hand resting in his, she stayed by his side.

Secret looked around the living room with an opening to the dining room and kitchen. It was full of guys. Some were sitting on the couch and chairs playing video games. Some were at the table playing a game of cards. All were either drinking or smoking. As a matter of fact, there was so much smoke that Secret could barely see two feet in front of her.

There was a second television other than the one the guys were playing video games on. A porno was showing on that one. So there was a sound mixture of shooting from the video games, moaning and groaning with an acoustic guitar string from the porno along with cussing and fussing from the heated card game.

"I see you brought us a new toy to play with." A guy walked up to Lucky, rubbing his hands together. He looked Secret up and down like she was his next meal. Or more like his last supper.

"Oh, no, no, no," Lucky said, pushing the guy back. "This one is mine."

"Aw, come on, man. Since when don't you share? You know the saying: it ain't no fun if my homies can't have none."

"Down, boy," the young guy with a mouth full of bling told his friend. "You heard what my man said."

The friend put his hands up in defense. "All right, my bad. My bad. It's all good." He held up his hand to high-five Lucky.

"Fo' sho." Lucky gave him a hand slap. "But I got you. I'll bring a little somethin' around your way. Got this nice Dominican chick I know you'll have fun with."

The guy's eyes lit up. "Now that's what I'm talking about." He gave Lucky another high five and then walked away, but not before eyeballing Secret with silent thoughts of wishing he could have her right now.

Lucky looked to Secret. He was about to say something to her but his phone began to ring. Lucky pulled his phone out and looked at it. His eyes lit up like Times Square at night. "Yes!" he said quietly and did a little fist pump in the air. He then quickly looked to Secret. "Hey, I gotta take this call. I'll be right back." He started to walk away as he hit the talk button to answer the phone. "This is Lucky." He spoke in a professional business manner. There was none of that "wasup" and "yo, my man" he greeted all his other workers with. This time Lucky spoke as if he was speaking to his boss instead of worker bees.

Secret was only two steps behind Lucky as he walked down a small hallway, heading toward the bathroom at the end of the hall. It wasn't until he got to the bathroom and went to close the door that he realized Secret was behind him. He briefly took the phone away from his ear and whispered. "Hey, I said I have to take this call."

"Then I'm taking it with you," Secret whispered right back with attitude. She then pointed to the living room. "If you think you're leaving me out there in the lion's den, you have really lost your mind." The look in Secret's eyes let Lucky know she was not about to back down on this one. He had a very important call on the line and didn't have time to argue with her.

Agitated, Lucky mumbled. "All right. Just wait right here then." He pointed to the spot right outside the door and then closed it.

Secret stood right outside the door with her arms folded. At first she wasn't paying any attention to what Lucky was saying, but then with nothing else to focus on, his words began to penetrate her ears. And what he had to say made Secret's ears perk up. Although she could only hear one side of the conversation, she could hear enough to know that this coming Friday, something big was going down. A shipment of "ice cream." Secret recalled the day back at the dungeon with Quasi. The men carrying boxes said they were bringing a delivery, that the ice cream man or something like that had arrived. Secret put two and two together. The boxes had the drugs in it that the girls at the pool tables had to do their thing with. That was the ice cream.

Secret pressed her ear to the door and this time she clearly heard Lucky set up a meeting time for this Friday, three days from now, at six p.m. The meeting spot was Lucky's garage.

Now it was Secret pumping her fist in the air. She had what she needed. No mistake, she was sure once she relayed this information to Detective Davis that would be all he needed to take Lucky down. Game over.

Chapter 26

"Girl, what the hell happened to you?" Secret said as she let Kat into her house.

Lucky had dropped Secret off a couple hours after they'd left the trap house. He'd cut their training day short. He was amped up on ten and told Secret he had to go take care of some private business, set some things up. She figured he had to get his crew ready for the shipment. He told her that if it wasn't too late, he would shoot back through to her place tonight.

"I think I'm going to go pick up Dina from the babysitter's, go home, take something for these cramps, and knock out," Secret had told Lucky. She put her hand across her lower abdomen for emphasis, even though her period wasn't expected until next week. She was done with Lucky and this whole drug thing. She had what she needed, and based on Detective Davis's excitement over the phone when she shared the details of Lucky's upcoming shipment, he now had what he needed as well. Secret had been feeding Detective Davis little appetizers here and there, keeping him in the loop of everything Lucky was showing her. Secret had relayed locations and everything to Detective Davis. Clearly this last bit of information was the main course.

"You did good, Secret," Detective Davis had said before hanging up the phone.

"I did well, Detective," Secret corrected him. She no longer had to fit in or speak improper English either.

Detective Davis chuckled and ended the call.

Secret had felt so relieved and at peace, too. No more training days and no more giving her body to Lucky. But now Kat had showed up at her door disturbing the peace.

"Your face . . ." Secret went to touch Kat's bruised eye. It wasn't a fresh bruise. Looked like it had been there a minute, but it looked painful all the same.

Kat flinched and pulled away. "Nothing, I'm good," Kat said, walking into Secret's house. "Just got into it with some hating-ass bitch is all. Just some he said, she said shit." Kat shot Secret a stern look. "Apparently some bitch is running around lying on me." She was looking at Secret as if she was referring to her.

Secret closed the door behind her. "Well, it looks like y'all's fist did all the talking."

Kat walked over to Dina who was in her swing. "How's auntie's babe?" she said to her niece.

Secret had just fed Dina milk and infant cereal. Once Miss Good started feeding Dina solids, Secret was forced to follow suit because Dina would still fuss like she was hungry after taking in just milk. Secret had really wanted to be a mother who followed the doctor's orders by the book, but Miss Good had thrown a monkey wrench in that.

"I haven't talked to you in a minute," Secret said. "What's been going on with you?"

"Nothing too much. A little bit of this. A little bit of that." Kat pushed the swing just a tad bit. "Oh, yeah, the twins want to see you. I figured we could all go out to eat or something."

"That would be real nice," Secret replied. She'd love to see her half twin brothers. "How are those knuckleheads doing anyhow?"

"Thuggin'. They ain't gon' be shit, just like they daddy."

Secret cringed at hearing those words. The same had been said about Secret in reference to her mother. She knew that people didn't have to be a victim of their circumstances. She'd keep hope for her brothers that they wouldn't end up on the same path as their father, in and out of jail. "Well, y'all just let me know when and where and I'm game."

The two women stood in the living room. Finally Kat spoke. "So, what have you been up to?" She looked at Dina. "Talk to your baby daddy?"

"Yeah." Secret nodded.

"About what?" Kat went and sat down on the couch. Her legs were open and she rested an elbow on each knee. She was leaned in like she was interrogating Secret.

Secret shrugged. "You know, about Dina, and just stuff."

"Stuff, huh?"

"Yeah, stuff." Secret walked over and fixed Dina's head that was starting to tilt to the side. Secret stuffed a blanket on each side of Dina's head to keep her head from wobbling. "Why are you asking like that?"

"No reason. It's just that . . ." Kat's words trailed off.

"Finish." Secret went and sat down next to Kat. "It's just that what?"

"I just want to make sure you are not getting caught up in no bullshit is all. I know how Lucky is. Trust me. I've been under that nigga's spell since I can remember. I get that he's your baby daddy and all. But that's where you need to draw the line." Kat had spoken that last line more like she was giving Secret an order.

"Look, sis." Secret took Kat's hand into hers. "I know you are just trying to look out for me, and I appreciate that. But you can best believe that Lucky is not and will never be a part of my life in that way again."

Secret's pledge seemed to have relieved Kat to some degree. Kat exhaled and put her other hand on top of Secret's. "I hope that's the truth, Secret." She searched Secret's eyes for confirmation.

The way Kat was coming at Secret made Secret feel a little strange. It was almost as if there was an underlying threat in Kat's words. To Secret it felt as if Kat was warning her not to mess with her man.

"Kat, is everything okay?"

Kat stood up and wiped her hands down her jeans. "Yeah, sure. Of course. Why wouldn't it be?"

"I don't know. You walk in here with a black eye, questioning me about Lucky."

"Like I said, I'm just looking out for you. If protecting you from that piece of shit means I have to be all up in your business, then so be it. In all honesty, I wish to God he wasn't even your baby's daddy so that he wouldn't have no reason to come sniffing around over here in the first place." Kat clenched her fists while looking at Dina. "It just breaks my heart that you had a baby by Lucky." Kat shook her head as her eyes watered.

Secret felt so hurt and sad to watch her sister enveloped in such heartbreak. What made Secret feel even worse was that she could rid Kat of that heartache in a matter of seconds if she told her the truth. If she told her that Lucky wasn't actually Dina's biological father. Secret thought about it as she watched Kat wipe the tears at the rims of her eyes before they could even fall. She already hated the fact that she'd kept so many secrets from Kat as it was. What would be the harm in revealing this truth? So Secret decided she would share the fact that Lucky wasn't Dina's biological father. She wasn't, though, going to tell her who really was. There were just some secrets that had to go to the grave.

"Kat, there's something I want to tell you," Secret said.

Kat sniffed. "What is it?"

"It's about—"

Secret's phone rang before she could finish her sentence. She looked down at the caller ID. She didn't recognize the number. She held her index finger up to Kat, telling her to hold on a minute.

"Hello," Secret answered. "Hey, Shawndiece." A huge smile covered Secret's face. "I'm so glad to hear from you." Secret truly was glad to hear from her best friend. Not only because the last time they'd seen each other they'd had sort of a spat, but Shawndiece was the piece of the puzzle Secret had forgotten all about.

Shawndiece was part of Lucky's crew now. If he went down, nine times out of ten she was going to go down with him. Secret had to keep that from happening. She needed to find a way to talk Shawndiece out of the dope game, at least with Lucky.

Secret walked past Kat over to the dining room table. "I need to hook up with you. I really need to talk to you about something." Secret sat down at the dining room table. "It's really important," Secret said. "As soon as possible. Tonight if possible." Secret paused for a moment. "Well, how about tomorrow? I have to work tomorrow. Let me check my schedule and then I'll get back with you. This number that showed up in my caller ID, is this your cell phone?" she asked. "Cool, then I'll call you back as soon as I check my schedule. All right," Secret said, and then ended the call.

Secret let out a sigh of relief. She had three days to meet up with Shawndiece. Hopefully she could find a way to convince her to call it quits with her connection with Lucky. If not, she might be forced to tell her the truth: that Lucky was going down and that she didn't want her to be on the ship with him when it sank. But would she be able to trust her enough to tell her that?

Secret laid the phone down on the table prepared to finish her conversation with Kat. She stood up from the kitchen table and turned around only to find Kat gone and the door cracked open from where she'd left.

Looked as though that truth would have to wait.

"What y'all up to sitting on the porch cackling like y'all up to no good?" Secret asked Miss Good's granddaughters who were sitting on the porch steps staring at an iPhone. Sometimes the teenage girls would come over to their grandmother's house after school to visit. They only lived a couple blocks away.

"Just some ol' ghetto mess. These two chicks fighting," the youngest granddaughter, who was about fourteen, said.

"What is it, a television show? Let me guess, one of those ghetto reality shows?" Secret stopped at the steps and put her hands on her hips.

"No, this is for real," the older sixteen-year-old grand-daughter replied. "There's this Internet site that be showing people fighting."

Secret was curious. "Let me see that mess." She sat down next to one of the girls and watched the video. All she could see was two chicks on the ground with a death grip on each other's weaves. It was all hair. There looked to be a group of dudes standing around laughing. The person recording the fight was commentating.

"That's right, slam that lying-ass bitch's head into the ground," the cameraman cheered on as the girl on top began doing just as he'd said. "Bitches who run dey mouth get punched in dey mafuckin' mouth," he spat.

Secret could only stand to watch about a few more seconds before she stood up. "So that's today's youth's entertainment?" She shook her head. "Guess it ain't no better than grown women watching other grown women do it on reality shows."

The girls paid Secret no mind as they continued watching the fight. Secret shook her head again and walked up on the porch to go knock on the door.

"Oooooh," she heard the older girl say. "Shawndiece got her good."

"Yeah, but Kat punched her in the face."

Secret was just about to hit the doorbell when she heard the two teenagers speak. She turned back around to face the girls. "What did y'all say?"

The younger girl replied, "I think Kat won. Shawndiece got in more licks, but Kat got them power punches." The girl play boxed the air.

"Let me see that." Secret stormed over and snatched the phone from the girls.

"Mmm, hmmm. Addictive ain't it?" the older girl said, then crossed her arms in an "I told you so" manner.

Secret watched the video. Still all she could see was lots of hair, but after hearing the two teenagers say the names of the girls, she looked closely for resemblance to her best friend and sister. Honestly, what were the odds? The women in the video continued to wrestle on the ground as Secret waited impatiently for their faces to be shown. Her eyes wandered and she caught the title of the video. It read Lying-Ass Bitches Get Stitches. Shawndiece vs. Cat.

Even though Kat was short for Katherine, Secret was sure that was just a typo by the person who uploaded the video. Secret watched a few seconds longer before someone finally separated the girls.

"These bitches ain't gon' do nothing but pull hair," the guy who separated them said.

"Yeah, I ain't trying to waste my battery recording this shit," the camera guy said. "But I bet that bitch won't lie again."

Once the two women were separated each proceeded to try to fix their hair, and that's when their faces showed. Secret had a look of horror as she looked at the faces of her sister and best friend. The images were a little grainy, but it was them. She was certain.

Secret thought back to the day Kat had come over to her place with her face all bruised up. She was so agitated. She kept questioning Secret and fishing. The words Kat had spoken popped up in Secret's head.

"Apparently some bitch is running around lying on me."

Then Secret remembered the look Kat had given her. It was almost as if Kat was insinuating that she was the one who had lied.

But what was it she could have lied about, and to who? Secret pondered. Then she recalled the conversation she'd had with Lucky when she was trying to persuade him to put her on.

"I want in. Just like Shawndiece," Secret told Lucky. "I've been thinking about all this for a minute now. And to keep it real with you, it was something I was going to do with or without you. But I'd much rather do it with you."

"Trust me, ma, you wasn't gon do it without me." Lucky chuckled. "Ya boy got the streets on lock. So whoever you thought you were gonna get put on by, trust me, nine times out of ten, they work for me anyhow."

"Maybe so. It's some dude Kat was telling me could put me on. Some dude named Pain, or something like that."

Secret recalled the way Lucky had shot up off of the bed. He had been so angry that his nostrils were flaring. Having Shawndiece beat Kat down must have been his and Major Pain's way of teaching her to keep her mouth shut.

Clearly the lie Secret had told to Lucky about Kat hooking her up with Major Pain had been the cause of this brawl. That must have been Major Pain behind the camera, which explained his comment about her not lying on him anymore.

Secret put her hand to her forehead. She couldn't believe this.

No longer hearing a sound coming from the phone the older girl said, "Is it over?" while extending her hand for Secret to hand her back the phone.

Secret was too deep in thought to pay the girl much attention. So when she didn't extend the girl the phone back, the teenager stood up and took it from Secret's hand. She and her sister proceeded to search the site for the next fight to watch.

Secret just stood there dumbfounded. Why hadn't Kat told her about what happened? Why hadn't she just called her to the carpet on it? Why was she keeping it a secret? And why had Lucky cared enough to seek her out and question her about the situation? Question after question went through Secret's head, but she had not a single answer. Clearly Kat wasn't going to give her the 411 or else she would have when she'd come over her house. Secret wasn't about to confront Lucky about it. That left only one person for Secret to get answers from. In all of their years of being best friends, Secret and Shawndiece had always been honest with one another. She'd soon find out if that was still the case.

Chapter 27

"It's been a minute," Secret said as she and Shawndiece walked through the park side by side. "I was glad you were able to find the time to meet up with me today." Secret strolled Dina along the trail in her stroller.

"Me too," Shawndiece replied. "Yesterday just wasn't good for me. I had some business to handle."

"With Lucky I suppose," Secret said.

Shawndiece just kept walking, not confirming Secret's statement.

"I guess that answers my question," Secret said under her breath, but not low enough where Shawndiece couldn't hear her.

"Well, from what I hear," Shawndiece said, "you've been handling a little business of your own with Lucky."

"True," Secret admitted. "Call it temporary insanity."

Shawndiece stopped and looked at Secret. "Does that mean that you're no longer interested in being part of the crew?" Shawndiece used her fingers to put quotation marks around the word "crew."

Secret turned to Shawndiece. "I won't beat around the bush. Like I said on the phone, I really need to talk to you about something important. And that something important is me changing my mind about getting all mixed up in this whole dope thing."

Shawndiece chuckled and started walking again. "I take it you've met Quasi," Shawndiece said. "She has the tendency to change a bitch's mind about wanting to be in the game."

"No, it wasn't Quasi," Secret said. "It's you."

"Me?" Shawndiece stopped walking again and questioned Secret.

"Yes. The only reason why I even got mixed up in all that was because of you."

"Girl, please." Shawndiece waved Secret off. "Don't even try it. I have never put it in your head to do something like that. As a matter of fact, remember how I was all up in your ass the day Lucky brought you to the garage?"

"I know, but since I've been out of jail, I don't get to talk to you, I don't get to hang out with you," Secret said. "Every minute of your time was occupied by your so-called hustle. I just wanted my friend back. If becoming part of the crew"—now Secret was the one putting the word "crew" in quotation marks—"was the only way things could go back to normal with us, then that's what I was willing to do."

"But things aren't back to normal."

"But they can be. That's what I'm trying to say." Secret threw her hands up and allowed them to fall to her side. "The hell with this. Let's just go back to the life we lived pre Lucky coming into our lives. It's all just been downhill since."

"What, and me go back to being a gold-digging ho?" Shawndiece said. "Rocking with guys I don't give two shits about just to keep clothes on my back and a little chump change to throw at my moms for rent? The hell with that," Shawndiece said. "Do you know how much money I have made in just these few months?"

"Let your momma tell it, not enough," Secret said. "That day I went looking for you shortly after I got out of jail she said you were dodging her to keep from paying rent."

"I wasn't dodging her," Shawndiece was quick to say. "I had been in that fucking dungeon with Quasi for days making mad loot. I practically slept there. I got my mom's mortgage paid up six months in advance plus a nice savings for myself."

"That's great," Secret said. "Then you definitely don't need to keep doing it. Live off of your savings. You graduated high school. Heck, you don't have any kids. You can go to college. You still live at your mom's address right?"

Shawndiece nodded.

"You still pay her rent. Girl, you can get financial aid for college and end up going for free. Just get your mom to cosign that all of this is true." Secret was telling Shawndiece to get her mother to do what Yolanda would have never done for Secret. As far as Secret was concerned, Yolanda never wanted to see her only child make it. "I can even get you a job at the grocery store with me." Secret shrugged. "Who knows, we can end up being roommates and just—"

"Will you stop it with that whole fairytale shit?" Shawndiece snapped. "You always did live in la-la land. Well, haven't you figured out yet that this is the real fucking world?" Shawndiece looked and sounded so exasperated. "That's your story, Secret, not mine," Shawndiece told her best friend.

"But it can be your story too. It can be our story. You've always been so strong and so smart, Shawn," Secret said. "I don't even know how you got caught up with Lucky like that in the first place. I mean, you rolling with ballers is nothing new. But usually it's just for their money."

Shawndiece exhaled. "I've been fucking with these niggas for so long I just got exhausted and jaded. Yeah, I have some nice jewelry, designer clothes, shoes, purses, memories of some nice trips, but where has that gotten me? The day I caught up with Lucky, I followed his ass out to the burbs. Do you know he has a five thousand–square foot home with two nice-ass cars parked in his driveway?"

Secret didn't know that. If she'd really given a damn about Lucky, that probably would have pissed her off, that she was supposed to be his so-called woman, yet he had her living in government housing while he lived in the lap of luxury, but she didn't care anymore. That still didn't hide the surprised look on her face when Shawndiece told her.

"I thought so," Shawndiece said. "And I wouldn't have known either had I not seen it for myself. By the time I approached him, I no longer gave a shit about cussing him out." She paused and said, "But I did cuss his ass out though."

Secret half smiled.

"But when all was said and done, I had dollar signs in my eyes. I wanted to know how I could get that. Being put up in an apartment or condo by a dude would no longer suffice. I wanted to bring shit to the table on my own. My mother always said make sure the only thing you ain't got to eat is what another nigga done brought to the table. And that's how I had been living my entire life. Eating whatever was handed to me. Well fuck that. After snagging a baller hadn't seemed to be working to my benefit anyway, I figured, if I can't beat 'em join 'em."

Secret looked down at Dina. So far her trying to talk Shawndiece out of the drug game wasn't working. She had to come up with something else. She thought for a moment and then looked back up at Shawndiece again. "Can I be honest? I feel a certain way about you working with Lucky," Secret said. "After what he did to me and you go into cahoots with him."

Shawndiece twisted her face up. "But you wit' that nigga now, so what's the difference?"

"The difference is . . ." How could Secret tell Shawndiece what was really going on without blowing her cover? She couldn't. Shawndiece was her best friend from the cradle to the grave, but she worked with Lucky. As much as she hated to say it, Secret could not 100 percent trust Shawndiece with the full truth. "Look, I was stupid to forgive Lucky."

"No, that's just who you are. You've got a good heart."

"Yeah, well, my heart can get me trouble. You always taught me to listen to my head. Well my head is telling me that I should have never even start messing with Lucky again, and you should have never started in the first place."

"Well, looks like it's too late now, huh?" Shawndiece shrugged her shoulders and started to walk again.

Secret stopped her. "No, it's never too late." Secret had to think fast. She needed to say something to convince her best friend that hanging around with Lucky could cost her her freedom. Secret was tired. It was time to end this game. It was time to deliver him to the police and move on with her life before everybody got in too deep.

"Lucky is supposed to be stopping by my house tonight. I'm breaking things off with him. I need you to do the same."

Shawndiece sniffed. "Damn, you acting like I'm dating the nigga. I'm just putting in a little work."

"And has putting in work really gotten you any further than giving blow jobs did?" Secret snapped.

Shawndiece raised an eyebrow.

"I'm sorry, Shawndiece, but it's the truth. You still don't have a house on the hills or anything like that."

"It takes time," Shawndiece said.

"Come on, you're smarter than that."

Shawndiece put her hands on her hips. "Not everybody is as smart as your college-bound ass."

"Well, my college-bound ass is working in a grocery store, on welfare raising a baby. Might I add low-income housing?"

"Yeah, but you still don't have to want for nothing with Lucky in your corner. So I have him in mine too, in a different way."

Secret was becoming desperate. Nothing she seemed to be saying was registering with Shawndiece. Lucky was about to get set up, and anybody in his crew at the wrong place at the wrong time could go down with him. Secret wouldn't be able to live with herself if one of those people ended up being Shawndiece.

"How about we just be in each other's corner?" Secret suggested. "Just me and you. Fuck the world. After all, what has the world done for either of us?"

Shawndiece didn't reply. She looked to be taking in Secret's words.

Secret continued to strike while the iron was at least warm. "You once told me yourself that the streets don't give a shit about anybody. It will chew you up and spit you out. So is that what our fate is?"

"Maybe mine, but not yours," Shawndiece replied.

"If it's yours, then it's mine as well. I'm following your lead. You've never steered me wrong before, so I don't think you would now. So if you think being in the game is worth it, then fuck it; let's do this. We're in the game, together."

"Come on, Secret, you're talking crazy." Shawndiece was half taking her friend serious. But the longer Secret stood there with a straight face, the more serious Shawndiece began to take her friend. "Secret, what you're asking me to do isn't as easy as it sounds. I mean for you it is because you play a different role in Lucky's life than I do."

"Then I'll tell him for you that you're out." Secret wiped her hands as if to say it would be as easy as taking out the trash. "He'll listen to me."

"Secret, you don't understand."

"No, Shawndiece, you don't understand." And that was no exaggeration. She didn't even know half the truth as to why her friend was so desperate for her to quit Lucky's crew. "I've trusted you for years." She took Shawndiece's hands into hers. "Don't you think it's high time you start trusting me?"

Shawndiece stared down at their hands. The two had had such a strong connection since they were young girls. They'd always been there for each other and had each other's backs. Secret was right; she had always allowed Shawndiece to take the lead, to be the teacher. It had been draining Shawndiece over the years, always feeling that, as the decision maker, if things went wrong it was her fault. She'd even blamed herself for Secret being locked up in jail. And now even today Secret still wanted to follow Shawndiece, even after how all that had turned out. Shawndiece just couldn't lead her friend down that same path again.

"Okay," Shawndiece said in an almost inaudible tone.

"What?" Secret asked, leaning her ear in closer.

"I said okay," Shawndiece shouted into Secret's ear, trying to be funny.

Secret laughed, let go of Shawndiece's hands and then hugged her friend. "Oh, God, thank you, Shawn. Thank you so much." She pulled away and said, "Because if Quasi stuck her finger in me one more time . . ." Secret's words trailed off as she stuck her tongue out in disgust.

Shawndiece pulled Secret in for a hug. "I know, I know. No more dungeon, no more nothing."

Secret pulled away. "So when are you going to let Lucky know?"

"Well, I just have to handle one last piece of business on Friday, and then after that—"

"No!" Secret yelled. Her joy was short-lived. "You have to tell him now and just be done with it."

"I will tell him, Secret, but it's kind of like I need to earn my last paycheck, so after payday on Friday, I promise you—"

"No, no, no, no, no." Secret just kept shaking her head and repeating those words.

"Secret, please stop. I promise you that will be the last time. Come Saturday morning I will officially be out of the game."

Secret took a deep breath. "Please, Shawndiece. I just have a bad feeling. I don't want what happened to me to happen to you. And you end up in jail. Please. You said you would start trusting me and following my lead from now on. Well, I need you to do that starting now, not Saturday. Okay?"

Shawndiece just stood there. Secret could see dollar signs in her friend's eyes. She knew how important money and any type of come up was for Shawndiece.

"I know leaving money on the table is not something you do," Secret told Shawndiece. "But all money is not good money, and in this instance, that is truer than ever." Secret thought for a minute. "Lucky dropped me a stack for the little bit of work I put in. You can have it. I don't want it." Secret still had the wad of cash in her purse as she spoke. She dug down into her purse that was hanging on Dina's stroller. She pulled the money out and began to stuff it into Shawndiece's hands. "Here. Just take it. I don't want it anyway. It's blood money as far as I'm concerned."

"Secret, stop it," Shawndiece said as passersby began eyeing them. "You trying to get us knocked over the head and mugged out here?"

"Please, Shawn, I'm begging you." By now tears were streaming down Secret's face. Her shoulders began to heave and she was starting to make a scene out in public.

"Calm down, Secret. Just calm down." Shawndiece pulled Secret in for a hug. She could feel her body trembling. She'd never seen her friend like this before. "Okay, okay. I'll do it. I'll meet up with Lucky tonight and tell him I'm out."

"Promise?" Secret sniffed.

"Promise," Shawndiece said.

That was good enough for Secret. Never in their entire friendship had Shawndiece ever broken a promise to Secret, so she had no reason to think she would start now, especially one as serious as this.

Shawndiece used one hand to pat Secret on her back to calm her down and comfort her. She kept the other hand on the small of Secret's back, with her fingers crossed.

Chapter 28

Shawndiece ended up leaving the park before Secret. Secret strolled Dina around a few more minutes and then ultimately made her way back to the parking lot. Secret was truly on cloud nine, that was until she noticed her car hooked up to a tow truck about to be towed away.

"Hey, wait! That's my car," Secret yelled out as she began a light jog with the stroller, trying to make it over to her car before the tow truck driver pulled off.

He hadn't even turned her way when she yelled out. He looked to be on his truck radio, more than likely calling in the tow.

"Please wait!" Out of breath, Secret made it over to the driver's door before he pulled off. "This is my car. What's going on? I wasn't parked in handicap or anything."

"No, but you are parked with expired tags."

"Expired tags?" Secret thought she would just die. With all that had been going on, she'd forgotten to go down to the BMV and get new tags on her birthday a while back. She'd remembered mentioning her upcoming birthday to Ray. But with so much drama in her life, celebrating her nineteenth birthday had been low on the totem pole. "Damn it," she said under her breath.

"Where are you taking my car to?" Secret asked.

"Police impound. You're gonna have to go get new tags first. You got a ticket." He pointed to the ticket on her windshield. "So you're going to have to go pay that as well. Show proof of both to the police impound lot and your car will be all yours. That is after you pay them for any tow and storage fees."

Just listening to him tell her everything she had to do gave her a headache. "Won't I need my registration? It's in the glove box." She pointed to her car.

He looked at Secret, looked down at the baby stroller, thought for a moment and then looked back up at Secret again. He let out a loud huff and then opened the door and got out of his truck. He climbed up to the passenger side of Secret's car. "Hey, unlock it."

Secret pulled her keys out of her purse and hit the key fob to unlock the doors. The tow truck driver dug through her glove box and found the registration. He snatched the ticket off the windshield and then went and handed them both to Secret.

"Thank you," Secret said.

He tilted the dingy Michigan State snap back he was wearing then drove off.

"For nothing," Secret said. She looked down at Dina. "How in the world are we going to get home?" Secret pulled her phone out of her purse real quick, dialed, and then put the phone to her ear. "Hey, Shawndiece, are you still around the park area? My car got towed," Secret said. She let out a sigh of relief when Shawndiece told her she'd be there in ten minutes to pick her up.

Shawndiece picked up Secret and Dina from the park. Secret had to sit in the back seat with Dina because she'd forgotten to get the car seat from her car before it was towed away. From there they headed to the BMV. They'd have to spend the day beating the clock before everything closed. Thank goodness they had that wad of cash Lucky had given Secret. No telling how much it was going to cost altogether to get Secret's car back.

From the BMV, Shawndiece drove Secret downtown to pay her ticket. She wasn't sure if she needed to go to traffic court or the police station. She hadn't thought to ask the person who helped her at the BMV. Heck, she might have even been able to pay it there for all she knew. She'd start with traffic court first. Fortunately she was able to pay at the district listed on the ticket. All of that took another forty-five minutes.

Secret walked to the elevator bank and rode down to the lobby. The elevator felt like it had stopped on every single floor letting people on before it finally reached the lobby. Secret couldn't wait for those elevator doors to open. Someone on that elevator hadn't showered in days, maybe weeks according to the smell that almost suffocated Secret. She raced off the elevator, heading to the exit doors when something caught her eye. Someone.

Over at the entrance doors, where security was set up, Secret saw someone who looked familiar, someone who she hadn't seen in a while. She watched as the person lifted the jacket they were wearing and removed a gun from a holster on their waist. Next they pulled out something and showed the security. It looked like it was an ID or something. Secret saw the person open the other side of their jacket and flash. From the distance Secret was at, she couldn't tell exactly what it was, but it sure as heck looked like a badge.

"What the . . ." Secret said as someone trying to exit bumped Secret out of the way and kept going. Not fazed by their rudeness, but more concerned about the scene playing out before her, Secret made her way over to the entrance.

By the time the familiar face went through the security formalities, Secret was standing there waiting, looking at them eyeball to eyeball.

"Who the fuck are you? Who the fuck are you?" Secret screamed with tears falling from her eyes. It didn't even register in her mind where she was and that this is the last place she should be making a scene.

"Secret?" This person was clearly just as caught off guard with seeing Secret as she was at seeing them. The surprised and startled tone was a dead giveaway.

"Officer Maxwell," the man at the security post called out. "You okay?"

"Yes, yes. I'm good," she answered, and then took Secret by the elbow and walked her over to the women's bathroom. As soon as they entered, she locked the bathroom door and went to make sure no one was in there.

"What is going on?" Secret said, tears running down her face. Today had just been too hectic. Too much for her to face yet another situation that would probably pan out to be even more betrayal.

The woman who Secret stared down took a deep breath, washed her hands down her face then squeezed her eyes closed tightly. It was as if she was gathering her words before she spoke. She opened her eyes and let out the deep breath she'd been holding in. Next she finally spoke. "I'm Officer Olivia Raygiene Maxwell. Special duty undercover agent for the city of Flint, state of Michigan."

"Ray? Raygiene?" Secret threw one hand over her mouth and the other over her stomach as if a sharp pain had hit her. She hunched over. She opened up her mouth to let out a crying yelp, but nothing came out. She had no air. She couldn't breathe. Anything she thought wanted to come out of her throat was stuck.

"Secret, please." Ray went to walk toward Secret and place her hand on her back.

Secret quickly removed her hand from her mouth and shot straight up, pushing Ray back. Secret began to shake her head from side to side. "No," she finally managed to get out. "Don't you come near me. Don't you touch me. You are a liar. You were never there to help me, you were always there because you were getting paid to be there. You never cared about me or my daughter," Secret cried.

"First my mother, now you. Who the fuck else is on Team Detective Davis instead of Team Secret?"

"Secret, I am on your team. Can't you see that? That's why I wanted to make sure you were all right. That I took care of you."

"Is that so?"

"Yes, that's so."

"So then eating my pussy is what you call taking care of me?"

Ray had no comeback for that one.

Secret put her hands to her head. "I can't. I mean, I don't understand. Is everyone willing to sell their soul just to get Lucky?" She sucked her teeth. "I guess I have some nerve asking that question seeming I've done the same thing." She looked to Ray. "But I have a good reason. That son of a bitch got me locked up. Had me damn near having my baby in a jail cell. He has done nothing but turned my life upside down. Just killed my spirit." Secret squatted down and just bawled.

"He killed my spirit too," Ray said, "when he killed my sister."

Secret looked up at Ray. Suddenly her wound didn't seem as deep as Ray's. "Your sister?"

"Yeah, my baby sister," Ray began to explain. "She, uhh, you know how it goes, started hanging out with the wrong crowd. Long story short, she ended up messing with an old friend of Lucky's. Lucky turned against his friend and my baby sister ended up getting caught in the crossfire. So when it all boils down to it, I wanted Lucky just as bad as the next person," Ray said. "I've been working the case for a couple of years now. I thought I'd blown my cover that day at the house when he thought he recognized me." Ray gave Secret the opportunity to speak, but she said nothing, so Ray continued. "My sister was everything to me."

Now all of a sudden Secret felt bad for going off on Ray like she had done. She was still pissed, but the good heart she had had empathy for Ray as well. "What was your sister's name?"

"Ivy," Ray said.

Secret looked at her bug-eyed. "So Ivy is your sister, not your girlfriend?"

Ray nodded. "Those pictures you saw, that was me and Ivy. Pictures are all that I have left of her and Lucky is responsible for her death. The day I buried my sister I made a vow and a promise to her that I'd get his ass no matter what it took and by any means necessary."

"Even if it meant using me?" Secret asked.

"I wasn't using you, Secret. I was protecting you. And I know you might not believe me, but I didn't even look at that as part of a job. I wanted to be there for you."

Secret could have stood there, been angry, hurt, and deceived by Ray, going back and forth with her over and over. But what did it matter now? Still, Secret could not believe what she was hearing. Everyone who she ever thought wanted to help her, to truly help her, had had their own hidden agenda. Everyone had used her and she'd been too dumb, naïve, and blind to see it.

"Well, thank you for being there for me, Officer Maxwell," Secret said sarcastically. She then walked over to the bathroom door and unlocked it. Before exiting she turned around and said to Ray, "Like Detective Davis told me, 'you did good.'" And on that note, Secret exited the bathroom.

As she walked to the exit door of the building, she couldn't help but think about how everyone seemed to have played a part in this whole mess. Everyone seemed to be a piece of this crazy puzzle, even Secret herself, so who was she to judge? Everyone had something to gain out of this. But for some reason, Secret felt that she was the only one who had something to lose.

Chapter 29

Secret's stomach had been twisted in knots ever since she woke up this morning. Today was the day. It was Friday; the big drug buy was going down today and thanks to Secret informing Detective Davis of all the details, the police would be there to witness Lucky's participation. He would be caught with his hand in the cookie jar so to speak. For once and for all Flint's most wanted would become the property of the State of Michigan.

All day long Secret had been brushing off the guilt of having set up Lucky. She asked herself why she couldn't be more like Shawndiece when it came to her feelings. Had she just told the cops that the dope had belonged to Lucky in the first place, none of this would be taking place. Lucky would have been the one who got hauled off to jail and he would have been nice and comfortable in prison by now. This would all be over with. Had it been Shawndiece getting hauled off to jail for dope that wasn't hers, she would have told the police the drugs were Lucky's without them even having to ask. But Secret was human with a decent heart. Perhaps a good characteristic to have, but it had always seemed more like a flaw, never working in her favor.

But even Shawndiece had managed to get caught up. Money and material things had always been Shawndiece's guilty pleasures. She felt that was her ticket out of the hood, while Secret had always felt it was her education that was her escape route. Thank God Secret had talked

Shawndiece into giving up the life. Maybe hearing about Lucky's forthcoming downfall would have her thanking Secret for getting her out of the game.

Secret had just finished feeding Dina and was burping her when there was a knock at her door. With baby on shoulder, Secret walked over to the door, looked out of the peephole and saw that it was Kat. Secret hadn't spoken with Kat since the whole video of her and Shawndiece fighting. She'd decided to table that conversation until everything went down. Definitely since the whole Ray thing and not knowing who she could trust and who she couldn't, she didn't want to say the wrong thing to the wrong person. Therefore Secret had kept to herself the last couple days.

"Hey, momma, what's up?" Kat said all happy go lucky as she walked up into Secret's apartment.

"Hey," Secret said dryly.

Kat kissed Dina on the head and started doing baby talk. "How's auntie's baby? How is auntie's little girl? I've got something for you." Kat held up a Macy's shopping bag.

Dina lifted her head and started smiling.

"I was trying to burp her, do you mind?" Secret snapped off.

Kat pulled back and stared at Secret. "Damn, what's wrong with you?" She set the bag down on the coffee table.

Secret sighed. "Nothing I'm sorry. I just . . ." Secret went and sat down in the chair.

"Something's bothering you. It's written all over your face," Kat said as she sat on the couch. "And you just bit my head off for nothing. That's not like you. Come on, talk to me, sis. What gives?"

Secret felt as though the weight of the world was on her shoulders. It would be nice to finally lift some of the weight by sharing what was going on in her life. Her mother had given her the right name for sure, because it seemed like all she did was keep secrets and live a secret life. But today it would all be over with. She would start things anew. She would forget all about the day she ever met Lucky. Secret closed her eyes and thought for a minute until tears began seeping out of her eyes. Everything was just too much. Far too much to bear, alone.

She felt Kat's hand rest on her knee. She opened her eyes to see a concerned pair staring back at her.

"What is it, sis? You can talk to me," Kat said.

Kat was right, Secret thought. They were sisters and if Secret couldn't share her feelings with anyone else she could certainly share them with Kat. At first she'd felt skeptical about what she could say to Kat and what she couldn't say because of Kat's own connection with Lucky. But Lucky was pretty much history now so none of that mattered. What did matter, though, was Secret getting things off of her chest and be able to breathe again.

"It's Lucky," Secret finally said.

Kat twitched a little as if she was uncomfortable. But then again it could have been a cross between being anxious. "What about Lucky?"

"Well, you know I've been seeing him," Secret said.

"Honestly you didn't have a choice. He is Dina's father so—"

"No, it wasn't like that."

Kat paused and swallowed hard. "Wha . . . what do you mean?" She began tapping her foot on the ground. "Like seeing seeing him? Like him not just coming over to see Dina, but to see you too? Like y'all getting back together again type of seeing?" Kat waited with baited breath.

Secret nodded.

It looked as though all the blood had drained from Kat. She balled a fist and then stood up pacing. "That son of a—"

"It wasn't just on him," Secret interrupted, seeing how teed off Kat was with Lucky. "It wasn't him talking sweet little naïve Secret into getting back with him," Secret admitted. "I wanted to get back with him."

Kat stopped pacing and looked at Secret like she was crazy.

"Correction, I had to get back with him."

"What do you mean had to?" Kat had an apparent attitude with her baby sister. "You act like somebody had a gun to your head."

"Something like that," Secret said.

"What do you mean something like that? Is he threatening you? Is that what it is?" Kat was getting agitated. Secret was taking too long to spill the beans.

"The police, it's why they let me out of jail. To get back in good with Lucky. Get him to trust me, find out what he had going on, so that I could . . ." Secret paused. She still hated the fact that she'd been a part of setting Lucky up. That wasn't who she was but it was who she had become.

"So that you could what, Secret?" Kat sat back down and glared at Secret with such intensity. She started shaking her head. She had a look on her face that read, "Lord, please don't tell me what I think you are about to tell me." She started bouncing her knee.

"They said it was the only way they would let me out of jail," Secret said. "They came to the hospital when I had Dina. They told me they were going to throw me back in jail and put Dina into the system." Secret felt like she did when she had to tell her mother she was pregnant. She just couldn't understand why Kat was making her feel that way. "I couldn't let them do that, so I agreed."

"Agreed to what, Secret?" Kat asked sternly.

"To help them set up Lucky."

"Jesus Christ!" Kat said, standing and throwing her hand on her forehead. "Secret, do you know what Lucky and his crew are going to do to you if they find out you're playing for the other team? And what about your girl, Shawndiece?"

"I saw the video of you and Shawndiece," Secret admitted. "I know what they made her do to you, that they made you two go at it, and I'm sorry."

"I'm not talking about that," Kat interrupted, shooing her hand like she couldn't have cared less about that situation. "What about Shawndiece getting caught up?"

"Shawndiece is out. She doesn't work for Lucky anymore."

Kat let out a sinister laugh. "Oh, is that what she told you? Because five minutes before I came here she was with him. As a matter of fact, they were about to go handle some business."

If Secret didn't know any better, she would have thought she was dead. She was almost certain if she looked down on the floor every ounce of her blood would be at her feet. That's what she felt like, as if all the blood had drained from her body. She'd thought her heart had stopped beating as well if she couldn't hear it pounding furiously through her eardrums. And her brain felt like it was going on the blitz trying to process what Kat had just said.

"You must be mistaken," Secret said to Kat nervously.

"Damn it, Secret, what have you done?" Kat pulled out her cell phone.

"Who are you calling?"

"Lucky," Kat said as she beat the numbers into her phone. She put the phone to her ear after dialing.

"Why? What's going on?" Secret stood. "I thought you didn't talk to him anymore."

"I don't. I mean . . ." Kat's words trailed off as she focused on the ringing in her ears.

"And how did you know Shawn is with him? When did you see him, and why? I thought you weren't—"

"Lucky, it's me, Kat," she said into the phone while raising her hand to silence Secret. "Please call me back. It's important. Oh, my God you don't know how important it is. Please, baby, call me back."

Secret was thrown back by hearing Kat refer to Lucky as, "Baby?" Secret questioned out loud. "Kat, what is really going on?"

Dina started whining. The poor baby could feel all the tension in the room. Secret began patting her back trying to calm her.

"Secret, please. You wouldn't understand," Kat said, almost in tears. "I wish I knew where they were." Kat looked at Secret accusingly. "How could you do this? To your baby's father? To your best friend? You might be out of jail now, but what is your best friend going to say when the tables are turned and you're the one visiting her in jail?" Kat shook her head.

"I didn't know," Secret swore. Her heart ached just thinking about the fact that her best friend was about to get caught up and end up in jail. In this particular case, unlike with Secret, Shawndiece really did have dirty hands so she was more than likely going to spend a lot of years behind bars. "Oh, God, what have I done?" Secret began to pace as tears flowed down her cheeks. All of a sudden she stopped in her tracks. "Wait! I know where they are at. I know where things are about to go down."

Secret immediately went and grabbed her car keys. She didn't even have to say a word to Kat, she was right on her heels out the door. Secret buckled Dina into her car seat and then hopped into the driver side while Kat hopped into the passenger side.

"Where are we headed?" Kat asked.

"To the garage they work out of," Secret told her as she started the car and pulled off.

Kat stared at her for a minute. "You know where the spot is?"

Secret looked over at her. "You don't?" she shot back.

Kat swallowed and just looked straight ahead as the two drove like bats out of hell. At the moment Secret didn't have a care in the world about her deal with Detective Davis. She had a best friend to save.

Chapter 30

"They're here! There's Lucky's truck!" Kat exclaimed as they pulled into the front entrance of the warehouse. She looked around anxiously. "And it doesn't look like the police are here yet. We have time!" Kat shot out of the car before Secret barely had a chance to put it in park.

"Kat, wait!" Secret yelled out the open window. All of the windows were rolled down except for the back ones. Secret didn't want the air to be too much for Dina.

Kat ignored her sister and proceeded into the warehouse.

"Damn it!" Secret snapped, jumping out of the running car. She had only a split second to think about Dina and taking her inside. She had no idea what was going down in there. She had no idea what they might do to her. Whatever it was, she didn't want it done in front of her daughter.

Secret raced inside the warehouse and through the door. She saw Kat clearing the hallway. Secret got halfway through the room to the hallway before she stopped. She turned back around and looked at the toolbox she'd recalled Fonda making mention of. She said a quick prayer that the gun was in that box. She exhaled as she lifted the box. It was there. She removed the black piece of steel from the toolbox.

Secret had only been to the shooting range once, but she had enough confidence in her abilities to handle business with the weapon if need be. She hoped it didn't come to that though.

With the weapon down to her side, Secret made her way toward the back room. She could hear voices and all kinds of commotion coming from the room. But the sound of a toilet flushing startled her.

Secret panicked, looking from left to right. There was a door beside what looked like a huge storage cabinet to Secret's left. She tried the knob but it was locked. Her only other option was to try the storage cabinet. Secret was relieved to swing open the door and find it practically empty. To the left was a row of shelves that had a few automobile-related items positioned for show. The other side was where work uniforms probably would have hung if there were actual real mechanics working there. There was one lone jacket hanging up. It was navy blue and had a patch on it that matched the sign out in the lot: Lucky's Garage. Secret jumped into the larger side of the cabinet and closed the door.

No sooner than Secret closed the door had a door down the hall opened and Secret could hear footsteps coming in her direction. They then sounded as if they were heading in another direction, like back in the main garage area.

All of a sudden the loud voices from the room got louder and louder.

"What the hell you talking about? Slow the fuck down. Where she at?" That was Lucky.

"Yo, Lucky, everything all right back there, man?" Secret recognized Fonda's voice.

"Where the fuck you been? How she get back here?" Lucky's voice was right up on the cabinet.

"I had to take a shit real quick," Fonda said.

"Did you lock the front door, or did your dumb ass forget like the last time?"

There was silence. Secret imagined Fonda giving Lucky the doofus "uh-oh" look.

"What I tell you was gon' happen the next time you did that shit? Huh?"

"Lucky, plea—"

A large booming sound blasted through Secret's ears. She threw her hand over her mouth to hold the scream she wanted to let out inside.

"Arggh."

Secret cringed herself at the painful-sounding yelp. She heard a thud and figured it was Fonda on the ground taking his last breath.

"Fuck!" Lucky said, almost sounding regretful.

"We've gotta go," Kat warned.

"Go where?" That was a male voice Secret didn't recognize. It must have been one of the guys Lucky was doing business with.

"Mafucka, you tried to set us up?" That was another male voice Secret didn't recognize.

"Please, do I look like I'm in on this shit?" Lucky snapped.

"It's Secret," Kat said. "She's been playing you the whole time since she got out of jail."

Secret's mouth dropped open. She couldn't believe her sister was turning on her like that.

"We have got to go." Kat's voice was shaky and full of fear. "Hell, for all you know, they five-oh and part of this setup too."

There was a moment of silence then gunshots could be heard. Secret covered her ears and kneeled down. It sounded like she was front and center at a Fourth of July fireworks display.

It was a matter of seconds and it was all over. The sound of gunfire ceased.

"You okay?" Kat asked.

Secret had no idea who she was asking though. Then she heard a reply.

"Yeah," Lucky said. "You know I'm good with this thang. But it doesn't look like Shawn is good though."

Shawndiece! In that moment in time all Secret could do was picture her best friend lying there shot, bleeding to death. Without even thinking she pushed all her weight against the cabinet door and rushed out. She felt a huge weight and then saw Lucky on the ground. The gun he had been holding fell from his hand. He went to reach for it and instantaneously Secret pulled the trigger of her gun.

"Fuck!" Lucky shouted as he grabbed his side.

Kat had the nerve to run over to Lucky and check on him.

Secret began to tremble when she saw Shawndiece lying face down. There were two guys next to her. A pool of blood seeped underneath all of them.

A shrilling cry escaped from Secret's lips.

"You shot him," Kat looked up at Secret and yelled.

"Fuck him!" Secret snapped. She couldn't care less if Lucky lay right there on that floor and bled to death. That's exactly what Shawndiece was doing. How had Secret gotten them all mixed up in this mess? This was all her fault. Why did she even take Lucky's phone number the day they met? If only she could turn back the hands of time.

"It's just a graze, a flesh wound," Lucky managed to say, still trying to keep his cool. But the agony in his tone gave him away. It might have been just a graze, but it was hurting him like hell.

"Oh, just a flesh wound, huh?" Secret spat. "Then it looks like I need to finish the job."

"Secret just cut it out," Kat snapped. "You know this ain't even you." Kat, not taking Secret seriously, helped Lucky up off the floor. Once he was to his feet, Kat started walking him into the main garage area.

"What do you think you're doing?" Secret asked, following them.

"I'm taking him to get some help." Kat continued walking.

"I can't even believe you, Kat. Do you really have that low of self-esteem? He's been playing you like some bottom bitch whore for all these years and you're still concerned about whether he lives or dies." Secret let out a tsk. "Did not having Daddy in our lives fuck you up that much? You're going to just let him keep playing you?"

Kat let go of Lucky's arm. He continued hobbling toward the door while Kat addressed Secret with a pointed finger.

"He loves me." Kat rammed her index finger into her own chest. "Can't you see that you're the one he's been playing all along?" Kat shouted at her sister. "He's been bragging about his secret little weapon for over a year now. That day I picked Lucky up when you were arrested, that's when I found out just what this secret was, or should I say who?"

Secret looked to Lucky who was halfway to the door. "Stop or I'll shoot your ass again."

He hobbled around and faced Secret. "Don't listen to her, Secret," Lucky begged, gripping the wound where the bullet had grazed his side.

"Shut up!" Secret yelled, her hand trembling while she now held the gun aimed toward Lucky. She turned her attention back to Kat. She wanted to hear everything Kat had to say, no matter how much it hurt her. What would it matter anymore anyway? Any minute now the cops would be showing up. This time they'd be hauling Lucky off to jail. There would be no pleas or deals for him to get back on the streets. He was the kingpin the police had been trying to nail for years. Well, before they took him to prison and threw away the key, where Secret would never talk to him a day in his life, she wanted to know just who the real Lucky had been all this time.

Kat looked over at Lucky. "Why don't you man up and tell her the truth? What do you have to lose now anyway? She's about to blow both our brains out. Die with the balls of keeping it real. It's over."

Secret looked to Lucky. Her eyes pressed him to come forth with the truth.

"It wasn't all a lie," Lucky admitted. "When I first met you, I really liked you. I thought you was going to be the one I wifed and brought to my home." He gritted his teeth in pain. "No broad has ever laid her head in my home."

Secret looked over to Kat.

"Not even Kat," Lucky confirmed what he knew Secret's eyes were questioning. "But once you tried to set me up, I knew I couldn't trust you."

"And when he can't trust you, he can groom you," Kat jumped in.

"Bitch, shut the fuck up," Lucky snapped, causing a pain to rip through his side. He looked down at the blood seeping between his fingers. "Please. I need a doctor."

"Just talk!" Secret yelled, waving the gun.

"Kat is right," Lucky said, hunched over in pain. "I've learned you can only give a person one chance at trust."

Secret looked at him with complete shock. All that talk about giving him a second chance after he showed her his true colors. Even though she had forgiven him mostly because she had to according to her deal with the state, a part of her had felt for him and felt he deserved a second chance. Now come to find he hadn't truly given her a second chance after finding out her initial intentions with him. He'd just been playing on her emotions and personality all along.

"I'm not like you, Secret," Lucky told her. "You have a good heart. You haven't dealt with some of the shit that I've dealt with to know that when a person shows you who they are, believe them the first time. So when you told me how you was going to try to scheme me, I knew you had it in you to scheme. The fact that it was in your blood let me know I couldn't trust you on that tip."

"Then why did you continue to fuck with me?" Secret asked.

"Because on the flip side, you were loyal to a fault. I knew eventually, after you had the baby and all, I could get you on my team. And then when you went down for me on that drug charge, I knew I had to have you. You were the diamond in the rough I'd been looking for all my life."

"Your secret weapon," Secret said, her eyes filled with tears.

Lucky shrugged. "What can I say? We was all in it for our own reasons." He looked at Kat and then back at Secret. "I really was done fucking with Kat up until I saw her with you in the restaurant." He looked at Kat regretfully. "Sorry, shorty, but I only start fucking with you again because you was close to her." He nodded toward Secret. "I needed you to watch her, to be my eyes and my ears. I knew that no matter what, you'd always have my back."

Kat's mouth dropped. Kat's heart dropped.

There was a tornado of emotions going through Secret's head. She thought she'd heard it all until Lucky put the nail in the coffin.

"Then Major confirmed your story about what you did for your pops, and that convinced me even more," Lucky added.

"Our pops," Kat chimed in. She looked to Secret and shot her a "what is he talking about?" look.

Secret's mouth dropped. "Major? What does he have to do with this?"

"Come on, Secret." Lucky rolled his eyes. "It's all over. Like Kat said, everybody might as well come clean. You know exactly what Major has to do with all this."

The humiliation and the shame she felt the night she slept with Major Pain for her father all came back to her. Bits and pieces of the night her father begged her to atone for his mistakes ran through her head.

"Remember when you said you'd do anything for Daddy?" Secret's father had asked her. "Well, baby, right now I really need you to make good on your word." He squirmed a little in the driver's seat while he looked over at his seventeen-year-old daughter in the passenger seat. "You see Daddy is having it real hard right now. I been off that stuff a little bit now, but you know I did that bid in jail, too."

Secret didn't know exactly which bid he was talking about. He'd done several. As a matter of fact, that's one of the reasons why he'd been out of her life so much, because he was in jail so much.

Her father continued. "I just need you to do me this one solid. Please, Secret, and I promise I won't ever ask you to do anything like this again." He nodded over his shoulder to the man standing outside the window. Then in a whispered tone he said, "Just a couple hours with him and I swear to—"

"Daddy, no!" Secret yelled out, her eyes filling with tears. "How could you?" She turned to try to get out of the car but her father stopped her by grabbing her arm.

"Just wait, Secret. Please, Daddy needs you to do this. Look, keepin' it one hunnid; Daddy owes some really bad people a lot of money. If I don't pay them, baby girl, you probably won't ever see your daddy again . . . alive that is. And I ain't just talking shit either, Secret. They

gon' kill your daddy if I don't get them their money." He fought back tears of his own.

Secret became so emotional that she wrapped her arms around her father and began to cry just as hard as he was. She hated seeing him like this. The way he looked, he was already dead. And how Secret saw it, his blood would be on her hands. How would she be able to live with herself? So she gave in and agreed to sleep with the man for money to help pay for her father's debt.

Secret thought she would throw up right there in the warehouse just thinking about that night. And at the time she had no idea that the man waiting to bust her cherry was Major Pain. She never thought in a million years she'd ever see him again. Even so, she never thought in a million years he would even remember her again if he ever saw her, but apparently he had. That day Lucky had introduced the two at the warehouse he'd looked at her with familiarity. Clearly he must have eventually remembered her all too well.

"Major pulled me aside a couple days after he saw you here in the warehouse," Lucky said. "Honor among brothers. He had to let me know he'd hit that. He told me the scenario. I put two and two together."

"Is he trying to say that you got down with Major and Daddy set it all up?" Kat asked.

The lone tear escaping from Secret's eye gave Kat the answer.

"Secret, honey," Kat said empathetically and then took a step toward Secret in an attempt to comfort her.

"Don't move!" Secret yelled. She put the gun on Kat and Kat froze.

Kat had a look of hurt in her eyes. She couldn't believe her sister was standing there aiming a gun at her.

"What?" Secret said unsympathetically. "You think you're the only one who can say fuck blood and stab 'em in the back?" Secret looked into her sister's eyes. "You were my blood, and you played me for him?"

Kat looked over to Lucky as she spoke to Secret. "Like I told you, he was like my kryptonite. Something about him. I just kept going back."

Secret had to realize that even though she and Kat had this instantaneous inseparable bond when they were little girls, it was only temporarily. That bond had obviously deteriorated over the years they had been apart. But always looking at the glass half full and wanting that fairytale life, Secret thought they could just pick up where they'd left off. She though Kat had felt the same way about her. Looked like she couldn't have been more wrong about her and Lucky. The two were made for each other, definitely cut from the same cloth.

"And by the way," Lucky said. "He knows about Dina."

A look of horror covered Secret's face. Not so much because Major Pain now knew that Secret had given birth to his child and she had no idea what he would try to do about it, but because Dina was still out in the car.

"Oh, my God, Secret," Kat said, shaking her head. "I didn't know."

"And would it have mattered?" Secret yelled. "You're just like him." She now pointed the gun at Lucky, shaking and in just complete hysterics. She felt like the world was against her, tumbling down on her. Both Lucky and her own sister had betrayed her. No wonder they'd been connected for so many years. The two were just alike and meant to be together. Well now they would die together. Certainly this wasn't part of Detective Davis's deal, but Secret had made one too many deals with the devil already. And nothing was ever what it seemed. Well, she was no longer willing to take that chance.

"I hate to say it, baby girl," Lucky said, growling in pain, "but you brought it all upon yourself. Like you said yourself, you are the one who made the choices."

"You're right," Secret said, "and now I'm about to make another one." She cocked the gun. "And by the way, you don't need a doctor," Secret said to Lucky, aiming the gun right at his head. "You need Jesus."

"Secret!"

Shawndiece coming from down the hallway into the garage area startled everyone, especially Secret, who swooped her arms in Shawndiece's direction and accidentally pulled the trigger.

There were multiple screams. It was hard to tell if it was Secret, Kat, or Shawndiece, but considering Shawndiece was the one lying on the ground, chances were it was her.

"Oh, God, Shawn!" Secret dropped the gun and ran over to her best friend who lay on the ground not moving. She was covered in blood. Secret didn't know if it was the old blood from the puddle she'd last seen her lying in, or fresh blood as a result of the shot Secret had just fired. "Shawndiece, please. Oh, God. I'm so sorry. I didn't mean to shoot you."

"Good," Shawndiece said, lifting her head. "Because you didn't."

Secret was in shock, but at the same time relieved. "Then why the hell are you on the ground?" Secret spat.

"Bitch, ain't I taught you nothing? When you hear bullets flying, you're supposed to hit the deck. Not stand there and wait to get hit. Didn't you see my ass lying back there on the ground? I wasn't hit then either. But a bitch hit the ground as soon as the first shot was fired."

Secret could have strangled Shawndiece, but the sound of a gun shooting made Secret hit the deck as well. That's when she looked up and saw Kat aiming the gun and shooting it at the garage entrance door. She looked at the door just in time to see Lucky clearing the doorway to the outside.

"Shit," Secret said, Kat running toward the door still shooting.

Finally there was nothing but clicking sounds as Kat was out of bullets. Just then Secret heard tires screeching while at the same time hearing sirens. It was the sound of the screeching tires that put the most awful feeling in the world in the pit of Secret's stomach.

Secret scrambled up from the ground. "My car. No, no, no. Dina! Dina!" Secret ran out the door, pushing Kat aside. Kat was still aiming and trying to shoot the empty gun at Lucky, who was driving off in Secret's car just as police cars pulled up.

"Freeze!" cops yelled, exiting their cars and drawing their guns on Kat.

Kat dropped the gun and put her hands behind her head.

Just then Secret saw Detective Davis getting out of the first squad car that had pulled up. "He's getting away, and my baby is in the car. He's getting away." Secret pointed just as Lucky pulled out of the side exit of the lot. No sooner than Detective Davis turned to look, there was the sound of screeching tires, a loud crash and all that could be seen was a semi truck pushing Secret's car out of view.

A piercing scream escaped Secret's mouth as she dropped to her knees. "Oh God! My baby! My baby is in the car."

Officers began running toward the accident. Secret was still in shock and couldn't move.

"Get up, Secret. Come on, let's go." Shawndiece pulled on Secret's arm trying to get her to her feet. Secret was dead weight and Shawndiece was unable to get her to budge. "Get the fuck up!" Shawndiece yelled. "That's your baby. We gotta go see about your baby."

Secret looked up to Shawndiece. She was in a daze. She had a puzzled expression on her face as if she didn't understand what Shawndiece was saying her.

Shawndiece used a calmer tone. "Let's go see about, Dina, Secret." She tugged her arm. "Come on."

Secret began nodding in agreement. "Dina. I gotta go see about Dina."

"Yes. Come on." Shawndiece was able to get Secret to her feet.

In a slow pace Secret began following the path of the police officers. Within seconds her slow pace had turned into a light jog, then a run. When she cleared the corner all she could see was the mangled up car pinned to the front of the semi.

Secret threw her hand over her mouth and gasped. There was no way anyone could have survived this accident. Her car was mangled, crushed like an aluminum can. Secret searched for air. There was none. She couldn't breathe.

Both Secret and Shawndiece stood frozen. When Secret took a step toward the truck, Shawndiece grabbed her arm. Secret looked back at her. Shawndiece shook her head. "No, Secret." Shawndiece had changed her attitude in just that short of time. A few seconds ago she was urging Secret to go see about Dina. Now she wanted to save her friend the despair of having a vision embedded in her head that might never go away.

"Son of a bitch," Shawndiece said in awe as she looked past Secret.

Secret turned to face the scene of the accident. She saw Lucky emerged from the car through the passenger window, as it would have been impossible for him to escape through the driver side that was smashed into the truck's grill. Seeing Lucky gave her hope. Things might not have been as bad as it looked.

Secret broke loose from Shawndiece and went running toward the car. A huge explosion sent Secret shooting back toward Shawndiece. She slammed into her best friend as they both hit the ground. When Secret looked up the car was in flames. There was a cloud of black smoke hovering over top of it. The same black cloud that had been following Secret her entire life.

Chapter 31

For the past two weeks Secret hadn't been able to peel herself from off of her couch. She'd been lying there staring at the television that hadn't been turned off and remained on the same exact channel. There was no need to channel surf. She wasn't paying attention to anything being aired anyway.

Her cell phone hadn't even been turned on since the memorial service Secret had at the funeral home. It was private, not printed in the daily newspaper. There was no funeral program, no slide of pictures of Dina, no singing, and no eulogy. Just Secret and her baby girl who lay in the tiniest coffin. Burned beyond recognition, the casket remained closed. For two hours straight, Secret wept beyond the depth of grief.

Honoring her best friend's request, Shawndiece had allowed Secret her time alone inside the funeral home with her daughter. Shawndiece remained out in the car waiting for her friend.

Secret hadn't seen Shawndiece since she'd dropped her off at her house after the service. Shawndiece had wanted to stay with Secret. She was worried about her friend. She was in a deep state of depression. But Secret insisted on being alone. And alone is exactly what Secret had been. She hadn't seen or talked to anyone.

Her mind was consumed with the fact that her baby was dead, and she'd watched her die. Visions of her car being demolished right there in her face knowing Dina was in that back seat helpless haunted her. It had paralyzed her to the point where she hadn't cleaned herself or her house since the private memorial service.

Her house stunk because she hadn't taken the trash out. She stunk because she hadn't showered. She only got up off the couch to use the bathroom, several times contemplating urinating on herself. Climbing those steps had taken up energy she didn't have.

She no longer had a job, having not returned since Dina's death two weeks ago. The store manager understood, though. Upon hearing about the loss of her baby, he even sent her a flower arrangement. He had given Secret the assurance that whenever she was ready, she could come back to work anytime. Her position would be waiting for her.

She told him how much she appreciated that, but knew in her heart she was never going back there to work. The way Secret felt, she could stay right there on that couch forever and die. With Dina gone, she had nothing to live for. It would take a miracle from God for her to find the strength to want to go on.

The mail falling through the mail slot onto the floor turned Secret's attention away from the television and to the pile of envelopes on the floor. The mail looked like a pile of dirt sitting next to a freshly dug grave. She hadn't opened it the last few days, tired of the cards of condolences and poems that only seemed to make her break down more instead of lift her up.

She hadn't cried in about an hour. She felt guilty when she wasn't crying and mourning Dina. Misery loved company, so maybe cracking open a depressing card or two would make Secret feel better. She was comfortable wallowing in her own misery. Secret lifted herself off the couch as if she weighed a ton. In all actuality she'd lost almost ten pounds by not having eaten. She lost her appetite when she lost her baby.

She stood up and dragged her feet over to the door. She slowly bent over and scooped up all the mail. As she walked back over to the couch she flipped through the usual cards, utility bills, and advertisements. She got to one envelope in particular that made her pause. Secret placed all the other mail on the table, but kept that one particular piece of mail in her hand. She sat down on the couch and stared at it for a minute before opening it. Finally she tore it open and pulled out a piece of white paper. She read the little yellow sticky that was stuck on the piece of paper out loud. "Sorry it took so long."

She unfolded the white piece of paper and allowed her eyes to scan it from left to right. Tears began to fall from Secret's eyes as she read the words on the paper: "Congratulations, Secret Miller. You've been awarded a full scholarship to The Ohio State University."

She went on to read about how her scholarship included tuition, books, room and board as well as food vouchers. It was everything she'd worked so hard for. A free higher education and then some. That piece of paper had been her ticket out of Flint. She crumbled it in her hand and began to cry hard. Her shoulders heaved. The anger she had toward her mother for destroying what could have been rose up in her all over again. Balling up that paper had been like balling up her life. All that hard work she'd done in high school was for naught. There was no turning back the hands of time now. Over a year had passed. Surely some other student was living the life that should had been Secret's.

No longer wanting to sit there and wallow in misery for fear she might drown in it, Secret stood up. She shook her head and looked down at the balled up scholarship award that was in her hand. A piece of paper that had once been worth thousands, priceless to Secret, was now worthless.

"Oh, well, there's nothing I can do about it now." There was nothing she could do about much of anything. She just felt so useless. She shrugged, tossed the paper up, and caught it back in her hand. She headed to the kitchen in order to throw it away. Just like the day Ray had brought her back to the apartment for the first time, an odor assaulted her nose the closer she got to the trash can. He stood over the trash can. "I threw my life away a long time ago. This just makes it official."

She was just about to put it in the receptacle but then she paused as a sudden thought entered her mind and froze her actions. She slowly unrumpled the paper. A smirk forced its way on her lips then she said to herself, "Then again, maybe there is something I can do about it."

"I truly appreciate you coming with me today, Mrs. Langston," Secret said as she met her former high school counselor inside the lobby area of a downtown Columbus, Ohio office building. They'd driven almost four hours from Flint to get there.

"Oh, Secret, honey, no need to thank me." Mrs. Langston hugged Secret. "I'm so sorry dear. I can't imagine how you must feel. What you must be going through."

"Thank you," Secret said.

Mrs. Langston pulled out of the hug. She looked into Secret's eyes. "Why didn't you tell me, sweetheart? That day you saw me in the store. I feel so awful. I was going on and on about the scholarship and you being off at college. I didn't know. I could have maybe helped you then. Then maybe you wouldn't have even been in town for . . ." Her words trailed off.

"It's okay, Mrs. Langston. You're helping me now."

"It was just a phone call."

"A phone call that got the scholarship board to at least meet with me. The rest is up to me I suppose." Secret's voice sounded doubtful.

Mrs. Langston took Secret's hands. "You can do it, Secret. You didn't come this far to give up now. You've been through a lot. And after all you've been through you've still gotten this far."

Secret smiled. "That reminds me of something my grandmother used to say."

"What's that?"

Secret's smile got bigger thinking back to her grandmother's words. "God didn't bring me this far just to leave me."

"Amen," Mrs. Langston said.

Secret smiled.

"Well, shall we?" Mrs. Langston asked.

"Yes, we shall." Secret looped her arm through Mrs. Langston's and the two women headed to the room they were told to meet the scholarship committee in.

Secret took in a deep breath as she entered the room. For all of her life it felt as though her fate was always in somebody else's hands. As she looked at the two men and three women waiting at the long conference room table, this once again proved to be true. Overcome with nerves, Secret stood frozen at the door.

"Go on, you can do it," Mrs. Langston whispered in her ear. "You're a fighter. It's what makes you different."

Secret looked to Mrs. Langston as if she'd just had an "ah ha" moment. It was as if Mrs. Langston had just solved a hundred-year-old mystery. In Secret's mind she had. So many people for so many years had continued to tell Secret that she was different, but no one could ever give her a reason why; not one that made sense or resonated with her anyway. For the first time ever someone had.

A fighter. That's what made her different from everyone else she knew. Everybody else accepted life for what it was. They adapted. Secret had always fought against the current instead of going with the flow. And that truly was what made her different.

A huge grin spread across Secret's face as she walked over to the conference room table, greeted each member of the scholarship committee, and then put on her boxing gloves prepared to fight for her life.

Chapter 32

Secret loaded the last of the last into her rented U-Haul truck. "Well, that's everything," she said brushing her hands together. She then looked over to her best friend.

"I'm gonna miss you, girl," Shawndiece said staring down. She'd just helped her best friend since she could remember pack up everything she owned into a U-Haul truck. In less than five minutes she'd be watching her pull off.

"I keep telling you to come with me. Detective Davis had the state drop all charges against you since you were a cooperating witness in putting Lucky away. So it's not like you're on probation or anything."

Shawndiece looked around. "Might as well have gone on to prison. I'm a prisoner of these streets anyhow."

"But you don't have to be," Secret said. "Once upon a time, I thought the same thing. But after that call to the scholarship committee and pleading for them to grant me a meeting before the board. After hearing my story, and of course Mrs. Langston agreeing to come for support and tell them about my character, they reissued the scholarship. They said they'd never ever done that before. I was a first. So you see, anything can happen, Shawndiece."

"That's because you went to church when you were little. You had faith."

"I had faith, but faith wasn't enough. I had to put some action behind it, otherwise I'd still be lying in there on that couch."

"Smelling like death." Shawndiece turned her nose up and pinched it with her fingers.

"Girl, I felt like death. I lost my child." Secret bit her lip to keep from crying. "I lost my baby because of some old street bullshit I got caught up in."

"And I feel so guilty about that," Shawndiece admitted.

"Why in the world would you feel guilty? You weren't the one who left your baby in a running car, the dude you were messing with jumped in it and drove off into the path of a semi truck. That was my doing."

"But you had no business even being caught up in this life. But I taught you how. I groomed you to be something you were not instead of telling you that even with a baby you could have made it. I think a part of me didn't want to lose my best friend. I knew you'd run off to college and forget all about me, just like you are about to do now. So all this fucking shit was in vain?" Shawndiece yelled and then broke down in tears.

"Shawn, don't." Secret went and hugged Shawndiece. "Don't blame yourself. No one had a gun to my head. I'm responsible for the choices I made. I can't bear leaving knowing you are carrying this burden."

Shawndiece lifted her head up and smiled. "Oooh, then it worked? 'Cause, girl, you know I don't be crying."

Secret play slapped Shawndiece on the arm.

"I'm just kidding," Shawndiece said, wiping tears away. "You go on off to college. But, girl, I am going to miss you."

Secret's eyes watered. "I'm going to miss you too." Secret swallowed her tears. "Well, I guess I better go lock up." Secret looped her arm through Shawndiece's and they headed to her apartment. They took one last walk-through to make sure Secret had everything then they made their way back down to the door. Shawndiece walked out onto the porch while Secret took one more look around the place and then closed the door shut. She locked it and then dangled the key in front of Shawndiece. "You'll drop this to my landlord for me?"

"Yep," Shawndiece said, taking the key. "And since I did help you clean up the place, can I get that deposit?" Shawndiece laughed.

Once the laughter died down there was a moment of silence. It was obvious neither girl wanted to say that final good-bye. But the clock was ticking and Secret had about a four-hour drive ahead of her.

"Good-bye, friend." Shawndiece spoke before Secret did.

"Will you not say it as though we are never going to see each other again or talk again?"

"I'm just being real," Shawndiece said. "Keeping it one hundred, like I always do. I believe I served a time and a purpose in your life, Secret. I was there to hold you down, to teach you what you needed to know for such a time as this."

Secret pulled her head back and looked at Shawndiece with surprise. She'd remembered that scripture from the Bible.

"Mmm, hmmm. Didn't know I knew a little somethin' somethin' about the Bible, did you?"

"You go, girl," Secret said.

"But anyway, what I taught you, you don't need any-more. You are about to live the life you are supposed to live. Five years from now when you are living it up in some suburb, your life in Flint and everything about it will be like some bad nightmare you are going to forget all about." Shawndiece's face saddened. "That includes me."

"Shawn—"

"No." Shawndiece put her hands up to halt Secret's words. "It is what it is, Secret. But it's all good. I get it. And like always, I've only wanted what's best for you.

What's best for you is getting your ass in that U-Haul truck and getting to that campus before they take that scholarship again."

Secret laughed, wiping her fallen tears away. "You're right. I need to get going." She gave Shawndiece a hug. "I love you, girl."

"I love you too," Shawndiece said.

The two best friends separated. Secret went and got inside the truck as Shawndiece stood off on the sidewalk watching.

The truck started and then slowly pulled off into the street. Shawndiece stood on the corner waving as the truck drove away. After the truck was about four houses down, Shawndiece stepped off the curb to cross where her car was parked. There was the loud screeching sound of tires. The last time that sound had been heard, someone had died.

"Secret, don't forget, study group is tonight at seven," said the geeky-type girl with long blond hair and black-framed glasses.

"I know, I know. I'll be there," Secret replied then headed her separate way across The Ohio State University campus.

Secret took in her surroundings. She admired the campus halls, bike racks, other students coming and going from class, right down to the landscaping of the trees and grass. She'd made it. She'd fought her way through to her dreams and was now living them out. Shawndiece had been right: Flint life had been just a nightmare so that she could wake up and appreciate what she had just that much more.

"Shawndiece." The name of her best friend floated across her lips. There was a girl walking in the distance who looked like Shawndiece. Secret squinted at the uncanny resemblance. The closer she got to the girl, the more and more it looked like Shawndiece.

"Shawndiece," Secret said again as she got closer and could recognize her completely. "I thought that was you. Girl, what are you doing over here?"

"Duh," Shawndiece said, throwing her hands on her hips. "Did you forget that you were supposed to tutor me at the library?"

Secret thumped herself upside the head. "Ugghh, that's right. You didn't want to do it back at the apartment because of Trina."

"Honey, yes. That girl is so nerve-racking. I can never get any real studying done when she's around. She talks loud, she plays her music loud, her television is loud." Shawndiece rolled her eyes.

"Well, you do remember she has a hearing impairment, right?" Secret reminded her about their third roommate.

"How can I forget?" Shawndiece sucked her teeth. "Damn upgrading her cell phone, she needs to upgrade her hearing aid to the Galaxy 6 or something."

Secret tried not to laugh but she couldn't help it. Perhaps she'd convinced Shawndiece to move out of the hood, but clearly the hood took up permanent residence in Shawndiece.

"Beggers can't be choosey," Secret said. "I begged the scholarship committee to reinstate my scholarship. They'd already given out the ones for this year so there were no dorms. My only option was apartment housing. Part of my dream had been to live on campus in a dorm, but I'm willing to give that up if it means having my best friend here with me."

"Aww really," Shawndiece said fake blushing.

"Cut it out," Secret said, play hitting her on the arm.

"Seriously, though. Girl, I appreciate all you've done for me." Now Shawndiece was the one looking around, taking in and admiring her surroundings. "I can't believe I'm a frickin' college student." She looked back at Secret. "Well, not at this college. But the community college will help me get here one day."

"That's the spirit," Secret said. "Now aren't you glad that day I was leaving Flint I slammed on my breaks and came back and forced you to come with me?"

Shawndiece smiled. "I really am. You told me I could get an education and make something of myself just like you. And I really appreciate you helping me and my mom fill out the college app, the financial aid forms, studying for those placement tests and everything. It was a lot."

"What can I say? Remember all the time you took teaching me what I needed to know? Let's just say now I'm returning the favor." Secret winked.

It was ironic that once upon a time Shawndiece had made it her own special task to take Secret up under her wing and teach her how to operate in the hood life. Well now Secret was making it her own special task to take Shawndiece up under her wing and teach her how to operate in the good life.

"It's funny how everything worked out, huh?" Secret said. "Now I'm the teacher and you're the student."

"Yep, pretty funny indeed."

The two best friends headed toward the library.

"I bet you never thought in a million years all my school smarts and girlie ways would ever come in handy, huh?" Secret said to Shawndiece as they walked side by side.

"I can honestly say I didn't. And I'm so glad all my ghettoness, hood and ratchetness I taught you didn't take the place of who you really are, your own super powers. 'Cause even though they drove me crazy over the years, looks like they truly came in handy."

The girls looked at each other and said in unison, "For such a time as this."

"Amen," Secret said to her friend. "Amen."